"Was that a compliment?"

"Yes, well, you're going to have to try to look a lot less beautiful if you expect me to keep those things from slipping out."

She cocked her head to the side. "You managed so successfully for years. What's changed?"

"Nothing. Or maybe everything." He took a step toward her, and the look in his eyes reminded her of the one he'd had in the kitchen the night he'd tended to her foot, the night she'd been certain he'd been about to kiss her.

Her mouth went dry as she stood frozen in place, a million thoughts running through her mind. The hallway felt as though it were closing in around her as he came closer. Her breath caught and held in her throat, and her eyes were unblinking as she continued to stare at the crystal blue eyes staring right back at her, giving nothing away…and saying so much at the same time.

ALSO BY JENNIFER SNOW

Maybe This Kiss (novella)

Maybe
THIS
TIME

JENNIFER
SNOW

FOREVER

NEW YORK   BOSTON

Copyright © 2016 by Jennifer Snow
Preview of *Maybe This Love* copyright © 2016 by Jennifer Snow
Excerpt from *Maybe This Kiss* copyright © 2016 by Jennifer Snow
Cover design by Elizabeth Turner. Cover photography by Claudio Marinesco.
Cover copyright © 2016 by Hachette Book Group, Inc.

Forever
Hachette Book Group
1290 Avenue of the Americas
New York, NY 10104
forever-romance.com
twitter.com/foreverromance

First Edition: November 2016
Forever is an imprint of Grand Central Publishing. The Forever name and logo are trademarks of Hachette Book Group, Inc.
The publisher is not responsible for websites (or their content) that are not owned by the publisher.
The Hachette Speakers Bureau provides a wide range of authors for speaking events. To find out more, go to www.hachettespeakersbureau.com or call (866) 376-6591.

ISBNs: 978-1-4555-9486-3 (mass market), 978-1-4555-9485-6 (ebook)

Printed in the United States of America
OPM
10 9 8 7 6 5 4 3 2 1

ATTENTION CORPORATIONS AND ORGANIZATIONS:

Most Hachette Book Group books are available at quantity discounts with bulk purchase for educational, business, or sales promotional use. For information, please call or write:

Special Markets Department, Hachette Book Group
1290 Avenue of the Americas, New York, NY 10104
Telephone: 1-800-222-6747 Fax: 1-800-477-5925

To my husband, Reagan, who has come to terms with the fact there will always be pictures of other hot men hanging on my office wall and every date night will involve me saying, "Hang on, I have to write this down." Your love and support amaze me.

Acknowledgments

Writing a hockey-inspired romance series was an inevitability for me. Growing up in St. John's, Newfoundland, "the good old hockey game" was a big part of my Saturday night. My dad and I would sit in our Toronto Maple Leaf jerseys with our matching troll dolls (wearing their Leaf jerseys) and yell at the screen for three periods plus overtime. So, for my love of the game and many wonderful memories, thank you, Dad.

Thank you as always to my agent, Stephany Evans, who attempted to sell this series chapter by chapter, and my wonderful editor, Madeleine Colavita, who fell for my hero. As usual, this story is so much better for your feedback.

Thank you to everyone at Grand Central, especially the art department, who created a cover any author would be thrilled to have, and to the cover models for being so damn perfect as Abby and Jackson.

A big, big thank you to Brijet and Ray Whitney—an inspiring couple who answered all of my hockey-related questions and more. I appreciate your help, and any errors in this book are mine and mine alone. Congrats again to you both on Ray's retirement. I wish your family all the best.

Thank you to my readers who have waited patiently for this series, especially my SnowAngels Reader Club members, whose support truly amazes me. I am so fortunate to do what I love and to have readers who love what I do.

XO,
Jen

Maybe
THIS
TIME

CHAPTER 1

◦◦◦

*O*f all the mistakes she'd made in her twenty-nine years, Abigail hoped her decision to move back to Glenwood Falls wouldn't be the biggest one.

The silent treatment she'd received from her daughter on the exhausting fifteen-hour drive from California to Colorado made her think that maybe it was.

She waved to Dani from the sidewalk as the school bus pulled away from the curb, but her nine-year-old ignored her.

Great.

As the bus rounded the corner, Abigail pulled her cardigan tighter around her and turned to walk back toward her family home. The mid-September mountain breeze felt even cooler to her, having spent so many fall seasons living in sunny Los Angeles, where the palm trees and green grass never gave way to the gold and red leaves crunching beneath her feet as she walked.

The wind blew her long blonde hair across her eyes, and

she tucked it behind her ears. The sunshine reflected off of her solitaire diamond ring, nestled safely next to the platinum wedding band that used to hold a promise of forever.

She'd have to take them off soon. She probably should have already.

Dean's wedding band had been sitting on the nightstand on his side of the bed for almost ten months.

Some people had an easier time letting go and moving on.

She took a deep breath as she opened the front door. The smell of coffee and blueberry pancakes greeted her, and she forced a smile, hoping it would dull the constant aching in her chest.

Time to face another day.

Another day in Glenwood Falls—her former hometown. Another day with her parents trying to make her feel better about her divorce. And another day she had to get through with a heaviness weighing on her whenever she thought about her future.

Hers and Dani's.

Following the smell of coffee, she went straight to the kitchen.

"Good morning," her father said, pouring her a cup.

"Hi, Dad," she said, glancing around the kitchen that hadn't changed in years. The same harvest gold fridge and stove that had been popular in the seventies and that her father miraculously managed to keep running, the round glass-topped table near the window that seated four, and the same butterfly-patterned curtains she'd sewn one year in home economics class—the only thing she'd ever successfully made. In ten years, nothing had changed, and she'd expected that sense of familiarity to make her feel better.

Instead it made her feel as though her attempt to move on with her life had taken her two steps backward.

"Dani got off to school okay?"

"Yes, although she still refuses to speak to me," she said, sitting in her old familiar place at the table. She took a sip of the tar-like coffee and winced, but immediately took another one. She used to hate how strong her father made it, but the last three mornings, she'd needed the strength it provided to deal with Dani's anger at her for moving them away from her father in L.A.

"She'll come around," he said.

Abigail knew it was true. She just hoped it was before her little girl started college.

On the table was that day's *Glenwood Times*—the local newspaper. Picking it up, she opened it to the classified section as she had the day before.

Nothing new added. Still just three open positions in the town of five thousand residents—the deli counter at the supermarket, early morning flower delivery, and sawmill operator.

"Dad, how hard is it to operate a saw?" she asked with a sigh.

He chuckled. "Just the fact that you need to ask means you probably shouldn't apply for that one, sweetheart."

Her mother came into the kitchen and her expression said it all.

"Yes, Mom, I'm looking for a job," Abigail said.

"I didn't say anything."

She didn't have to. Isabelle Jansen's face was the most expressive her daughter had ever seen. Every emotion, every thought could be conveyed by the small furrow of her brow or the twitch of an eye…

"I know you think I need time to get settled, but the sooner I can find work to keep myself busy, the easier that will be."

"You know yourself better than anyone, sweetheart. I'm just saying there's no hurry."

"I appreciate that." And Abigail did. After leaving Glenwood Falls, she'd only gone back to visit a few times, instead sending plane tickets to her parents to come visit her and Dani in L.A. Her decision to move home as her divorce was being finalized had surprised her parents, but they'd opened their door and arms to her and Dani. They were making this transition as easy on them as possible. And she knew how valuable their support was. She also knew she couldn't use them as a crutch. She needed to get back on her feet and prove to herself this was the right decision, that she could move forward without Dean, as soon as possible. And Dani needed to see that, too.

Abigail hesitated, wondering if she should tell them about the one job in town she *was* interested in. She cleared her throat. "I was actually thinking about applying for a teaching position at the elementary school."

Both of her parents stared at her.

"What? I do have a teaching degree." She'd completed the degree after Dani started school, realizing she might someday want a career of her own.

"Yes, but…you've never actually used it," her mother said.

"Don't they expire?" her father joked.

"Very funny, Dad," she said. "When I registered Dani on Monday, I heard one of the other teachers say they were looking for a substitute teacher that could turn into a full-time fourth grade position when Kelli Fitzgerald goes on maternity leave next month."

"Oh, that's right! I saw Kelli at last month's town meeting—she looked ready to deliver then. She's such a sweet girl, and her husband is one of the nicest men—he helped your dad with the deck last spring…" Her mom's voice trailed on, but Abigail wasn't listening.

Her mother raving about Kelli and other of her former high school friends was something she heard often. Apparently they were all living wonderful, successful lives in Glenwood Falls. None of them had fallen in love with a star athlete or left town six months pregnant…or had to crawl back home nine years later after a bitter divorce.

Nope, no one else. Just her.

Abigail's cell phone ringing was her escape, and she was relieved to see her lawyer's office number lighting up the screen. "I have to take this," she said, heading upstairs to her old bedroom. "Hello?" she said, closing the door behind her.

"Hi, Abigail. How are you?" her lawyer, Olivia Davis, asked, sounding far too busy to really care.

"I'm fine. Everything okay?" The divorce was almost finalized after six months of back and forth with Dean's lawyer. There were just a few things left to sign off on—her proposed custody arrangement and the financial settlement terms. She knew Olivia was fantastic at her job and she'd come highly recommended by several other divorcées she'd known as a hockey wife, but she still worried about whether she'd made the right decision hiring her. Deciding who to put her trust in these days was like deciding between the devil you knew and the devil you didn't.

"Well, I have good news and bad news."

Her marriage of nine years was almost officially over— she wasn't sure there was any real *good* news to be had, but she asked for that first.

"I just received an uncontested document to the custody file," Olivia said.

That actually was good news. She'd been worried Dean would try to fight for custody of Dani, even though she knew with his travel schedule with the L.A. Kings and her history of being their daughter's primary caregiver, his chances of getting it in court would have been slim.

Maybe he knew that, too.

"That's great…"

"Actually, he's even stated that the visitation time is too much, and he is relinquishing all of the time to you."

Abigail frowned. "What does that mean—he doesn't want to see Dani at all?" she asked, sitting on the edge of the bed.

"Hopefully that's not the case. It just means he is leaving the power to decide when and how he sees Dani in your hands. The two of you can arrange something that works… without involving a legal, binding visitation schedule."

Great. So, it would all rest on her shoulders. She would have preferred it didn't. Her own feelings toward Dean were sure to cloud her judgment, and she knew she was going to have to put them aside and do what was best for Dani. "Okay," she said. So much for good news. Now she really didn't want the bad.

"So, the bad news is—he's contesting the settlement. He is claiming that because you decided to move back to Glenwood Falls, where real estate and the cost of living are cheaper, he shouldn't have to pay what we're asking."

No doubt in most situations, this would be the bad news, but the truth was, Abigail didn't care about the money. Yes, she expected Dean to pay child support to help raise Dani, but she'd never been the materialistic type who enjoyed the flamboyant perks of being a hockey wife. She'd bought the expensive clothes and spent the small fortunes on her hair and makeup because it was what Dean expected, what was needed to fit in with the other hockey wives.

At first, she hadn't felt the need to be part of the group,

but she'd quickly learned how lonely life as a professional athlete's spouse could be. Other hockey families understood the sacrifices and the often-stressful lifestyle, and she'd found comfort and security within the close-knit group.

At least she *had* until a few weeks ago, when she hadn't been able to bring herself to log in to the Hockeywives.com site. She was no longer one of them, and she needed to stand on her own two feet now. Reaching out for their support didn't seem right. And she also didn't want any information about her new life traveling back to Dean through their hockey-playing husbands.

"Look, don't worry," Olivia said when Abigail was quiet. "I'm sure it's just a delay tactic. He can't possibly believe the courts will rule in his favor on this. The longer he can delay things, the longer he doesn't have to pay the divorce settlement or alimony and child support."

"So, what's next?"

"Well, I'll file the counter and see what happens. But in the meantime, try to feel good about the uncontested custody—you wouldn't believe how often that causes the biggest delay. You're lucky."

Lucky, she thought sadly as she disconnected the call. Strange, she didn't feel lucky. How was she supposed to explain all of this to Dani, who'd had a say in outlining when she wanted to spend time in L.A. with her dad? How could she tell the little girl that her father hadn't wanted to commit to a schedule, to time with her? The last thing their strained relationship needed was Dani thinking this was somehow her fault. Neither did she want to paint Dean as the villain, as much as she resented him for what he'd done, for tearing their family apart and putting her in this situation.

No, *lucky* definitely was not a word she'd use.

She stared at the rings on her left hand. Her mother had

said there was no rush, she'd know when she was ready to remove them. She struggled to recall the memories attached to each one—the joy, the love, the excitement she'd felt the day he'd proposed and then six months later at their wedding—but too many other memories—of nights alone, of fights that had left her crying herself to sleep, of his betrayal—had caused the good ones to fade.

She stood and walked toward the dresser, where an old wooden jewelry box with her initials and a flower carved into it sat—a gift from Dean he'd made in woodworking class senior year. She opened the lid and removed the rings, then placed them inside.

Her mother was right. She did know when it was the right time.

* * *

Sitting on the tiny bench outside the principal's office at Glenwood Falls Elementary two days later, Abigail felt like a kid who'd been caught skipping class. Everything around her was so familiar, yet once again, she didn't take comfort in it. Years before, she couldn't wait to leave Glenwood Falls, and she'd been filled with illusions of a fantastic, exciting life in L.A.

Things hadn't quite worked out the way she'd planned, and the media attention given to her divorce and the circumstances around it left her no hope of saving face among her former friends and neighbors in the small town. Hell, she suspected half of them had known Dean was cheating on her based on the tabloid photos long before she'd even realized something was wrong.

God, she'd been so blind.

Loving him as much as she did—*had*—had clouded her

judgment about everything. She'd just felt so lucky that Dean Underwood had chosen her to ask to the school prom, had picked her to be his girlfriend, and then had proposed when she'd told him she was pregnant. The star athlete could have had any girl in town, but he'd chosen her.

And the offer of an exciting life as a pro athlete's wife had been a dream come true for her. She could be the stay-at-home mom with their daughter while Dani was young and they could travel with him around the world...it had all seemed too good to be true.

And it was.

For the first five years, things had been wonderful, but then Dani started school and Abigail went back to college for her teaching degree. She'd also become more active in the hockey wives' charity for the local hospital, Dreams for Life, and soon they were barely together as a family. Dean traveled with the team. She raised their daughter and helped fundraise for various causes.

And somewhere along the line, he'd started having affairs, and she'd been too busy to notice.

"Abby?" Liz, the principal's receptionist, said as she came out into the hall. The woman had been the school's receptionist when she'd been a student.

She stood. "It's Abigail now." She hadn't been Abby in a long time...and she doubted she'd ever see that girl in the mirror again.

"Okay...well, Principal Breen is ready for you," Liz said, holding the office door open. "Just head on in."

"Thank you." Running a hand along her charcoal pencil skirt, Abigail went inside, feeling exactly as she had years before when she'd been sent to the office for talking too much in class. Her palms damp with sweat, she forced a deep breath.

"Wow. I wasn't sure I was reading it right when I saw you on my schedule this morning—but here you are. Abby Jansen back in Glenwood Falls—no one will believe it," Principal Breen said from her seat behind the big mahogany desk.

Nope. No one. Not even her.

Abigail forced her best smile. "Nice to see you, Principal Breen."

"Have a seat, please," she gestured to the chair across from her.

She sat, looking around the office. The same bookshelf along the wall, the same file cabinet near the window, and the same bamboo tree growing in the corner. Nothing had changed in the office. Everything was exactly the same.

"So...you're interested in the substitute teaching position?"

"Yes." Abigail folded and unfolded her legs, shifting in the seat. This was her first real job interview, as the Dreams For Life charity work had kept her far too busy to apply for a teaching position in L.A. Her heart echoed in her ears and her mind raced. What was she doing here? She wasn't even remotely qualified for this position.

"Do you have a recent resume?"

She swallowed hard. "Actually, I don't have one with me..." She did, but not one she was comfortable producing, despite hours trying to make it sound better. Her mother's "maybe they won't need to see a resume" comment when she'd shown it to her said it all.

Principal Breen's eyebrows joined behind her seafoam-green rimmed glasses. "Okay, well, why don't you start by telling me about any previous teaching experience you have." She reached for her notepad and pen and waited.

How about none? How could she somehow turn her

treasurer role on the Dreams for Life charity and her stay-at-home mom position into something this woman would consider an asset? "Well, I haven't taught in any schools… but I do have a degree and I did home-school my daughter, Dani, for a while." Three months while they tried to make traveling with Dean work.

"Okay…"

"And I was involved with the Dreams for Life charity, which helped a lot of children…" God, she sounded like a moron. She wasn't qualified for this job. Nowhere near it. She might as well mention her after-school newspaper delivery job as well.

"Right." Principal Breen set the pen down and clasped her hands in front of her on the desk. "Well, we were really hoping to hire someone with actual teaching experience."

Shit. She needed this job. She needed something to make her feel like she could actually start building a life for herself and Dani there in Glenwood Falls. She needed her confidence to return. And she needed to know they would be okay without Dean. *She* would be okay without him.

"Principal Breen, please," she said, clutching her hands tightly in her lap. "I know my lack of experience isn't ideal, but I can do this job. Please let me prove that to you." And herself. She hated the sound of begging in her voice, but she wanted—*needed*—this job. It was hard enough moving back home, having everyone in town know the sordid details about her failed marriage, and trying to gain her daughter's confidence in her; she really didn't want to be forced to take the flower delivery position in town. Her already low self-esteem couldn't handle it.

The woman hesitated. "I'd like to help you Abby…"

Please don't say *but*…

She paused and studied her for a moment. "How long are

you planning to stay in Glenwood Falls? Is this a permanent move? Or just until you get back on your feet?"

She swallowed hard. "It's a permanent move." She refused to uproot Dani again. Leaving L.A. and her friends had been tough enough. They were here to stay and to start over.

"Okay. The substitute position will only be a few days a week…as needed."

Her breath caught and she tried to hold her excitement. The woman hadn't quite said yes yet.

"When are you available to…"

"Any time," she said quickly.

Principal Breen nodded, looking as though she already regretted the decision. "All right. We'll try this…but there's no guarantee you'll get the full-time position at the end of next month."

"I understand," she said, but there was no way she wasn't getting it. She'd do whatever it took to prove to Principal Breen she was the right person for the job.

She released a breath, tension seeping from her shoulders. This was a good start to getting her life back on track. Maybe not the one she'd planned, but hopefully one she could someday be proud of.

CHAPTER 2

⤛✣⤜

*A*nother school year. Another season.

Jackson Westmore stapled the new hockey tryout schedule on the bulletin board outside of the gym at Glenwood Falls Elementary.

"Hey, Coach, ready for another championship?" his buddy and the school's gym teacher, Darryl Sutton, said as he passed with a group of ten-year-olds returning from a warm-up run around the school track.

"You bet," Jackson said, stopping one of the bigger boys. "As long as James is still planning to try out."

The taller-than-average, skinny kid nodded.

"As long as he keeps his grades up," Darryl—also the boy's father—said.

"Yes, sir," the boy said, disappearing inside the gym with the rest of the class.

Jackson sympathized. He knew what it was like to have a parent as a teacher. His mother had taught at the Glenwood High School for over twenty years. It sucked. He and his brothers couldn't get away with anything. And then they'd catch shit at school *and* at home. His sister had had it easy, being the only non-troublemaker of the group.

"I hear the team is going co-ed this year," Darryl said, glancing at the sign-up form where the announcement was posted.

"Yeah…We'll see how it turns out. I'm not sure there are many eight- to ten-year-old girls who will be interested, but you never know," he said with a shrug.

He was actually thrilled by the Junior Hockey League Association's decision to make the Atom/Novice teams a co-ed division. So far in Glenwood Falls, they hadn't had the funding for a girls league, and he knew one in particular who was dying to play. His niece, Taylor, had been on skates since before she could walk; with two uncles in the NHL and him coaching the local Junior team, it seemed only natural for her to be interested in the sport. She was ten, and this would be her last year to play on his team. He couldn't wait to get her out there; she could skate and puck handle better than any boy he'd ever coached.

"I assume Taylor is guaranteed a spot?" Darryl asked.

Jackson grinned. "She'll have to try out like everyone else, but I have a feeling the Glenwood Falls Lightning will have a new female defenseman this season."

"Well, I've seen her play, so I'm all for it, but not everyone feels that way."

Jackson frowned. "Who's having an issue with it?"

Darryl lowered his voice. "James mentioned that some of the boys…and I suspect it's the boys' fathers' words they're repeating…are not as open-minded about this."

He nodded slowly. Not everyone liked change. He knew that. He just hoped that once the team was finalized based on who could play the game, and not their gender, everyone with reservations would start to feel better. They were kids after all, and the Atom league was the place to have fun while learning the sport. They would start to be more competitive once the talented, promising players moved up to Peewee and then Bantam. "Thanks for the heads-up."

Darryl looked past him down the hall, his expression changing. "Speaking of a heads-up…"

Oh no. He knew in his gut before he even turned around who would be standing there. He'd already heard the rumors she was back. Yet, nothing prepared him for the sight of Abby Jansen, dressed in a slim-fitting suit, her long blonde hair loose around her shoulders, her three-inch heels clicking on the tiled floor, walking toward them.

In ten years, she hadn't changed a bit.

And obviously neither had his feelings for her.

Damn.

* * *

Keep walking. Don't stop. Just keep walking.

One expensive Gucci pump in front of the other…Shit. They were both staring at her. "Hi, guys," Abigail said tightly, keeping her gaze on Darryl and ignoring the other man she'd gone to school with.

Wow—what an understated way to describe their relationship, she thought.

"Hi, Abby. How are you?" Darryl asked, looking uncomfortable as he glanced at his friend.

Jackson's gaze was burning a hole through her forehead, but she plastered on the fake smile she'd perfected since news of her divorce had spread all over the country and continued to pretend he didn't exist. "I'm great." Okay, that might be stretching things a little, but she'd just gotten a job, so that counted for something. "How are things?"

"Good…still teaching phys ed."

She nodded politely. He'd inherited the job from his own father when the older man had retired.

"Well…Better get back in there." The awkward tension seemed to be making him squirm, and he opened the gym door and ducked inside. "Great to see you," he said quickly, as the door shut.

Jackson's panicky gaze left her just long enough to glance at his disappearing friend.

Leaving them alone together in the hallway.

She cleared her throat and waited for him to speak first. She had nothing to say to her soon to be ex-husband's best friend, who'd never disguised the fact that he disliked her. All through high school, he'd treated *her* like the third wheel whenever the three of them went anywhere together. She'd even tried setting him up with countless friends, but he'd scared them all off with his jerkish I'm-better-than-everyone attitude. Obviously, he was still chasing them away. She'd heard he was single, and it couldn't be his tall, dark, and handsome looks keeping the women at bay.

She hadn't seen him in years, other than to peek over Dean's shoulder sometimes when the two Skyped. He was taller than she remembered, towering over her, even in her heels, and his broad shoulders and chest revealed he was a lot more muscular than he looked on the computer screen. His midday five o'clock shadow seemed Photoshopped to perfection, and his square, strong jawline erased any trace of the boy she used to go to school with. All he and Dean ever talked about was hockey, and she often wondered if there were any other layers to the friendship besides a shared passion for the sport.

Obviously without hockey as the subject, the guy had little to talk about, she thought as she continued to wait for him to say something.

He stared at the floor, his hands shoved deep in his pockets, rocking back and forth on his heels.

Silence.

Okay then.

Moving around him, she continued down the hall.

His voice stopped her. "I don't believe everything they're saying about Dean in the papers."

Neither had she, but actually seeing her husband in bed with two women was proof enough.

Of course she didn't expect Jackson to see her side. Slowly, she turned back. "Believe what you want, Jackson. I really don't care."

He moved toward her and her spine stiffened. His light blue eyes were dark and judging. "Adultery? Abuse? Come on. We both know Dean is not that guy."

She hadn't believed him capable of the emotional and verbal abuse, either. That had changed the day she'd confronted him about pictures of him and a Dallas Stars cheerleader she'd seen on the front of a supermarket tabloid. He'd gone on the defensive, saying nasty things to make her believe she was the one at fault for even accusing him of anything. Paranoid, stupid, delusional…just some of the angry insults that played on repeat in her mind.

"I'm not having this conversation with you. Or any conversation." They'd barely spoken before, why start now? "Glenwood Falls is big enough. I think we should be able to make these run-ins few and far between if we try hard enough." Though, that might be harder now that she would be spending time at the school, which was right next door to the arena.

"Oh, believe me, I'll try hard enough," he said, his ice-cold stare making her shiver.

The sound of the lunch bell prevented her from saying anything more as instantly they were swarmed by groups of children heading toward the school cafeteria.

Her eyes skimmed the crowd for Dani. Spotting her coming toward them, Abigail smiled—for real for the first time that day. She waved a hand, relieved to have the perfect excuse to end the intense, uncomfortable conversation.

"Mom? What are you doing here?" Dani asked with a frown when she reached her.

Not exactly the warm greeting she'd been hoping for, but at least her daughter was speaking to her. That small victory was short-lived as she noticed Jackson still standing there watching them. Dani had never actually met Jackson, only saw him occasionally on the computer and in Facebook pics. And Abigail wasn't about to make the introduction. If in nine years the two men hadn't felt it necessary, neither did she.

"I came to talk to Principal Breen about a substitute teaching position," she said, wrapping an arm around her daughter's shoulders.

Dani shrugged away.

Her arm fell to her side. She knew none of this was easy on her daughter. Dani was close with her father, despite his frequent long absences, and she was more like him, which made common ground for bonding with her a challenge. Her daughter was too young to understand everything going on, but Abigail had done her best to explain the situation to her. She didn't want her to rely on the tabloids for information. However, she sensed Dani blamed her, at least for the move, and she was determined to make things right with her. "She said I can start next week…whenever they need a substitute." She glanced toward Jackson. Why was he still standing there—listening? "Isn't that wonderful?"

Dani shrugged.

Heat rushed to her cheeks, and she forced herself not to look at Jackson. Moving her daughter farther away, she knelt in front of her. "I'm sorry you're upset, and I know this move is hard on you," she said. "But, I promise things are going to get better now." How often had she said those words to Dani in the last three days? She wondered if it was only her daughter she was trying to convince. "Soon we'll move into our own place, and before long this will start to feel like home." She brushed her daughter's whip-straight dark hair—her father's hair—away from her face and searched her expression for any sign of understanding.

Dani didn't look convinced, but finally, she nodded. "Fine. Whatever," she said simply.

She'd take any agreement she could get at that moment. "Come on. We'll go to the diner on Main Street for lunch." The cafeteria food sucked. Soon enough they would both have to get used to it. But not today.

And she suspected soon enough she would have to get used to seeing Jackson Westmore. But that, too, was something she was more than willing to postpone for as long as possible.

* * *

"Keep your hands away from your body...that's it. You don't want to be looking down at the puck, or you won't have it for long," Jackson said as he skated backward, watching Taylor move across the ice toward the net with the puck.

Tryouts were the following week, and he wanted to make sure his niece would be ready. Darryl's warning about the other dads still troubled him, but what had him off his game was his brief—yet far too long—glimpse of Abby Jansen earlier that day.

She was going to be teaching at the school. Fan-freaking-tastic.

He shook his head, banishing the image of her in her expensive suit, looking more beautiful than ever. He didn't need any new memories of her competing with the old ones.

He moved closer to his niece to steal the puck, but she moved her body between him and the biscuit the way he'd taught her. He smiled. The kid was a natural. "That's good. Where did you learn that?"

"From Uncle Ben," she teased.

"Ha! I taught both of your uncles everything they know." Ironically, that was true. He'd been the first of the three of them to develop an interest in the sport at age four. His older brother, Ben, and his younger brother, Asher, hadn't started playing until several years later.

But, as it turned out, they were both better than he was. That's why they were playing on major league hockey teams and he was still coaching in Glenwood Falls.

Taylor skated faster and shot the puck. It hit the right post.

"You released it too soon," he said, skating up to her and patting her helmet. "Just hold on to it a little longer. You're overeager to score without an assist—maybe you have been learning a thing or two from your Uncle Ben." Ben played for the Colorado Avalanche. He was the top scorer for the team for the last three years, but he didn't know how to share the puck.

Jackson skated by it and scooped it up. Checking his watch, he saw it was after five. They'd been practicing for almost two hours. "Come on, let's go get something to eat."

"Can we go to Slope and Hatch?"

"Craving a Big Valley Mac?" he asked as they sat on the bench to remove their skates.

She took off her helmet and shook her short dark hair. "Is there any other hot dog worth eating?"

He laughed. "You make a good point, kid. Go grab your stuff." As she rushed off toward the locker rooms, he stood, staring out at the ice. Above the center line hung the local team's championship flags and across from him on the wall was the banner that read WELCOME TO THE HOME OF THE WESTMORE BROTHERS!

Ben and Asher—the source of community pride.

They were the stars of Glenwood Falls—he was just everyone's favorite coach.

CHAPTER 3

～∾～

The Slope and Hatch was one of the best family-friendly restaurants in Glenwood Falls, and that night's choice of dining establishments to celebrate Abigail's new job. Since being back in town, she'd avoided the popular restaurant, not wanting to run into any of her former high school friends or extended family yet, but after that day's encounter with Jackson, she'd thought, *What the hell?* She'd already faced the person she wanted to avoid the most. Any others should be easy in comparison.

"Are you really going to eat all of that?" Dani asked, staring wide-eyed at the large plate of nachos in front of Abigail, loaded with ground beef, chicken, cheese, and hot peppers.

"You bet I am," Abigail said. Her stomach growled; the sight of her favorite comfort food was the first familiar thing she'd appreciated since arriving in town.

"But it's all carbs," her nine-year-old said as she devoured a French fry.

Right. No doubt her little girl was confused considering

she'd never seen her mother consume a carb a day in her life. Well, that was going to change. "Sweetheart, remember all the stuff I said about pasta and potatoes and nachos?"

She nodded, her mouth full of hot dog.

"Forget everything." Abigail picked up an ooey-gooey chip and popped it into her mouth, grateful that her daughter seemed to be in a better mood. Closing her eyes, she almost moaned. The cheesy jalapeño burst of flavor on her tongue was better than any sex she'd had in the last few years.

Probably because Dean had been saving the good techniques for other women.

Pushing all thoughts of her ex away, she reached for her diet soda and extended the glass toward her daughter. "To starting over."

The little girl just shrugged, reaching for another French fry. "Sure."

Guess that was about as much excitement as she was going to get from the kid. "So, tell me about your first week at school. How was it?"

"I don't know."

"Well, do you like your new teacher?" Kelli Fitzgerald was Dani's teacher until her maternity leave started, and then Abigail could potentially be in that position. She wondered how Dani would feel about that.

"She's okay."

Wow, had she been this vague as a child? Well, if Dani still didn't feel like talking, she would. "I'm excited about the new position and if things go well…"

But Dani wasn't listening as her gaze drifted past her. "Oh my God, there's my new friend!"

Okay then.

Abigail turned in the seat to look where her daughter was pointing, but she didn't see anyone Dani's age—just Jackson

Westmore. Again. She knew this was bound to keep happening, but it still irritated her. The sight of him reminded her of all the times he'd tried to get between her and Dean. He'd always tried to exclude her, claiming their annual Super Bowl party was "guys only" and their weekend camping trips in the summer were women-free. She often wondered if maybe Jackson Westmore might be hiding a secret about his sexuality. He was just a little too attached to his best friend.

Well, he could have Dean now.

He glanced their way and she turned quickly, hoping he hadn't seen them. She just wanted to enjoy a nice dinner with her daughter. "Where's your friend, honey? I don't see anyone," she said quietly.

"Right there. Taylor!" she called, waving her arms to get her friend's attention.

Abigail turned again to see a little girl a few inches taller and maybe a year older coming toward them. She wore a hockey jersey, and her short dark hair was tied back in a messy ponytail.

"Hi, Dani, Dani's mom," the young girl said.

"Hi, I'm Abi—Ms. Jansen," she said, realizing she could have this girl in class someday. "You and Dani are friends?" The girl was definitely too old to be in the fourth grade.

"Yes. I'm a new student helper at school."

"Oh." She remembered being one of those at that age. Students were assigned to new classmates to help them adjust to the new school, help them make friends. She was glad they still had the mentorship program. This might be her hometown, but Dani had grown up in L.A. Transitioning to a new school was tough. It was great that her daughter had a friend already in the older girl.

"Do you want to sit with us?" Dani asked. "Is that okay, Mom?"

How could she possibly say no when her daughter looked happier now than she had in a week. "Of course. Are you here with your parents?" She glanced around, wondering if the girl's family was anyone she knew and instead caught sight of Jackson coming toward their table.

Oh not now.

She shot him her best "fuck off" look, but he still continued toward them.

What the hell did he think he was doing? She refused to get into it with him again in front of her daughter and her friend. The few times Jackson had visited Dean in L.A. during the off-season, he'd insisted on staying at a hotel and only spent time with Dean. Now wasn't exactly ideal timing for Dani to meet her father's best friend. Their earlier conversation didn't inspire confidence that any interaction between them would be easy, and she didn't want Dani feeling the awkward tension.

"Actually I'm here with my hockey coach…and uncle," Taylor said with a giggle.

Abigail's eyes widened as she swung her attention back to the girl. "Your hockey coach uncle?" Seriously?

Jackson stopped at the table and draped an arm around the little girl. "Hello again."

Or for the first time. She couldn't remember actually exchanging pleasantries earlier that day. Nope. She was pretty sure he'd gone straight for the jugular.

"Can we eat with them, Uncle Jackson?" Taylor asked, looking hopeful.

He shook his head. "Oh, I don't think…"

"My mom said it was okay," Dani said quickly, moving in a seat to make room for Taylor on her side of the table.

Which meant Jackson—the world's biggest a-hole— would be sitting on her side. Wonderful.

Abigail wanted to say no, but Dani was already chatting happily to her friend. "It's fine. Please, have a seat." Her teeth were clenched so hard she'd need to start wearing her night mouthguard again.

Jackson looked just as happy about it as he sat in the empty chair beside her, moving it as far away as possible.

Ha! As if *she* was the one who smelled. It was he who'd obviously just come from the arena—the faint smell of sweat mixed with his soft aftershave…an all too familiar one, making her stomach tighten. She'd always loved Dean's fresh-from-practice smell, but she hadn't expected it to cause her pulse to race now on account of Jackson.

Damn.

Reaching for her glass, she took a sip of her drink, appetite gone. She looked longingly at the nachos, but there was no way she could polish them off now.

To starting over, she thought wryly. Yeah right. More like—To picking up right where she'd left off.

* * *

With his niece ignoring him across the table, Jackson took out his cell phone and opened a game of Candy Crush, while they waited for the food he'd ordered at the counter. He had no desire to make small talk with Abby, and he suspected she'd prefer the awkward silence as well.

Damn, why had she come back here? With a nice divorce settlement—which she would no doubt get from his friend—she could have moved anywhere…or stayed in L.A. But no, she'd moved back to Glenwood Falls to make his life miserable. Being around her before had been tough enough; now it would be torture. The only thing more off-limits than your best friend's girl was your best friend's ex-girl. And besides, the shit she was putting Dean through wasn't easy for him, a loyal lifelong friend, to swallow.

But damn, she looked good...And smelled better than the scent of apple pie baking in the restaurant's kitchen. Her soft, delicate perfume tickled his nose, and he hoped it helped to mask his sweaty self. He should have showered, but he hadn't expected to be sharing close quarters with the woman he'd never been able to get over.

"Mom says we're not allowed to use phones at the table," her little girl said, glancing at him.

His first instinct was to respond, *Your mom's not the boss of me,* but before he could say anything, Taylor spoke up. "Yeah, Uncle Jackson. You know the rules."

He was getting schooled by preteens. He sighed and tucked the phone away. He glanced around the nearly empty restaurant. Nearly empty. They could have had any table in the place.

Beside him, Abby cleared her throat. At least he thought that's what she was doing. She might have been choking on pride. It was hard to say.

She did it again and he turned to face her. "Need a drink?" Man, that sound must have driven Dean nuts.

That's it—focus on the one flaw you can find in her.

She glared at him briefly, then after a deep breath, said, "So, you're still coaching the Junior team."

His jaw clenched. She could make that statement sound casual, but he heard the meaning behind it. What she was really saying was *So, you still haven't made it as a professional hockey player like your brothers and best friend.* "Yes I am. And you're back living with your parents." He couldn't help it. She'd touched a nerve. Correction: she *had* nerve.

"Only temporarily. Once the di..." She stopped. "It's a temporary thing."

"Until you can find another ticket out of here?"

When her expression changed to one of raw hurt, he immediately wished he could suck the words back in. That was too far. Damn it. They should have just let him play Candy Crush.

Recovering quickly, but not fast enough, she turned in her seat ready to argue. "Are we really going to do this?" she asked, her eyes the color of the blue circle at center ice and just as cold.

He sighed. "No. Let's not." Best to leave things unsaid.

As usual.

* * *

"How was school?" Becky Westmore asked her daughter as they entered her home an hour later.

"Fantastic. I scored twice on Uncle Jackson, and he says my drills are faster than any of the boys on the team last year," his niece said, tossing her backpack into the hall closet.

His sister rolled her eyes at him. "I asked about school, not hockey. Man, can we talk about anything else in this family, just once?"

He kissed her cheek. "Sorry, sis. The curse of having all brothers, I guess."

"Yes, I know. I just thought I was getting a break from all of it when the ultrasound revealed I was having a girl," she said.

"Well, maybe this time you'll actually get a *real* girl," Taylor said, hugging her mother's pregnant belly. "Hello, in there," she said to the stomach.

Becky laughed and kissed her daughter's head. "Start your homework."

"Don't have any," she said, opening the fridge and grabbing a soda.

Jackson opened the closet door and retrieved the backpack. Tossing it at his niece, he said, "If your grades drop, I can't let you be on the team, so start studying. I plan on keeping the championship trophy in the school's display case." Three years in a row, he'd coached the Junior league team to a win and with his niece on the team this year, he expected an easy fourth victory.

"Fine," Taylor grumbled, grabbing an oatmeal chocolate chip cookie from the counter and heading upstairs before her mother could stop her.

When she was out of earshot, he said, "She really is doing great, though. Even better than last year." He, too, reached for a homemade cookie cooling on the rack, and his sister slapped his hand, forcing him to drop it. "Hey!"

"Those are for the school bake sale on Sunday." She collapsed into a chair, looking exhausted. "They're back to school two weeks and already they have a fundraising event." She shook her head. "Don't they know some of us are pregnant and exhausted?"

He sat across from her and grinned. "Mom of the year, as usual," he said, his thoughts immediately turning to Abby and the odd, somewhat strained relationship he'd seen between her and her daughter in the school hallway and again at dinner.

It was the first time he'd even met Dean's little girl, and he felt guilty that over the years he'd basically gone out of his way to avoid Abby and Dani. It wasn't that he didn't want to get to know the child; he just wasn't sure he could handle seeing the family together. Up until nine months ago, when news of a suspected divorce hit newsstands, his buddy had had it all: the successful NHL career, the beautiful wife and family…everything Jackson had wanted for himself. Exactly everything.

The little girl looked just like Dean. It was hard to find traces of her mother in her at all, and according to Taylor on the way home, Dani's personality matched her father's as well. Taylor had gushed about how great it was to finally have another girl friend who loved hockey and knew as much about the game as she did.

He was happy his niece had a cool new friend; he just wished it wasn't Abby's daughter. Coaching next door to the school meant he would see her far too often already.

"Are you even listening to me?" his sister said across the table.

"Yeah, of course. You were saying you were exhausted…" And that was the last thing he'd heard.

"Yeah, about three minutes ago. I just gave you a complete run down of the *Desperate Hearts* episode today, complete with plot insights from yours truly, and you missed it all." She stood and grabbed a cookie and took a bite.

He laughed as he stood and took the rest of her cookie. "As much as I love hearing about your daytime soap opera addiction, I do have a lot on my mind, you know."

"Like Abby Jansen?"

He coughed as he choked on the bite he'd just taken.

Becky reached into the fridge and grabbed a soda. Opening it, she handed it to him.

He took a gulp to wash down the piece of cookie stuck in his throat.

"I take that as a yes," his sister said with a smirk.

"You're wrong. I don't even know what you're talking about. Abby's back in town?" He tried to sound nonchalant, but he suspected his sister wasn't buying the act.

"Okay, I'll play along. Yes she's back in town. Taylor

is her daughter's student mentor and hasn't stopped talking about how awesome she is all week."

He nodded, giving up the act. "She may have mentioned that…and we may have run into them at the Slope and Hatch."

"Aha! I knew I'd seen that look on your face before." Taking an oven mitt from the counter, she opened the door and retrieved a chicken and veggie casserole.

Despite having already eaten, or at least having tried to eat in the awkward company of Abby, his stomach growled as the smell of her homemade garlicky white wine sauce reached his nose. Annoying as she was, his sister was still the best cook he knew. "What look?"

"That pathetic, lovesick look you used to get over…"

"I don't know what you're talking about," he said quickly. His sister was the only one who knew about his feelings for Abby, but certainly not because he'd admitted to them. Ever.

"Fine," she said with a sigh. "Keep on denying it."

He would. Till his dying day. He watched as she cut the casserole, his mouth watering.

"I suppose you want a piece to go?" she asked, pointing the knife at him.

"Yes. Why else do you think I came in here? Because I like your abuse?"

She popped a serving into a plastic container and handed it to him, adding a cookie on top of the lid. "Bring my containers back. I'm running out."

"You keep filling 'em, I'll keep bringing 'em back."

CHAPTER 4

❧

*W*hen her cell phone rang Tuesday morning at six thirty, Abigail lifted her head and fumbled around the bedside table for it, blinking the sleep out of her eyes. Seeing the Glenwood Falls Elementary number lighting up the display, she quickly sat up and forced her voice to sound as though she'd been awake for hours. "Hello?"

"Hi, Abigail, this is Liz calling from Glenwood Falls Elementary," the receptionist said.

"Yes, hi, Liz."

"I apologize for the short notice, but one of our second grade teachers called in sick this morning, so can you make it in?"

She was nodding. Second grade. She could do second grade.

"Abigail?"

"Oh, yes. Definitely. Not a problem. I love second grade." Shut up, Abigail.

"Okay, well, just stop by the office and we will give you today's lesson plan and everything you need."

"Great. Yes. Will do." She disconnected the call and jumped out of bed. Her first day teaching! This was…She paused. Absolutely terrifying. Her excitement faded to anxiousness as she grabbed a towel and headed for the bathroom down the hall.

In the shower a minute later, she tried desperately to remember back two years to Dani's second grade experience. Double addition…the introduction to chapter books…She could add. She could read.

She had this.

Three hours later she stood staring at twenty blank expressions staring right back at her.

She *so* did not have this.

She cleared her throat and forced a deep breath. "Hello, everyone. I am Ms. Jansen, your substitute teacher for today…" In movies, they always wrote their name on the board. Seemed like as good as any place to start, so she did.

And underlined it. Twice.

Good, she thought nodding her approval at her own name in white chalk across the black board.

Now what?

She opened the file from the office and saw the math tests on top. "Well, it looks like we have a math test today," she said.

A collective groan went through the classroom. A hand in the back shot up.

"Yes…" She glanced down at the seating chart with all the students' names on it taped to the corner of the desk. "Matthew," she said, glancing back up at the boy.

"I've seen you on TV."

Okay. "That's possible. I assume it was a commercial for

Dreams for Life?" She'd been the spokesperson for the charity for two years, and the television commercials were the things she'd enjoyed least. She preferred getting her hands dirty behind the scenes, raising money and organizing events.

"Yeah. My mom said you are married to Dean Underwood, the right wing for the L.A. Kings," the boy said.

A murmur went through the rows.

Technically that was still true until the papers were signed. "Um…yes. Anyway, back to this math test. Who will volunteer to hand them out?" She scanned the classroom.

A little girl—Ashley—in the front row raised her hand. "I will."

"Great, thank you." She handed them to her.

Matthew raised his hand again.

"Yes, Matthew?"

"Are you getting a divorce?"

Man, what was with this kid? "Do you have any other questions? About the math test maybe?"

He shook his head no.

"Okay then. Once you all have your tests in front of you, you may begin." A minute later, all heads were bent over their papers and Abigail sat in the chair.

Immediately, her skirt felt wet.

Her eyes widened as she quickly stood back up and glanced toward the seat. Red Jell-O was spread all over it and now covered the back of her three-hundred-dollar pencil skirt. She clenched her teeth as she reached for a tissue to wipe the globs of red goo from her butt.

Giggles could be heard in the room, but she silenced them all with one stern look.

Welcome to the world of substitute teaching, she thought. Though admittedly she'd take pranks over personal questions any time.

*   *   *

She'd survived.

Along with her students, Abigail watched the clock on the wall count down the final seconds to the end of day bell. When it rang, she almost joined them in the squeal of delight. This teaching shit was hard.

"Okay, dismissed. Thank you…" she said, gathering her things.

"Will Mr. Thompson be back tomorrow?" Ashley asked as she passed the desk.

God, she hoped so. She thought maybe she'd do better with older kids…or younger ones. Second grade children were brats. "Let's hope for a speedy recovery," she said with a tired smile.

When all the kids were gone, she breathed a sigh of relief, then straightened again as Principal Breen came into the classroom. "Hi," she said, forcing her voice to sound upbeat despite the mental exhaustion she felt and the aching arches in her feet. No more three-inch heels for teaching.

"How was your first day?" the older woman asked, glancing around the classroom.

Abigail rushed to collect all of the science worksheets from the desks. "Great. The kids are…"

"Monsters," she finished with a smile. "I assume that's Jell-O on your skirt?"

Busted. "Yes, I think so…I hope so." She stacked the worksheets into the file and handed everything to the principal.

"It's tougher than it looks, huh?"

She had no idea what the right answer was. She didn't want to appear arrogant and overconfident, when it was the last thing she felt. Nor did she want to give the woman the impression she couldn't handle it. Or that she'd made a mistake taking a chance on her. "It was definitely a challenge, but in a good way."

Principal Breen nodded. "Well, they are all still alive—and so are you—so I'd call that a win."

Abigail smiled at the unexpected kindness. "Thank you."

"The other reason I wanted to catch you before you left for the day was I wanted to see if you might be interested in taking over the fundraising committee. Kelli Fitzgerald is currently in charge, but with her maternity leave, we will be looking to fill that responsibility as well. Even if the teaching position doesn't work out, that would still be a way to be involved with the school."

Abigail hesitated. She was more concerned with having gainful employment than in being involved with the school, but if she agreed to take over the role, it could only help her chances of securing the full-time position at the end of the following month. "Sure. I'd love to." She was getting really good at exaggerating lately.

Principal Breen smiled. "Wonderful. The next committee meeting is tomorrow night at seven."

She nodded. "I'll be there."

As the principal left the classroom, Dani entered. Finally a kid she liked.

"Hi!" Abigail said, hugging her.

"How did it go?" her daughter asked.

"Good…except for the Jell-O," she said, turning to show her daughter her red-stained butt.

Dani's laughter made the ruined fabric worthwhile.

"You think it's funny, do you?"

"Hilarious. We used to prank substitutes at school all the time." She covered her mouth as another giggle escaped.

"You could have warned me," she said, grabbing her jacket and tying it around her waist. "Ready to go home?"

Her daughter hesitated, biting her lip and staring at her hands.

Uh-oh, something was up. "Dani, you okay?"

"I want to try out for the hockey team," she blurted out.

Her chest tightened. "Okay…" Her daughter wanting to play hockey shouldn't surprise her, but somehow it did, and not in a good way. She'd noticed the sports announcements on the bulletin board outside the gym, but this was the first she was hearing about Dani's interest in trying out for any teams. "When are the tryouts?"

"Tonight. Taylor is trying out, and she said I should, too."

Right, Taylor. And her hockey coach uncle. "Well, you don't have any gear." She didn't want to sound unsupportive, but hockey was one sport she'd had quite enough of for one lifetime. The idea of going from a hockey wife to a hockey mom made her gag.

"Taylor said her skates and helmet from last year should fit me. And she said the other gear is provided for tryouts. That way parents won't have to buy anything unless their kid makes the team."

Taylor had thought of everything, hadn't she? She hesitated, staring at her daughter's eager, nervous face, and it hit her how hard this must have been for Dani. Waiting until the last minute to ask was a sure sign she'd been dreading the conversation, and Abigail's chest ached. She never wanted her daughter to feel anxious about talking to her about anything. She forced a smile and bent lower to hug her. "Of course you can try out."

Dani hugged her back. "Really? Thanks, Mom. You're the best," she said excitedly as she took her hand and led the way out of the classroom.

Would Dani still feel that way if she knew Abigail was secretly hoping her daughter didn't make the team?

* * *

Shit, the kid was good.

One quick glance across the arena to where Abby stood watching revealed she was thinking the exact same thing. The mixed look of admiration, pride, and oh-fuck-no on her face was easy enough to read, even from that distance.

But despite everything, he begrudgingly gave her credit for bringing Dani to the tryout in the first place. When Taylor had mentioned that her new friend would be there that evening, he'd been tempted to tell his niece not to get her hopes up. He suspected Abby was no longer the die-hard hockey enthusiast she'd once been. But she was there to support her daughter; that was impressive.

Unfortunately so was her perfectly curvy ass in the skin-tight skinny jeans she wore tucked into knee-high leather boots. Damn, why couldn't her kid have sucked? Having Abby around the arena for practice and at the games would be torture. Or at the very least a distraction he couldn't afford.

But Dani was a natural on skates. Her puck handling needed work, as he doubted she'd had much experience with it, but she was keeping up with the drills, and she was small but fast on the ice. She moved around the boys with a delicate ease that seemed to confuse them, trip them up.

And she was determined. She was working harder out there than anyone else, and he always said hard work and determination outdid talent any day.

Just not in his case.

"She's good," Darryl said, coming up behind him with coffee.

He accepted one from his assistant coach and took a sip, the hot liquid burning his throat. "Yep."

"Like really good…almost better than some of the boys."

"Yep."

"So, I assume she's on the team?" Darryl asked.

He released a deep sigh. "Yep."

*   *   *

"I made the team! I made the team!"

Dani's high-pitched squeal almost sent the SUV off of the road. Abigail straightened the vehicle and shot a quick glance at her daughter. "How do you know?" They'd just left the hockey arena ten minutes before.

Her daughter held her phone in front of her face.

"Driving!" she said, looking above the phone. "Is that a message from Taylor?" she asked nervously. She wasn't surprised. From where she stood watching and not breathing, her daughter looked like a natural. She'd reminded her of Dean out there on the ice.

An image that had caused her stomach to twist and knot in more ways than she'd thought possible. Being at the old arena where she'd watched Dean practice and play, where they'd shared their first kiss in the parking lot, and where she'd told him she was pregnant, was hard. Old memories had a way of overshadowing new ones sometimes, making it difficult to remember why she was back in Glenwood Falls, divorcing him and building a new life without the man she'd thought she would grow old with.

Beside her, her daughter texted furiously.

"Well, congratulations, sweetheart," she said, hoping it

sounded sincere. Her little girl was genuinely excited and she wouldn't rain on her parade, even though she'd been hoping to leave all traces of a hockey life behind.

"Thanks for letting me try out, Mom. I know how you feel about hockey lately…" she said, suddenly quiet, her gaze out the passenger window.

Abigail refused to let her daughter feel one second of unhappiness over this. "Hey," she said, touching Dani's cheek.

Her daughter turned to look at her.

"I was only anti-hockey because I'd lost my favorite player for a while, but now it looks like I'll have a new one," she said with a wink.

Her daughter smiled. "I could skate circles around Dad," she said, and the two shared a brief moment of girl-power bonding that had Abigail's hopes soaring.

They were going to be okay.

* * *

After relacing his skates, Jackson stepped out onto the rink. The kids were gone and all of the arena employees had cleared out and it was just him and the blank sheet of cold ice between his thoughts.

Lou, the Zamboni driver, always had to clear the ice before the first skate of the day, but no one ever said anything to him about his late-night skates. It was his routine, his time to unwind, his chance to play the entire season out in his head and decide which players he was going to push, which ones would push themselves, and which of the group had that special something that would see them rise above the others.

As he picked up speed approaching the first corner of the rink, the charge of lightning through his legs he felt when he was on the ice, was slow coming that evening.

He was worried about the season.

Worried about the changes to the league and how they would affect not only the team but the individual players and their families. He knew some of these kids had bigger dreams and aspirations for hockey. Others just wanted to play the game.

And some would dream big and never quite make it.

Like him.

An old-school defensive player in a changing sport, he was doomed. On the ice he knew one job—get between his team's goalie and any opposing player. He watched the game unfold from behind the blue line. Tall, thick, and not the most elegant skater on the team, he blocked and shielded and stopped his goalie's visibility from being obstructed. But when he had the puck, he passed. He gave it to an offensive player whose job it was to score.

But major leagues were looking for dynamic players who could play both sides of the line.

Maybe if he'd realized that sooner. He'd been so close. Despite getting drafted at eighteen by the Avalanche, he'd decided to go the college route, agreeing with his parents that an education to fall back on was the right plan. But his low-scoring college years had landed him nowhere near the Avalanche training camp the year he graduated. Instead, he'd been sent to play for the Colorado Eagles—a holding team for the league in Loveland.

The next four years had been torture. While most players on the East Coast Hockey League team found peace with their situation, enjoyed playing for the $30,000-a-year pay-check, and picked up a side job to survive, he couldn't let go of the dream. The NHL was within reach, and his brother Ben, playing with the Avalanche, was proof that it was possible.

So he played with as much determination and heart as ever and it paid off. Four and a half years in, he was called up.

And benched for three games.

And sent back to Loveland.

The disappointment of being even closer to the goal and not getting a chance to prove himself on NHL ice had broken him. Then his father had gotten sick and worry about his family had stolen his focus completely. Once the ECHL season ended, he packed up, quit the team, and moved back to Glenwood Falls, grateful for his business degree backup plan and his construction skills learned from his father.

As he picked up speed, the blades of his well-worn skates cutting through the surface of the ice, he thought about his niece. She understood the game. She worked behind the blue line, stealing the puck from the opposite team's offense with ease, but then she flew across the ice with it, scoring when it wasn't her job to do so.

At first, he'd tried to remind her of her position on the team. "Stay back in your zone. Protect your goalie at all times," he'd said.

But she'd just smiled and said, "As long as I have the puck, my goalie *is* safe, right?"

And he couldn't argue. She'd been right. And as he watched his brother Asher, a defenseman for the New Jersey Devils, play each and every major league game, the little girl's words had been confirmed. Asher played the same way. It was his ability on both sides of the blue line that made him great. That gave him the highest scoring percentage among the list of defensemen in the league.

Jackson's own defensive-minded strategy of keeping guard, playing the role of the stay-at-home bruiser who rarely ventured beyond his zone with the puck, was the thing that had held him back. And slowly he was learning not to coach his players into that same limiting mindset.

As he did his tenth lap around the rink, his thoughts shifted to Dani and her ability to see where the puck was headed before it left her stick. Her spatial awareness on the ice was incredible...one of those rare traits that couldn't be taught...they had to be felt.

She was Dean Underwood's daughter, and she would be playing on his team.

And Dean's ex-wife would be around to remind him of the other things in life that had been slightly out of reach.

He was screwed.

CHAPTER 5

∽◦∾

*W*ith the official list of that year's team players posted and individual letters sent home to the parents, there was nothing Abigail could do other than embrace her daughter's new extracurricular activity with all the enthusiasm and support she could muster.

Yet staring at the price tag for the new hockey skates made her wince. Hockey was an expensive sport, one that wouldn't have been a big deal a year ago. Now as she was struggling to build a new life for them without Dean's support, the idea of spending three hundred dollars on hockey skates that would only last one season, if they were lucky, made her ill.

Up until that week, she'd never worked, focusing instead on raising Dani and working on the Dreams for Life charity. Dean's income had been more than sufficient in providing everything they'd needed. With his eight-year contract with the L.A. Kings, he'd been guaranteed stability and over $24 million for the term. Three million dollars a year should have been enough for them to never worry about money in their lifetime, but between the $2 million home in L.A. and Dean's car collection and other expensive hobbies, they'd barely put anything away. The following year, his contract would be up and he would be a free agent. She wondered what his plan was then.

She shook the thought away. It wouldn't be her problem anymore.

"Do you need help with anything?" a store clerk at Rolling's Sports asked, as he surveyed the stack of required hockey gear she'd collected so far.

"I think I found everything okay," she said, reaching for the items. One way or another, Dani needed this stuff. Practices started that Friday after school.

At the counter, she averted her eyes as the tally added up.

"Five hundred and eighty-six dollars please," the clerk said, admiring the elbow guards. "These are fantastic. I just bought a set and they are so much better than the other brands."

They better be. At seventy dollars more, she hoped they would protect her little girl from damaged joints. She bit her lip. She still wasn't sure how she felt about Dani playing hockey—she was so little, and the teams were co-ed. Surely the bigger, stronger boys weren't a fair match-up.

"Five hundred and eighty-six," the young kid repeated.

"Oh, right, sorry," she said, opening her wallet and retrieving her credit card. Dean's credit card.

The clerk swiped it and frowned a second later. "It says declined. Should I try again?"

She nodded, her stomach twisting. "Yes, please."

"Nope, sorry. Still declined," he said a second later.

Shit. Her ex had just taken douchebag to a whole new level. Reaching into her wallet, Abigail handed him her debit card instead. Please, God, let there be enough money in there. She'd never worried about it before. Dean would always transfer money into her account for her and Dani every month, and they'd lived worry-free, knowing there was always money there. The credit cards were different; they were in his name only, and she just had a card to access funds as needed—or *used to have* a card.

She punched in her account PIN and held her breath until the APPROVED notification appeared on the screen. Thank God.

"Receipt with you or in the bag?" the clerk asked.

"In the bag is fine," she said, accepting the heavy over-sized bag. "Thank you."

As she left the store, she reached into her purse for her cell phone, her hand shaking as she hit dial on her ex's number. He'd never answer when he saw her number on his phone, but she had a fully prepared earful to give his voicemail. If he thought he could just walk away with no responsibility to her and Dani, he was dead wrong.

"Hello?" Dean's gruff, unfriendly voice caught her by surprise, and she almost hung up.

"You canceled my credit card."

"It's my credit card, and yes, my lawyer suggested that I should," he said tightly.

"So, how am I supposed to support our daughter while you continue to drag out this divorce settlement?" She lowered her voice as a family walked past her into the store.

"Get a job maybe," was his cool reply.

"I have one. Teaching," she said, switching the phone to the other ear and changing hands for the heavy bag. The position wasn't a definite thing yet, but he didn't need to know that.

"So what's the problem?"

"The problem is I don't appreciate having my cards declined in the middle of a store."

"You're lucky the debit card still works," he said, and she could hear the sound of music and clanging dishes in the background. No doubt he was enjoying lunch on a beautiful patio somewhere overlooking the ocean.

God, she missed L.A., she thought as a cool breeze rustled the leaves on the sidewalk at her feet.

"Look, please just sign the divorce settlement papers and let's get this over with." Olivia Davis had told her over and over again she was asking for far too little in the settlement given the circumstances, but she didn't care. She just wanted out.

"I'm not signing anything until we can reach a better agreement."

Her anger rose. She couldn't believe the thing they were still fighting over was money. As relieved as she was about not having a custody battle to deal with, she couldn't not address the issue of the visitation schedule. "Olivia told me you're not signing the visitation arrangement. I can't believe you don't want to commit to time with Dani." She still hadn't told their little girl, and she was dreading the conversation. In the last few days things had started to get better between them, and she feared Dani would think this was her fault.

"Don't make me out to be some monster. You know I can't commit when I have no idea where I will be next year." As a free agent, he could get drafted to a different team. "Between regular season, playoffs, and summer training…"

"Yes, I know all about the schedule." She'd planned their lives around it for too many years. She reached her vehicle and rested the phone against her shoulder as she opened the back door and tossed the bag inside.

"Besides, have you even asked Dani what she wants, or is this all about you? Your way of forcing me to be more involved."

Her mouth fell and she stood frozen. Forcing him to be more involved? Was he kidding? If she had things her way, she'd never have to deal with him again. Unfortunately they had a daughter together, and what was best for Dani was her priority. Her chest tightened. She'd been the primary caregiver since the day she was born, but Dani adored her father and cherished the little time they did spend together. "Dani would be crushed if she knew you didn't sign the arrangement. Despite everything, she's still your daughter."

"Listen, I don't have time for the guilt trip. I have to go. If Dani needs something, tell her to call me and I'll send the money directly to her. I don't feel comfortable discussing all of this with you. That's why we're paying lawyers."

That's what their relationship had been reduced to—arguing through strangers. Despite the nasty circumstances surrounding the divorce, it saddened her to realize how quickly things could change from enduring love and commitment to bitter anger and hostility.

Abigail swallowed hard, her pride making her regret calling him in the first place. She would have to get used to that never being an option. "She's fine. We are fine," she said before disconnecting the call.

As she climbed into the SUV, she debated calling her lawyer. Unfortunately, her gut told her Dean had every right to cancel the credit cards, and she'd be smart to set up a new bank account in her own name here in Glenwood Falls as soon as possible as well. She was no longer tied to her ex emotionally, and she needed to sever all financial ties as well as soon as possible.

She checked her watch. It was almost six thirty. The

fundraising committee meeting at the school started in half an hour, and now more than ever she needed to make a great impression on Principal Breen. Money may have been something she hadn't stressed over in the past, but she suspected that was about to change—at least temporarily—and she needed to start taking control of this other aspect of her life.

*   *   *

The last thing Jackson needed to finalize for that year's team was the new Glenwood Falls Lightning jerseys. The school provided funding for them from the previous season's fundraising efforts once the team was announced. So walking into the school office to put in the request should have been easy. Instead, he found himself hesitating at the door. Abby had been appointed the new head of the school's fundraising efforts the evening before, his sister had informed him. She'd also informed him of how good she thought Abby looked.

"Amazing body for a woman who's had a child, and not a gray hair or wrinkle to be seen. I should have married a hockey player and not an Air Force pilot who's gone all the freaking time," she'd said, arriving home after the school meeting. He'd been hanging out with Taylor and trying to help out by folding the heaps of laundry on the sofa.

He knew not to take her comments about Neil seriously. He'd never seen two people more in love than his sister and her new husband. But her comments about Abby had been spot-on. She hadn't aged a day since she'd left Glenwood Falls nine years ago, and it would have made his life a whole lot easier had she had the decency to look a little less perfect.

Opening the door, he entered the office and smiled at Liz.

"Hey, Coach. When's the first game of the season?" she asked.

Liz and her husband, Mark, never missed a Junior league home game. Not since their son had played years before. "In two weeks." He hoped he was able to work out the kinks in his new team by then. The first practice was the next evening, and he was still a little worried about how the boys who'd been playing on the team for three years would feel about the new co-ed structure.

"We'll be there," she said, marking it on her wall calendar.

"Great." He glanced toward the teachers lounge where the door was propped open and he could see a pair of tanned bare feet with French manicured toes poking out behind the doorframe. Very few women had a beautiful sun-kissed glow in Colorado in the fall, and his palms sweat a little as he asked Liz, already knowing the answer, "Is…uh…Abby here?"

"You mean *Abigail*?" she asked with a look.

Ah, so she wasn't going by her old nickname anymore. Too bad. He'd only ever referred to her as Abby—in real life and in his inappropriate dreams about her—and he sure as hell wasn't about to stop now. "She in there?" he asked, pointing to the lounge. He'd recognize those ankles anywhere. It was pathetic, really.

"Yep," she said as the phone rang and she excused herself to answer it.

He took a deep breath and walked into the staff lounge.

Abby sat on the couch, several file folders on the seat next to her and test papers spread out on the coffee table, next to a coffee mug with a faded Glenwood Falls Elementary logo on it. She obviously didn't hear him enter as she continued to work, and he took a second just to look at her. She'd always been beautiful, and time hadn't changed that. Nor had it dulled the ache in his chest that killed him every time he saw her, knowing she wanted nothing to do with him. How many times over the years had he tried to forget about her? Telling himself holding out for a woman he couldn't have was pointless. But common sense and self-preservation went straight out the window the moment she walked back into his life…available once more, but still out of reach.

He cleared his throat. The hockey jerseys. He was just here for the hockey jerseys.

When she looked up, her eyes widened for a brief second before they took on a look of annoyance. She had no idea why he was there, and already she was irritated? Wow. Had he always had this effect on her? His jaw clenched.

"Hi," she said curtly.

"Hey…I need to put in the request for funding for the new hockey team uniforms."

"Oh, okay." She looked around her at the mess of papers.

Not exactly the most organized teacher he'd ever seen. But definitely the sexiest, he thought as she leaned forward and he was offered a glimpse down her blouse. The slight swell of her tanned breasts spilling over the top of her bra made his mouth go dry.

"Just a sec. I know that file is here…somewhere."

Stepping forward, he reached past her on the couch and picked up the blue file folder with SCHOOL FUNDRAISER ACTIVITIES written across the tab. "This one maybe?"

She took it. "That's it." She opened it and flipped through the pages. Locating the junior hockey league's funding spreadsheet, she scanned it quickly. "So, it looks like there is…"

"Seven hundred and forty-two dollars and sixteen cents

in the budget. Yes, I know." His own blood, sweat, and tears had gone into raising that money along with the team last year. Everything from bottle drives to chocolate bar sales, he'd been the one encouraging the efforts.

"Right. So, what do you need?" She picked up her pen and waited. Strands of her long blonde hair escaped the loose, messy bun at the back of her head, and she tucked them behind one ear.

So many times he'd imagined what that silky hair would feel like falling against his chest or under his lips…The temptation to touch it now, to tangle his fingers in it, messing it up even further, took all his strength to fight. He didn't know what it was about her that had him so completely, foolishly head over skates, but resisting her was getting harder and harder. The only thing holding him back from making a move was her obvious disdain for him whenever they were forced to share the same air.

She glanced up at him from the couch. "You still with me?" she asked, waving a hand in front of his dazed expression.

He cleared his throat and mind. "Yeah, we need three hundred and fifty-four of that for the new uniforms."

She jotted down the number and subtracted the total from their budget. "Do you need anything else?"

Yes, a lot more.

He shook his head. "That's it, thanks." He turned to leave, then swung back. "Actually, there was something." He reached into his back pocket for a rolled permission form. "We'll need this filled out before the first practice. You guys left the other night before I handed them out."

She took the release and scanned it. "Didn't I already sign one of these for tryouts?"

"That was just for tryouts. This one asks for more

information and needs to be signed by both parents or legal guardians," he said. He wasn't sure if Dean knew about Dani playing hockey yet, but the way Abby's eyes clouded made him think not. Which was odd. He would have thought she would have been excited to tell her dad. Were they not keeping in touch with Dean since moving to Glenwood Falls? Were things really that bad?

He hadn't spoken to Dean since his separation from Abby, which was odd, too. They usually Skyped several times a year, and he made the trip to L.A. each summer for a visit, but that year the timing hadn't lined up for both of them. He'd called him several times and left unreturned messages, but other than seeing his buddy's recent Facebook posts, he'd had little contact with him for almost a year. Though in the pics of Dean with that Dallas Stars cheerleader, it appeared his friend wasn't having too hard of a time with his recent divorce. Jackson shook the thoughts away. Not his problem or his business.

"Well, Dean's in L.A…" Abby was saying.

"We can scan and email it to him, and he can sign and return the same way."

"Okay. Fine. Thank you." She tucked the form into the purse next to her on the couch and returned to the work in front of her.

"Oh, one last thing. What name does Dani want on the back of her jersey?" He knew the answer for the other kids on the team, but hadn't wanted to assume on this one. He'd rush order Dani's jersey from the pro-shop to have it for her the following evening.

Abby blinked. "Her last name, I guess."

"Which is?"

She looked panicked, as though he'd just asked her a trick question. "Um…I guess it would be Jansen-Underwood."

No way. He refused to do that to the poor kid. "No. Hyphenating your child's name is just cruel. Pick one."

She didn't hesitate. "Fine. Jansen."

His jaw clenched. "Her name isn't Underwood?" That was where her talent came from. Dean deserved that much credit at least.

"Not for long…" she muttered. "Jansen's fine."

"Are you sure?"

"One hundred percent."

The staredown that followed could have made the entire building implode. Her hard, unreadable expression made him want to grab her and kiss the annoyance from her face. The tension lingered so thick between them it was hard to breathe, and his own resolve was quickly fading as the urge to shut the staff room door and give in to the impulse he'd been fighting since he was nine years old grew stronger.

"Maybe we should ask Dani," he said finally, the words coming out on a long sigh. She probably hadn't had much say in any of the changes happening in her life these days, but she should at least get a say in this.

"Ask me what?" the nine-year-old herself asked, entering the office as the final school bell rang. "Hi, Coach," she said with a wide smile.

He returned it. Perfect timing. She'd just saved her mother from being kissed senseless. "How's my newest offenseman?"

"Offensewoman," Abby corrected.

"It's a non-gender-specific term, Mom," Dani said.

Abby sighed. "Anyway, now that you're here, Coach Westmore was wondering what name you wanted on the back of your jersey."

Dani's gaze lowered. "Um…"

"Whatever you decide is fine," Abby said, and to her

credit she sounded sincere, even though seconds before she was pushing for the Jansen name.

"I'd like to have Underwood, if that's okay," she said.

If Abby was disappointed, she hid it well. "Great. Then Underwood it is," she said, avoiding his gaze and busying herself collecting the papers.

"I just think people recognize that name so it might help, you know, with the other kids," Dani said.

"It's a good choice, Dani," he said, his eyes still on Abby. "You can never go wrong with an Underwood."

When her gaze met his, it was unreadable, but it made him wish he could once again swallow his words. He had to get his emotions in check. He could blame Abby for a lot of things—including dragging his best friend's name through the mud—but he couldn't blame her for not ever giving him the time of day.

He was the only one to blame for that.

The first time he'd seen Abby Jansen was the first day of second grade. His family had moved from Denver to Glenwood Falls when his mother decided to go back to work full time after his younger brother, Asher, started school. There was an open teaching position at the high school in the town. His father was a self-employed electrician and was just as happy living in the smaller town, where he didn't have to compete for work with bigger companies.

Led by their mother, he and his three siblings had walked into the principal's office to register, and there she was—the closest thing to an angel he thought he'd ever see. Long blonde hair, crystal blue eyes, and a toothless grin that had made his little heart pound and made him forget his own name when asked.

"I'm Abby," she'd said, standing next to three other

students he barely noticed. "I'm your student friend. I'm going to show you around school and help you settle in."

Ben had nudged him and whispered. "Someone's got a girlfriend already…"

And that was when he'd realized his brothers had both been assigned other boys their age to be their student friends. Why had he gotten stuck with a girl? A pretty girl who made his stomach do weird things and caused his tongue to swell?

"I don't need your help," he'd said.

She hadn't seemed fazed as she'd shrugged. "Okay, well, we're in the same class, so if you need…"

"I won't need help from a girl," he'd said, earning him a punch to the shoulder from Becky, who was three years older. He'd shot her a look, as the principal had led them all down the hall, stopping at each of their classrooms to introduce them to their new teachers: Becky in fifth grade, Ben in fourth, Asher in kindergarten, and he in second, with Abby.

When his new teacher told him to take a seat, he did, as far away from her as possible.

His avoidance strategy had started that first day of meeting her. Funny how even at such a young age, he'd known a girl like Abby would never fall for a boy like him.

"Let's go home," she was saying now to Dani as she slid her feet back into a pair of flats that reminded him of the ballet slippers his sister used to wear. Obviously she'd gotten smart and ditched the heels. Too bad; they'd made her calves look sexy as hell.

He turned his attention to the little girl. "I'll see you at practice tomorrow?"

She nodded in excitement. "Can't wait. It's going to be awesome," she said, glancing between him and her mother.

"Awesome," they both repeated in unison, neither with the same enthusiasm.

CHAPTER 6

❧

"What do you think, Grandma?" Dani did a quick turn in the living room entryway, showing off her new team jersey.

From where she stood near the door, keys in hand, waiting to take her daughter to her first hockey practice, Abigail prayed Dani had yet to learn her grandmother's facial expressions. This particular scrunching of the nose and wrinkling of the forehead combination was one Abigail had seen growing up quite often—it easily translated to *Are you out of your mind?*

"Doesn't she look great, *Grandma?*" she asked tightly, hoping her own agree-or-I'll-strangle-you expression was just as clear.

Her mother seemed to take the hint. "Oh yes, wow. Hockey, huh?" Her look of irritation was now redirected at Abigail, but at twenty-nine, she no longer cared. If hockey made her daughter happy, they all had to suck it up.

"Yeah. There were only two girls that made the team, and

I was one of them," Dani said, packing her new gear into the oversized duffel bag.

"Well, isn't that lucky?" Isabelle said.

"Not lucky at all. She worked really hard at tryouts, and Coach Westmore was smart enough to pick her as the newest right wing for the team."

"Coach Westmore? *Jackson* Westmore?"

"Well, it's certainly not Ben or Asher," Abigail said. She still couldn't believe Jackson's bad luck. Having both of his brothers playing in the NHL—a dream he'd always had for himself—couldn't be an easy pill to swallow. Not that she was prone to feeling sympathy for the man. In fact, after the awkward tension in the staff room, it was taking all her strength not to question any of the feelings she was suddenly experiencing. Usually his opinion of her was written all over his face, but that day, there was a different expression in his blue eyes. One that she couldn't quite put her finger on, but definitely had her on edge. His challenge over the jersey had sparked an electricity that she hadn't felt in a long time…a sensual energy that had almost knocked the wind from her lungs. Thank God Dani had entered when she had. Though she had no idea what would have happened if she hadn't. "Let's go, Dani."

Her mother stood, setting her cross-stitch aside. "Can I talk to you for a second?"

Oh, here we go. "Actually, Mom, can it wait? We only have fifteen minutes to get to the arena."

"This will take two," she said, disappearing into the kitchen.

Abigail turned to Dani and tossed her the keys to the SUV. "You can head out. I'll just be a second."

In the kitchen, Isabelle said, "Hockey? She's a little girl."

"And she wants to play. I don't see the problem." She

wasn't about to admit she'd seen countless problems with it over the last week since Dani had brought it up.

Her mother sighed. "And Jackson Westmore? He is *not* your friend, you know that right?"

Quite well. He'd never been anywhere near friendly, and she knew his loyalty was with Dean. She didn't plan on talking to him about anything other than hockey or the needed fundraising for the team, especially not after the other day.

But damn, even that sounded like a lot of awkward, tension-filled conversations with the man. "Don't worry, Mom. I haven't forgotten who I'm dealing with." She leaned forward and gave her mother a quick hug. "We have to go. Please try to be supportive, for Dani's sake?" she said, leaving the kitchen.

"I'll try," she muttered behind her. "But you could have at least insisted on putting *Jansen* on the back of the jersey."

*   *   *

"Is this the reluctant hockey moms' section?"

Abigail turned her attention to the woman standing next to her. She'd been so tormented waiting for Dani to leave the locker room, she'd barely noticed her approaching. "Becky?" Her eyes widened as she took in her old friend from high school. Jackson's older sister hadn't changed a bit: same shoulder-length brown hair with the flyaway unruly side bangs, the same crystal blue eyes that ran in their family, and the warm, welcoming smile that reflected her personality. Unlike her annoying, arrogant brothers, Becky was the one Westmore Abigail had always liked, and she was genuinely happy to see her. "Oh my God—hi," she said, leaning in to hug her quickly. "How are you?" She knew her friend had lost her first husband in a search and rescue accident a few years before.

"Well, remarried and pregnant again," she said, motioning to her belly straining against the buttons on her red, down-filled winter coat.

Abigail smiled. "How far along are you?" She'd guess about eight months.

"Twenty-two weeks."

Her eyes widened even further. Five and a half months? Maybe it *was* true that you gain more on second and third babies than you did on the first. She probably would never know.

"I knew it. I'm huge aren't I?"

"No!" Great. Insult one of the nicest women in town, probably one of the few who would welcome her and Dani back to Glenwood Falls with no preconceived judgments. "No. You look wonderful."

Becky grinned. "I'm teasing. I'm twenty-nine weeks and three days and seriously counting."

Abigail's shoulders relaxed. "That was mean."

"Sorry. Just thought you might need a distraction from worrying about Dani."

She was right about that. Arriving at the arena, Dani had immediately disappeared into the locker room, refusing Abigail's offer to help her get ready, and she'd been left alone to wander out to the bleachers, where her nerves could take over and every bad thing that could possibly happen came to mind. "I'm so nervous for her. How are you so calm and cool about this?"

"I'm not, but what choice do I have? We're a hockey family." She took a sip from a thermal mug and reached into her oversized purse for a soft cushion, placing it on the hard wooden bench before sitting.

Wow, she came prepared. Abigail sat on the peeling bench and tucked her frozen bare fingers under her legs. She should have remembered how cold the arena was, but when outside was ten degrees warmer, it was hard to remember the chilled air that smelled sharp, thanks to the ammonia injected into the cold brine running through the pipes under the ice to keep it frozen.

"So, I hear you're teaching at the school," Becky said, reaching into her coat pocket and handing her an extra pair of gloves.

Abigail accepted the warm, stretchy gloves gratefully. "Thank you." She slid her hands in. "Actually, I'm just subbing for now. I'm hoping for the full-time position once Kelli Fitzgerald goes on maternity leave."

"Our due dates are a week apart, but this is her first baby, so I'm hoping to race her to the hospital. There's bets going around on the PTA committee if you want to get in on it."

Abigail laughed. "You're okay with people betting on your delivery times?"

"It's a small town. We find amusement where we can get it. Besides, I started the whole thing." She took a sip from her mug. "Hot chocolate?" she offered.

"No, thank you."

"Well, it didn't take you long to get back into things. How's the fundraising committee?"

"Principal Breen must have caught me in a moment of insanity. I never thought there would be so much work involved with elementary school fundraising." The Dreams for Life charity had required work, but most of it involved charity dinners and golf tournaments with the players, hospital visits for sick children, that kind of thing. The school fundraising efforts were frequent and time-consuming— bake sales every month, bottle drives all year round, chocolate bar sales in the spring…Luckily Kelli had kept accurate records of everything.

When she glanced toward her, Becky was grinning above her mug.

"What?"

"Nothing." She shrugged.

"That look was not nothing. Out with it."

"I was just thinking about how your involvement is probably driving Jackson nuts."

Working together would be a challenge, but Abigail was hoping the time they'd actually have to spend together would be kept to a minimum. "Well, I'll do my best to stay out of his way if he stays out of mine."

"I'm not sure that's what he wants, but okay," Becky said. They heard the team coming down the hallway and Abigail had no time to question what she'd meant as Dani appeared at the arena door behind Taylor, dressed in her hockey gear and Glenwood Falls Lightning jersey.

Abigail's breath caught at the sight. She was at least a foot shorter than most of the other players, and even the smallest sized jersey hung down almost to her knees and loose around her shoulders. To say Abigail was questioning her decision would be an understatement.

"Relax, take a breath, Mom. This is just practice. Save the anxiety attacks for the real games," Becky said next to her.

Abigail nodded, but her hands clutched the bench beneath her. She'd never felt so anxious in her life. Her knees bounced and her heart echoed in her ears. She was going to need to start bringing a thermos with something much stronger than hot chocolate in it.

"Boo," a voice behind them said, as Dani and Taylor skated past on their warm-up.

Both moms swung around. The father of one of the other kids was grinning, but his expression was cold when his gaze met hers.

What the hell? She shot him her best sympathetic I'm-sorry-you're-such-an-idiot look and then moved closer to Becky. "Who's the a-hole?"

"Kurt Miller. Dex's dad," she muttered. "Jackson warned me there might be some hostility from him."

He hadn't warned *her*. A heads-up that some of the other hockey parents weren't thrilled about the new co-ed structure would've been nice. She wondered if it would have affected her decision to let Dani play. Would her daughter have reconsidered? Just the thought that it may have altered either of their decisions made her more furious at herself. Why should it matter?

"I take it he thinks girls shouldn't play hockey."

"Or any sport. Taylor was on Dex's soccer team this summer, and he had a stick up his butt about that, too. I've gotten used to his comments, and so far, Taylor seems either to not hear them or she's choosing to ignore them. Either way, it's not affecting her, but the moment it does…"

Momma bear would appear. Exactly.

Abigail stole another quick glance over her shoulder. "I don't recognize him. Should I?"

"Probably not. The family isn't from Glenwood Falls. In fact, the mom and the little girl live in Springdale, half an hour away. During the school year, Dex and his dad live here."

"Separation?"

"No. Kurt just wants Dex to play on a team coached by Jackson. He thinks the boy is headed for the NHL, and he wants to give him the best possible opportunity to make the A list on the Peewee team next year."

"Wow—that's dedication."

"It's not fair to Dex. I've watched the kid—he's fantastic, but he doesn't seem like he wants to play." Becky shook her head. "And then there's players like Taylor, who won't get the chance to even try out for the Peewee team next year…not the one that gets noticed anyway."

As the kids lined up on the ice, Abigail's gaze fell to Jackson. Was he really that great of a coach that Kurt Miller and his wife would live in separate towns for nine months a year just so the boy could play on this team? She knew the players had to live within a certain area to be considered, but it just seemed extreme. How much pressure would that put on the family? On the kid?

Was Jackson Westmore's coaching style that fantastic?

She watched as he skated to the side and grabbed a stack of bright orange pylons, placing them in a row on the ice, then instructed the kids to line up at one end. Going first, he demonstrated what he wanted them to do. Gliding across the ice was as natural for him as walking. It had been the same for Dean—so effortless and sexy as hell. She swallowed hard. Not that Jackson was sexy. He was arrogant and irritating and…fantastic with the kids, which was a whole different level of sexy, she thought as he skated backward, watching now as they zigzagged around the pylons. Once they reached the end, they'd select one of the pucks scattered on the ice around the blue line and take a shot toward the net, before rejoining the line.

When it was Dani's turn, her expression was unsure, which made Abigail's heart race once more. Was she afraid? Was she nervous? Was she having second thoughts about all of this?

But then Jackson skated over to her and leaning closer, he said something and the hesitation disappeared from Dani's face, replaced by a look of determination almost too intense for a nine-year-old. She readjusted her grip on her stick and skated between the pylons, shooting her puck at the end, where it sailed effortlessly into the open net.

The beam of pride on her face when she glanced quickly toward her made Abigail smile in relief.

Until her gaze locked with Jackson's just above her daughter's head. His own expression of pride made her heart stop completely. His smile was wide and unexpected, and her mouth went dry and her grip tightened on the seat. Annoyed, judgmental looks from Jackson Westmore she was used to, those she could handle. This rare glimpse of a friendly, kind Jackson was not something she'd been prepared for at all. Nor was her body's reaction to it. The fluttering in her stomach was…inconvenient, and so was the pesky thought that he looked amazing when he smiled. If only those smiles were directed at her more often.

She looked away quickly, turning her attention back to Dani, who was receiving high fives from her teammates as she skated to the back of the line. And when she dared to glance at Jackson again, he'd already turned his attention back to the team.

She sat staring at him, trying to comprehend what the hell had just happened.

"He's not as terrible as he seems," Becky whispered.

She scoffed. "That was the first smile I've ever seen directed at me. I think I'll reserve judgment a little longer," she said. It was going to take more than one heart-stopping smile to get her to change her long-held opinion about her ex-husband's best friend.

* * *

"Hey, Abby, can I talk to you for a second?" Jackson said, jogging up behind mother and daughter as they walked toward their vehicle in the arena parking lot an hour later.

She turned with a look of surprise. "Yeah, sure."

He stopped as they reached their SUV, and glanced at Dani. "I just need your mom for a sec. Why don't you hop on in?"

"Okay, Coach."

"Great practice today, by the way," he said to the little girl as she lugged her oversized hockey bag inside the backseat and shut the door.

"Thanks," she said, wearing the same happy look she'd had all evening. She may have been a little nervous at first, but it hadn't taken long or much encouragement to motivate her.

"Everything okay?" Abby asked as soon as Dani was out of earshot.

Other than the fact that the way their gazes had held during practice had completely thrown him off his coaching that evening? Sure, everything was great. "Yeah. I just wanted to let you know we didn't receive the signed release form from Dean yet." He'd checked the folder twice that afternoon for it, but had only found the one with Abby's signature on it.

Her expression hardened. "Of course not," she said.

"I let her practice tonight without it, but I'll need to have it on file before Tuesday," he said, zipping his coat higher against the cool, evening breeze.

"Tuesday?"

He nodded. Obviously Abby had no idea of the time commitment Dani had just signed her up for. "Practices are Tuesday, Friday, and Sunday. Games are usually Saturdays."

"Tuesday, Friday, and Sunday." She nodded. "Okay. No

problem. I'll call Dean this weekend and make sure he emails the form back to the school," she said, fidgeting with her purse strap.

Obviously it *was* a problem. And he didn't get it. The hurt and anger he saw in Abby's eyes whenever Dean's name was mentioned was so foreign to him. So different from the look of adoration her younger face used to wear whenever he was around. Their love for one another had been on display for everyone to see.

Even those who'd rather not have had a front row seat to it.

Annoyance overshadowed his common sense as he said, "Does he know that she's playing hockey?"

Abby's eyes narrowed. "Dani called him and left a voicemail yesterday, and I sent him the release form, so I'm assuming he does, yeah."

He nodded. "Okay…" He turned to leave, but against his better judgment he turned back. "When does he even get to see Dani?"

Her expression was cold, hard as she let go of the car door handle and folded her arms across her body. "Excuse me?"

"You move back here and take Dani with you. You know Dean has to be in L.A. for the team. When exactly is he supposed to see his daughter?" He knew this was none of his business. Yet, that didn't stop him from waiting for a response. It was as though his jerkiness was on autopilot.

Abby glanced toward the SUV, where Dani was focused on her iPod. "Not that it's any of your business, but Dean wasn't exactly fighting for visitation time."

"Oh, come on. He may have been an asshole to you, and things may not have worked out, but he loves Dani." From the talks he'd had over the years with his friend, he knew that much was true. His last conversation with Dean had been just the month before when his friend had claimed Abby was doing everything in her power to exclude him from Dani's life. Of course, his buddy had sounded a little drunk…

"Look, I don't expect you to believe me, but quite frankly, I don't care. You and I have never been friends, and I used to think that maybe it was my fault—that I'd done something to you, or said something—but I'm not losing any sleep over it anymore. If you honestly think it's me keeping Dean out of Dani's life and not his own selfishness, then you don't know your best friend as well as you think you do, and you know absolutely nothing about me."

She was wrong about the last part. He knew so much about her, cared so much about her, it terrified the shit out of him. He knew her favorite movies were old eighties romantic comedies she'd watched a million times already. He knew her favorite season was the fall, when the leaves started to change to orange and gold and the first snowfall covered mountain peaks in the distance. He knew that she'd been loyal and dedicated to his buddy and the life they'd built together. And he knew she didn't deserve the hurt she may be going through now. He'd never have hurt her. He wished she knew that.

"What?" she asked, when he'd been silent too long.

He shook his head. "Nothing. Hey, why don't I just call him?" he asked. "I mean, I can just as easily call and ask him for it."

Her expression softened a little, and in it was a trace of whatever he'd seen in them when they'd locked eyes on the ice. A trace of something he couldn't define, but that could give him hope, which would be far too dangerous. He was going to be in trouble if she planned to attend each practice.

"That's fine," she said, turning to open the car door. "Was that all you needed to talk to me about?"

Not even close. "Yep."

"Okay. See you Tuesday…and Friday…"

"And Sunday," he finished. Seeing her and not being able to touch her was absolute torture.

She sighed as though she'd rather have an unmedicated root canal. "And Sunday," she said, climbing into the car.

CHAPTER 7

❧

$\mathcal{G}$ive me twenty minutes and they'll be ready for you,"
George Watson, the only man in town Jackson trusted
to sharpen his skates, said as Jackson handed them over the
next morning.

That evening, his own men's league was playing their
first game of the season, and he needed his skates in their
best condition. With his younger brother drafted to the NHL
as well, he was the last Westmore left to lead the local
team to victory. The other men were previous high school
athletes, most of whom now had a million things on their
priority list that came before a game of small-town hockey—
wives, families, real jobs.

As he walked the aisles of the sporting goods store, he
reached for his cell. He'd checked the team's email that
morning, and there was still no sign of the release form from
Dean. Dialing his friend's cell number, he scanned a row of
sticks. He really could use a new one, but his was broken in
and molded perfectly to the shape of his hand.

It was the same stick he'd used since his last season with the Colorado Eagles, the year after his younger brother was called up to the majors. It was then that he'd known it was time for him to quit chasing the dream. Ben had played three games in the AHL before being called up. Asher played two years.

He'd put in his time, and Jackson had known when to pack it in. He'd spent his savings on a fixer-upper house and flipped it, turning a $20,000 profit, and then bought another one, pretending he was okay with life in real estate, away from center ice.

And in three years, he'd gotten real good at both—flipping homes and pretending.

"Hello," Dean answered on the fourth ring.

"Hey, man, how are you?"

"Hey yourself. Long time, buddy," Dean said, sounding distracted.

The sound of a woman's voice singing in the background made him frown. "Did I catch you at a bad time?"

"Um…I got a minute," he said, before obviously covering the mouthpiece and speaking to someone else.

He heard female laughter, then the sound of a door closing. "So, it turns out your little girl is a better stick handler than you," he said, trying to keep the mood light and erase the nagging feeling in his gut. It could be Dean's housekeeper…

"I wouldn't doubt that," his friend said above the sound of wind and waves.

He'd taken the call outside. "Yeah, she's quite impressive. She made the local Junior team. It went co-ed this year." As he spoke, he wasn't sure if his friend was even paying attention as he heard the door open and close again, and then whispering close to the phone.

"Huh, huh. Yeah, I heard. That's great. Listen buddy, can I call you back?"

Jackson frowned. "Actually, Dean, I won't keep you, but I was calling about the release form to see if you could send it in the next day or two."

"What release form?"

"Abby said she sent you a release form for Dani to be allowed to play. Can we get that signed and emailed back before Tuesday's practice?"

"I didn't receive any email from Abigail." Dean's hardened tone matched Abby's from the night before. The hostility between them obviously went both ways, but something in Dean's voice gave Jackson reason to doubt what he'd said. He knew his friend well enough to know when he was lying, but he couldn't get why he'd be lying about this. To make Abby look bad?

"Are you sure? She said she sent it from the school's account. Maybe check your spam folder."

"Jackson, she didn't send it. Just another ploy to keep me uninvolved and out of Dani's life."

Shit. The last thing he'd intended was to get in the middle of their conflict. He wanted nothing to do with their arguing or pawn playing with Dani. Though, he'd like to smack their heads together to make them realize the effect their stupidity would have on her. "Well, no problem. I'll resend it this afternoon." He paused as he heard Dean cover the mouthpiece and say, "I'll be there in just a sec, darling."

Darling? So much for the housekeeper theory. Irritation seeped through him. Over the last few months, he'd refused to believe the crap the media was saying about Dean, but Jackson couldn't ignore what was right in front of him. His friend obviously wasn't as innocent in all of this, a victim of the tabloids' eagerness for scandal, as he'd hoped.

His jaw tightened when he thought about how hurt Abby must have been to see those photos of her husband with another woman. How could his buddy give up so much? For what? Random hook-ups with strangers who couldn't possibly come close to what he already had at home?

Unbelievable.

"So, I'll resend it and you'll sign and email it back before Tuesday?" he asked tightly.

"You'll have it sooner. You'd have it already if Abigail had sent it in the first place."

He swallowed the argument on the tip of his tongue. He had no idea what had really happened with the form. "Okay, great. Thanks, Dean." He hesitated. "Hey, man, you've got a fantastic kid." One who deserved her father's love and attention. Dani was so much like Dean, he wished his friend realized what he'd had and lost.

But his words were met with dead air. Dean had hung up.

* * *

"Mom!"

Dani's voice echoed down the stairs to the kitchen where Abigail was pouring coffee into a travel mug. "In the kitchen," she called back.

"Mom! Where are you?"

She pressed the cover firmly over the cup and left the kitchen. "I'm downstairs by the door," she called up the stairs.

Dani appeared on the landing. "I can't find my blue sweatshirt. The one with the Colorado Avalanche logo on it."

"I think it's in the wash," she said, opening the closet door to retrieve her boots.

"In the wash?" Her daughter's voice was shrill and Abigail winced as she turned to look at her distraught expression.

Wow, what she wouldn't give for her preteen's problems. "Yes. Why don't you wear your white one?" Half of the clothing her daughter owned had some sort of hockey logo on it. And she owned most items in both the home and away colors.

"Taylor's wearing her blue one to the sleepover," Dani said with a pout.

"Well, I'm sorry. I haven't gotten to the laundry yet." Between reviewing the divorce settlement counteroffer documents from her lawyer and going over her proposed plans for the next fundraising meeting, she'd barely had time for a quick shower before needing to drive Dani to a new friend's sleepover party. She'd been hesitant to let her go, but Becky had reassured her it would be fine.

"What's all the fuss out here?" her mother asked, appearing with a laundry basket full of their clean clothes. Sitting on top was Dani's blue Colorado Avalanche sweatshirt.

She felt like kissing her mother.

Dani flew down the stairs and grabbed it. "Thanks, Grandma!" she said, shooting Abigail a look.

"Put that look away or I'll be adding laundry to *your* list of chores," she said, zipping her boots. She slid into her jean jacket and lifted her still damp hair over the back. "Do you have everything you need?"

"I do *now*, thanks to Grandma."

Abigail suppressed a sigh. "Thank you for doing our laundry, Mom. Please just lay it in my room and I'll fold it as soon as I get back."

"Folding laundry on a Saturday night. How fun," her mother muttered.

Abigail ignored it. What else was she supposed to do? A night out on the town in Glenwood Falls meant going to the only real bar: the Grumpy Stump, where far too many faces from her past might be.

Besides, who would she go with? Walking into a bar alone on a Saturday night would be just asking for trouble.

Nope. Folding laundry was the extent of her exciting plans. And maybe a bubble bath with a good book. She might even get a little crazy and pick up a bottle of wine on the way back.

"Ready?" she asked Dani as the girl slid her feet into her running shoes without untying them, crushing the backs. No wonder she went through shoes so quickly.

"Ready. Bye, Grandma," she said with a quick wave, heading outside.

"Have fun, darling," Isabelle called, carrying the basket upstairs to Abigail's room.

"Be back soon," Abigail said closing the door behind her.

Ten minutes later, they pulled into Taylor's driveway. The little girl was waiting in the window and bounded outside as soon as the vehicle stopped moving. Becky followed much slower behind.

"Hello, Ms. Jansen. Hey, Dani," she said, opening the back door and climbing in next to Dani.

"Hi, Taylor," she said, but the girls were already chatting, oblivious to their chauffeur.

When Becky finally reached the passenger side, she opened the door and climbed in.

"Um…hi?"

"Hi. I thought I'd come along for the ride to drop off the girls," she said, struggling to reach for her seatbelt, stretching it across her belly.

"Oh, okay, sure." She knew Neil was an Air Force pilot who was often overseas for months at a time, and Taylor had told Dani that her stepdad would be gone until the beginning of November. Abigail knew what it was like to have an absentee husband—on a much lesser scale, of course.

As she backed out of the driveway, Becky added, "I was also hoping I could convince you to go for a drink. Not a real one for me, of course," she said.

"Oh, I don't know. I have some things to do tonight…"

"Yeah, like fold laundry," Dani said, rolling her eyes in the backseat.

Abigail shot her a look through the rearview mirror, which just made Dani grin and stick out her tongue.

"I know all about folding laundry on Saturday nights. I swear between cooking, cleaning, and laundry, that's all I do, but I could use a break, and I bet you haven't been out since you moved back."

That was true, but for good reason: she didn't want to. "No, I haven't, but I didn't even do my hair or put on any makeup. I was expecting to drop off the girls and just go straight home." She glanced at her reflection in the mirror. Without her foundation, blush, and eyeshadow, she felt naked. The wrinkles around her eyes had deepened in recent weeks, and her hair floated in unruly waves around her shoulders.

If this were L.A. she never would have left the house like this. She could just imagine the look of shock on her hockey-wife friends' faces if they saw her now.

Becky, on the other hand, eyed her enviously. "I'd give anything to look as good as you do with wet hair and no makeup," she said. "I'm not even sure I put on matching shoes." She leaned around her stomach to try to get a look at her feet. "Close enough."

Abigail laughed. "Really, Becky. I'd rather take a raincheck." Though she'd used it as an excuse, she really wasn't too concerned with what people might think of her un-made-up appearance. In fact, she didn't give a rat's ass about looking good. It wasn't as though she were looking to meet someone.

That day was a long way off. So far off in fact she wasn't entirely sure that day even existed. Her mother claimed her heartache was still too raw, the wound too fresh to see how maybe someday she could love again, and maybe she was right. But right now, she was happy planning a future that included her and Dani and no one else.

So the thought of Jackson Westmore popping into her mind at that moment made her stomach uneasy. Since the night before at the arena, she hadn't been able to shake the memory of his smile and then the tension between them in the parking lot. Why was every interaction with the man—good or bad—so electrically charged?

"Oh, come on, Mom. You should go," Dani was saying, surprising her.

She hesitated. Why was everyone encouraging her to go out?

"This may be my last free night…ever. Please?" Becky said.

"It would make me feel better about leaving her alone," Taylor added, glancing up from her phone.

"Jeez, I'm starting to feel like I was set up here," Abigail said, peering at her daughter through the mirror.

Dani just smiled.

She sighed. "Okay, why not?" It was just one drink with a friend who would be exhausted in an hour and have to call it a night anyway, she thought.

Or not.

Staring across the bar at Becky two-stepping with Old Man Wilson, the owner of the Grumpy Stump, two and a half hours later, Abigail couldn't remember the last time she'd laughed so hard. Watching her pregnant friend twirl around the floor at breakneck speed to a fast-tempo song with the town's self-proclaimed old-school cowboy, she couldn't see through the tears.

Becky mouthing the words "help me" each time they swung past the booth where so far she'd miraculously been able to stay, turning down several dance offers of her own, only made it all the more amusing.

This outing had been Becky's idea after all, and she'd tried to warn her about Old Man Wilson.

"Another round?" the waitress asked. She had blonde hair cut in a cute pixie style and a hummingbird tattoo on her chest, and she didn't look much older than Taylor.

"Um..." Abigail checked her watch as the song ended and Becky slid back into the booth.

"Yes, please," her friend said, out of breath and clutching her stomach.

The waitress nodded as she headed toward the bar.

Guess they were staying for another round. "You okay?"

"Yes, my sides hurt from laughing. This is fun."

When their drinks arrived, Becky asked, "Are you okay?"

"Of course." She forced a smile.

Becky nodded. "For what it's worth, I think you're doing a great job of hiding it."

"Hiding what?"

"The heartache and struggle you must be feeling."

An unexpected lump rose in Abigail's throat and she forced it back down. "Some days it's tougher than others, but Dani's been a source of strength, and I'm hoping once we settle into a new place and I secure the full-time position at the school, this place will once again feel like home."

"It will. And then you'll start making new memories. Better ones," Becky said, covering her mouth as a yawn escaped her lips.

"Ready to call it a night?" She was. She reached for her jacket.

But Becky glanced at the neon-rimmed tequila-bottle-shaped clock on the wall. "Um…not yet. Maybe another few minutes." She was avoiding her eyes as she glanced toward the door.

Something was up. "Becky, what are you doing?"

"Nothing. I just haven't finished my drink," she said, picking up her glass and taking the tiniest sip possible. The liquid barely dropped a millimeter. At that rate, she'd be ready to leave by morning.

"You're up to something…" Abigail stopped as the "something" walked in through the door.

Oh hell no.

She grabbed her jacket and purse and slid out of the booth. "Look! Your brother's here. He can drive you home," she said in mock surprise. "I'm heading out."

Becky struggled to reach for her. "No, wait, please."

"You set me up." Or was attempting to. And with Jackson? Was Becky out of her mind? Pregnancy brain was obviously a real condition.

"No, I didn't." She offered an innocent look that Abigail wasn't buying. "Okay, sort of, but I just think Jackson can help you with some things."

"Ha! Your brother hates me." Or at least she'd been fairly certain he did…until a few super awkward, tension-filled moments and an earth-shattering smile had given her reason to think she may not be entirely right in her assumptions.

Becky's look clearly stated she thought Abigail was the dumbest person on the planet. "Abby, you know that thing where little boys tease and are mean to little girls they like because they don't know how else to deal with the strange feelings they're experiencing?"

She wasn't sure she bought into that crap—she'd taught her daughter if a boy was mean to her to punch him in the nuts, not fall in love—but she sighed, hating that she was curious about where Becky was going with this. "Okay…"

"Well, most guys move beyond that immature, awkward stage. Jackson never has." She rolled her eyes.

"You're not making any sense. Are you sure those were virgin Bloody Marys?" She reached for Becky's glass, took a sip, and gagged on the heat level of the Tabasco sauce in the drink. That baby would be doing summersaults all evening after that taste explosion. "I can't feel my tongue," she said, quickly reaching for her own drink and sucking hard, desperate for the last little bit of alcohol mixed with melted ice at the bottom of the glass.

"Okay, fine, forget about that. But, the thing is, Jackson flips houses for a living. He may be able to help you with a place of your own."

That stopped her. Jackson flipped homes? That's how he made money? She'd heard he was a contractor, but she just assumed he did construction work for one of the local companies when he wasn't wearing skates. "He does? Really, Jackson?"

"I heard my name," he said behind her a second later.

Turning, she gulped at the sight of him in a pair of jeans, ripped at one knee, and a black T-shirt visible beneath his leather jacket. Once again, she figured it must be his personality keeping the women at arm's length. Maybe he was an acquired taste that most women just didn't stay around long enough to acquire. It certainly wasn't the ice blue eyes framed by long, dark lashes or the full lips that looked tempting as hell. She licked her own lips as her gaze fell to his chest muscles straining against the fabric of the shirt. Definitely must be the personality keeping them away.

He looked at her with a confused, amused expression on his face, and she realized she was staring. She looked away quickly, and he turned to his sister. "What are you doing out so late?"

She raised one eyebrow. "Seriously?"

"I'm just saying you're pregnant and…"

"Exactly. Pregnant. Not dead. Sit down," she said, gesturing across the booth.

He shifted from one foot to the other, looking as though he wished he hadn't approached them.

Well, that made two of them. She couldn't explain her recent attraction to him, but she didn't like it.

"I'm actually here with the guys. We just finished playing a game against Springdale."

That explained the fresh scent of musky body wash lingering on the air around him and the still damp hair styled in a spiky mess. It looked like someone had run their hands through it…She caught herself staring again and looked away.

What the hell was wrong with her?

"Sit for a sec," Becky insisted.

Jackson sighed but slid into the booth, raising a finger to the other men at the pool tables to indicate he'd just be a second.

"You, too," Becky told Abigail.

"You're bossy."

"Something we finally agree on," Jackson said.

"Fine. Move in." Abigail tried to shove her into the booth, but Becky shook her head and held firm.

"My stomach's too big. Go sit over there."

Next to Jackson. Great-looking, great-smelling Jackson. Great.

He looked about as thrilled as she felt, but he moved in

and she sat as close to the edge as possible. "You've got three minutes before I have to go steal some money from those guys," he told Becky.

"Well, Abby was talking about moving into a new place, and I know you've almost finished that three-bedroom bungalow you were working on."

He was shaking his head. "I wasn't planning to sell that one right away. I was maybe going to turn it into a rental…" He reached for her Bloody Mary and took a sip.

His lips were wrapped around the straw where Abigail's had been a moment before. She wondered how he'd feel if he knew that. Her eyes dropped to said lips, and she slid out of the booth quickly, before she could start to fantasize about what they might taste like. "No worries. Thanks anyway," she said without looking at him. "Are you ready to go now, or are you going to stay?" she asked Becky, desperate to escape the close proximity to the man. She must be feeling the lonely nights a lot worse than she thought to be experiencing this kind of attraction to a man she'd barely been cordial with before. Either that, or he'd gotten a whole hell of a lot hotter in the last ten years.

Becky waved a hand at her and continued to talk to her brother. "Maybe Abby might want to rent it for a while." She turned to her. "I mean, it will get you out of your parents' place, and you can take your time finding a permanent home for you and Dani."

Abigail shifted from one foot to the other, trying to think of an excuse. With the development of this unexplainable attraction, the last thing she wanted was more ties to Jackson. Having to spend time with him because of the school and hockey were bad enough. Him as her landlord, even temporarily, didn't excite her. In fact, the idea kind of terrified her. Unfortunately, she had been going on and on all evening about how she was dying to get a place in town soon, and how her well-meaning parents were driving her crazy.

She'd been looking through the available places to rent in the paper every morning and there were few houses, mostly basement suites and several apartment buildings. Nothing appealed to her. She may not be able to give Dani a home in a $2 million house, but she wanted something nice and comfortable. A place they could stay in for a while. She was hoping to find a house with an eventual buy option she could consider once the settlement was finalized. She hated to admit it, but Jackson's new investment might be just the thing she was looking for. Besides, it wasn't as though she'd be living with him. And how often did one see a landlord anyway? She sighed. "When were you hoping to rent it?" she asked him.

Surprise flashed across his face, and she knew how he felt.

"Well…" He released a breath. "Maybe by the end of the month."

For someone with a property he needed a tenant for, he certainly didn't seem eager to discuss it. "If you don't already have someone interested in renting it…"

"It's yours if you want it," he said suddenly, and his gaze locked with hers, the expression intense and unreadable.

Was she missing something? Her mouth went dry as she nodded. "Great. Thanks."

"Hey, Jackson, are you playing or not?" Darryl called from where he stood across the bar, holding a pool cue, the balls already scattered across the table.

Jackson broke the connection with her eyes and nodded. "Yeah, I'm coming. Excuse me," he said, and she moved aside to let him pass.

"Hey, can we play, too?" Becky said.

So much for her friend being tired. "If you want to stay, maybe Jackson could drive you home later." She checked her watch—10:35. Pathetic. "I really should go." *Yeah, 'cause the laundry won't fold itself,* she thought, suddenly not as eager to leave.

"Or you could stay and play pool," Jackson said, a hint of a smile playing on those oh-so-dangerous lips.

An odd feeling, one she refused to define, washed over her. *Or* she could stay and play pool.

* * *

There was nothing sexier about a woman than knowing exactly how she would look the next morning waking up in his arms. With no makeup and wavy unruly hair falling across her shoulder as she lined up to take her shot, Abigail looked so much like the young girl he used to know he had to remind himself that time had passed and a lot of life had happened since then.

"Ready to hand over all that cash?" she asked, peering up at him from her perch over the pool cue.

He was ready to hand just about anything over to her. Always had been. He leaned against the ledge next to the wall and tossed his cue between his hands, hoping he was giving off an air of nonchalance, despite the fact that inside he was a mess. And it had nothing to do with potentially losing the two hundred dollars in cash they were playing for. "You'll never make this shot," he said, reaching for his beer and taking a swig as she pulled back and hit the white ball.

No one moved as it spiraled toward the eight ball and hit it, sending both balls in the direction of the right corner pocket.

"Don't scratch, don't scratch," she was saying as she watched, biting her lip nervously.

He couldn't tear his eyes from her pretty lips long enough to see what happened, but her face lighting up in a beautiful smile a second later told him he'd just lost the game.

"Yay!" she said, turning to high-five his sister, whose belly had been her excuse for not pulling her weight as Abby's partner.

Setting the pool cue aside, he reached into his pocket for the cash. "Here you are," he said, handing it to her. "Good game."

She shook her head, refusing the money. "Keep it. Consider it part of my damage deposit on the house."

What about a deposit for the damage she'd done to his heart over the years?

He nodded, tucking the money into his back jeans pocket. "So, did you want to swing by and see the place?"

She frowned. "Now?"

He shrugged. "Sure. Why not?" There were a million reasons why not—the main one being that seeing her in a house he'd actually bought for himself might create even more unhealthy, irrational fantasies he'd never be able to escape. Like cooking breakfast together after a night of mindblowing sex…or mind-blowing sex in the kitchen while breakfast burned on the stove…

Damn. Just the thought made his jeans fit a little tighter in the front.

He thought about retracting the offer, but Becky was climbing down from the stool with a yawn. "Sounds like a great idea. We can all go in your truck and you can drop me off on the way." She linked her arm through his and rested her head against his shoulder.

He laughed. "Do *you* want to argue with her?" he asked Abby.

She shook her head. "'Cause that ever works," she said, grabbing her jean jacket and sliding into it.

Fifteen minutes later, he pulled into the driveway of his latest project. The bungalow had cost him next to nothing, as the previous owners had been looking for a quick sale. The place was an older home but structurally sound, therefore he'd put less than $20,000 into it so far, and mostly it was upgrades and cosmetic work. It was the first one he'd purchased that had all of the features he'd wanted in a home of his own—all one level, three bedrooms, three bathrooms, a large backyard—and it backed onto the lake, which was perfect for ice fishing and pond hockey in winter and taking his small boat out in the summer.

Now, Abby would be living there. For a few months at least.

"Wow, it's bigger than I thought," she said, unbuckling her seatbelt. "You're sure you're only asking five hundred a month for it?"

He nodded. "Let's go in." Unlocking the front door a moment later, he held open the screen door and stood back to let her enter first. "Be careful not to trip over the laminate flooring there in the hallway. I should have it finished early next week," he said, closing the door behind them.

Pulling off her boots, she flicked on the light and headed into the living room. "Wow. This place is beautiful."

He smiled as he followed her. He'd had an eye on this place for a while, knowing the moment it went up for sale, he would buy it without hesitation.

"I love the old wood-burning fireplace."

So did he. "It works. I had a new ventilation system put in, and the chimney's been inspected, so it's safe to use." He shoved his hands in his pockets and watched her as she made her way toward the kitchen. "All new appliances, and the countertop should be here next week as well. It's a dark marble to match the backsplash tiles."

She shook her head. "You did all the remodeling yourself?"

"Most of it. Frank Hillier did the electrical work."

She smiled. "Probably for the best. Remember that time you tried to wire a new stereo system into your dad's car while they were away on vacation?"

He laughed. Oh, he remembered. He was just surprised she did. "Yeah, who knew the wires for the brake lights looked so much like the ones for the stereo?"

"Your dad was so mad…" She paused, her smile fading slightly. "I was sorry to hear of his passing."

"Thanks." Jackson cleared his throat. "So, down the hall are the three bedrooms. They're all still furnished, except for the master suite." He'd sold those items as he'd planned to buy new bedroom furniture for himself once the place was ready to move into. The stuff he had currently in his apartment was the same stuff he'd moved in with almost eight years before. He was getting a little old for his Wonder Woman pole lamp and Doctor Who police box DVD holder.

"That's fine. I brought some things from L.A."

He stood in the doorframe as she scanned the closet space. "Great walk-in…" He heard her say as she went into the closet that connected the bedroom to the en suite bathroom. Then, "Oh my God, that Jacuzzi tub!"

He grinned. The new four-person jetted tub was his favorite new addition to the house as well.

"I know where I'll be spending my evenings."

His smile faded as an image of Abby submerged in a tub full of bubbles, her long legs draped over one side, the ends of her hair wet, hanging below her shoulders onto her chest made his pulse race and all the blood in his body rush to his crotch. She still had the ability to induce a hard-on with just his imagination. He forced himself to think of anything else as she reappeared.

"I love it. I'm definitely interested in renting it. In fact, once the di…" She paused. "I might eventually be interested in buying it."

Wonderful. He was potentially losing his dream home to the woman of his dreams. If she wanted the house, there would be no way he could say no. Besides, living in it without her, knowing she had been sleeping in the master suite, bathing in that tub, drinking her coffee out on the deck overlooking the lake, would be torture.

He could strangle his sister for this. He'd never be able to think of the house the same way again. And more disturbingly, he wasn't sure he wanted to.

The feelings he'd had for her years ago paled in comparison to the new ones strangling his common sense. Before, he'd been a teenager, fueled by hormones. He'd wanted to touch her, kiss her, hold her hand, wrap his arms around her. Now, it was a deep longing from the depths of his chest making him want to do all that but also so much more.

Now, he wanted to know what it would be like to wake up next to her, to be there for her during this tough time, and to make love to her until she wondered why she'd wasted any of her emotions on anyone else. These new feelings made him wonder if maybe his loyalty to Dean had a time limit. They weren't as close as they'd once been, and he was starting to question if he knew his friend as well as he'd thought. Maybe it was just hockey they had in common…that and falling for the same woman.

"You okay?" Abby asked, stepping closer and studying him.

He blinked and shook his thoughts away. "Yeah, I'm fine. Why?"

"I just said 'thank you,' but you seemed to have zoned out for a second. Where did you go?"

She didn't want to know. "Nowhere...You're welcome." He headed back down the hall and she followed.

Unfortunately, he turned the hall light off a second too soon.

"Ow, shit, ow!"

He flicked the light back on and turned to see her hopping around on one foot, holding the other in her hand. "You okay?" He frowned as he moved toward her.

"My toe. I hit it on that stack of laminate flooring you warned me about. Ow!" She continued to hop, blinking back tears.

"Let me look at it."

"No. You'll hurt me." She moved out of reach as he went to grab her arm.

"I'd never hurt you," he said hoarsely, with more emotion than he'd intended.

She heard it too as she stopped hopping and set her foot back down. "Uh, it's fine. I'm sure it's fine," she said, but she was wincing with every step toward the door.

"I don't think so," he said, noticing her sock turning red at her toe. Damn. He should have told her to leave her boots on.

She went pale as she glanced down. "I need to sit," she said quietly.

He led her into the kitchen and pulled out a counter stool. "Sit here."

She did and he bent to remove the sock, relieved to see just a small gash on the top of her big toe. Her beautiful, manicured, soft toe. The temptation to bring the small, delicate foot to his lips and kiss away the pain made him slightly tipsy.

"Is it horrible?" she asked, covering her eyes.

"No, it's perfect," he mumbled.

"Huh?" She looked.

"I mean, it's fine. Just a small cut. Give me a second."

A minute later, he was back with antiseptic, a face cloth, and a Band-Aid. Minor injuries were almost guaranteed when he was renovating, so he'd learned to keep a small first aid kit nearby.

"Here, let me," she said, reaching for it.

"No, because you won't apply the antiseptic."

"Yes, I will."

"No, you won't." He wiped the blood away from the cut gently, then opened the bottle. "I remember the summer we were jumping over logs in the forest and you slipped." He poured the alcohol-based liquid onto the edge of the cloth. "A sharp twig sticking out of one of the logs pierced your skin. It took three of us, Asher and Ben and me, to hold you down while Mom cleaned the wound."

She scoffed. "I was twelve. I'm not a kid anymore."

No shit. Every part of him had certainly noticed. "Take a breath," he said.

She did as she closed her eyes.

He applied the antiseptic quickly and blew on the cut softly to try to ease the sting, then he quickly applied the bandage. "There. Better," he said as he stood.

"Thank you," she said, accepting her bloodied sock from him awkwardly. "You know, you're kinda nice when you're nice."

"I'm always nice," he murmured, aware of just how close they were. One tiny step and a whole shitload of courage and she could be in his arms. He waited. Neither happened.

"Not to me," she whispered.

Damn it. His own legs refused to move, so he reached out and, grabbing her waist, pulled her off of the stool and into him. "Maybe it's time for that to change."

Her eyes widened, but she didn't move away from him, as his hands left her hips to cup her face. "Jackson..."

"You really think I'm an asshole, huh?" he whispered, searching her eyes.

"Yeah, I really do."

"Well, kissing you probably won't change your perception," he said, swallowing hard.

"Probably not," she said, her eyes wide. She looked as though she wanted to run away, but her feet were frozen to the floor.

He stared at her mouth. Damn, a kiss from those beautiful pink lips would be worth a slap in the face. One taste of her would be worth unravelling any progress they'd made in becoming friendly. Who the hell wanted friendly? Not him. He wanted wild passion in the Jacuzzi tub and his and hers towels hanging in the master en suite that she'd admired moments before. But her bewildered, hesitant expression told him to proceed with caution.

Reluctantly, he moved away, letting his hands fall away from her. "So, the place. You're happy with it?"

A look of disappointment competed with a look of relief on her face as she nodded. "Yes. The place is perfect. It was exactly what I was hoping to find to start over," she said softly.

He nodded. "Great." He wondered what else she might need to start over, and whether someday he might make that list.

CHAPTER 8

～৩৩০～

*W*ait! Stop. I need to get a snack for this," Becky said, starting to push herself up from the couch.

Jackson stopped pacing and shot her a look. "This isn't a movie. This is my life, which I have totally complicated in less than two weeks," he said, running a hand through his messy hair. He'd yet to sleep, driving around town into all hours of the night after dropping Abby back at her SUV. Driving always helped him think, but last night, he'd had to fight the urge to drive back in the direction of her parents' place and throw rocks at her bedroom window.

What exactly he'd wanted to say to her, he had no idea. Temptation mixed with an intense agonizing guilt over wanting to kiss his best friend's wife. *Soon to be ex-wife,* a voice in his mind reminded him. He silenced the hopeful annoyance because it didn't matter. Abigail was off-limits. The night before he'd let things get a little carried away. Thank God, things hadn't gone any further than they had.

Thank God? His body claimed otherwise.

"Help me," Becky said, giving up the struggle and falling back against the couch.

"Forget about food for a second and help me," he said. "This is your fault for suggesting she move into my house." He picked up a throw pillow from the couch and threw it at her.

"I made orange raspberry muffins."

His favorite. He sighed as he helped her up, then followed her to the kitchen. "Becky, come on. What am I supposed to do?"

She opened a container and retrieved two muffins. Handing him one, she said, "I don't know why you're so freaked out. You've been dying over this woman for years, since we were kids. You saw your chance last night, and you almost grew balls big enough to take it." She bit into the muffin.

"Last night was *not* my chance. I don't get a chance. Not with her," he said, popping a chunk of his own muffin into his mouth. His friendship with Dean may not be as strong as it had been when they were kids, but that wasn't a good enough reason to pounce on his ex-wife in a moment of vulnerability.

Dean had been the first kid to really include him after moving to Glenwood Falls, and their shared love for hockey had made them fast friends. His buddy was an only child, his parents wealthier than most families in Glenwood Falls. They'd spoiled their son, and he'd reaped the benefits as well, attending hockey games in Denver with Dean with the family's season tickets, getting to enjoy the family's mountain cabin.

But more than that, Dean had been the one to encourage him to stick it out with the Colorado Eagles. He'd helped him train and get ready for open tryouts, and he'd been the one to call bullshit when Jackson hadn't played a game once he'd been called up to the majors.

Bottom line: If roles were reversed, his friend would never be going after a woman he'd once been involved with.

Would he? The old Dean wouldn't. He wasn't so sure about the guy his friend had become recently.

Jackson shook his head. "Abby is not an option," he said but with a lot less conviction than he'd aimed for.

"What are you talking about?" Taylor asked, stumbling into the kitchen.

"How did you get home?" Becky asked. She glanced at the clock on the microwave. "It's only ten thirty. I thought I was picking you and Dani up at Angela's house at noon."

"Her mom decided to drive us all home."

"In other words you were all driving *her* crazy," Becky said with a knowing look.

Taylor shrugged. "Whatever. What are you two eating?"

"Orange raspberry muffins. Third container on the right."

Jackson leaned against the counter and tossed the rest of the muffin into his mouth. So much for getting advice from Becky. Unfortunately, he had no one else to go to for it. His brothers would only torment him about his undying childhood crush if they knew. And well, his best friend wasn't exactly an option. "I'm outta here," he said, rustling Taylor's hair and stealing the rest of her muffin on his way out of the kitchen. "See you at practice in a few hours."

Where he'd also be seeing Abby.

* * *

The sound of her cell phone ringing was met with a welcome sigh of relief. Finally, a valid distraction to take her eyes and mind off of Jackson standing, with his arms folded, near the players' bench, calling out instructions to the kids playing a practice game on the ice. He didn't seem to be struggling with the same problem as he'd barely glanced at her, shooting her a quick nod as she and Dani had entered the arena twenty minutes before.

She wasn't sure the source of her irritation, but she couldn't deny the way her nerves were standing on edge being around him after the night before's brief…what? What had occurred between them? He'd mentioned kissing her—to which she could only come to the conclusion that he must have been high—and then he'd quickly dismissed the idea.

Which she should be relieved about. Drop-kicking her daughter's hockey coach and her new landlord was sure to make things even less friendly between them…And that was what she would have done, right?

The phone rang again, stealing her focus, and she reached for it, checking the caller ID. It was Jocelyn, another hockey wife from L.A. She hadn't heard from the woman since they'd consumed three bottles of wine at her place the night she'd officially filed for divorce. Part of it was her fault; she'd distanced herself from the ladies as the divorce had dragged on, and especially after deciding to move to Glenwood Falls. Keeping in touch when she was no longer one of them felt odd. She hadn't been sure their friendships had run that deep.

Picking up her nearly empty disposable coffee cup, she moved away from the glass in the front row and went out into the hall near the locker rooms. "Hello?" she said, her voice echoing off of the concrete surroundings.

"I saw that you removed your contact information from the hockey wives site."

"Well, technically, I'm not a hockey wife anymore. How are you?"

"Fabulous." It was her standard remark. She claimed that even on her worst days, she could always find one fabulous thing about it to cling to. "How are *you*?" she asked, sounding as though Abigail should be hiding under a pillow, drowning her sorrows in more wine.

"Actually, things are going well. I have a job teaching at the elementary school. It's temporary for now, but I'm hoping it will turn into a full-time position next month." She was happy to have positive news to report. No doubt it would find its way back down the gossip chain to the other women, and for some reason, ego maybe, she really wanted them to know she was surviving and doing okay.

"Teaching? Like children?" Jocelyn said the word as though she were talking about rattlesnakes.

Abigail laughed. "Yes. You know, those little short people your company caters to." Jocelyn ran a successful high-end baby and toddler boutique in Beverly Hills. Baby Couture was located on Rodeo Drive, and frequent shoppers included celebrities and movie stars. It had shocked Abigail to learn the woman disliked children when she'd made a successful livelihood from their existence.

"My company caters to the mom-to-be with something to prove," she said. "So, what was the settlement?"

Blunt, direct, and completely oblivious to societal rules. That was Jocelyn.

"We haven't reached one yet." Abigail switched ears as she paced the concrete floor. She took a sip of the lukewarm coffee and glanced around for a garbage can, but didn't see one.

"Asshole is dragging it out. What a surprise," she said. "Is he also fighting for custody?"

"No."

"Well, that's good at least. Ashlyn's husband—Kyle, the left wing for Detroit—fought for the entire off-season in their divorce. She's devastated every June when she has to ship her kids off to Detroit for the summer."

Abigail bit her lip. Being away from her daughter for three months every year? That would be awful. Maybe she had been lucky.

"Well, if he's not taking time with her, you should be entitled to a great child support and alimony settlement."

Abigail sighed. She wasn't at all opposed to making Dean pay as much financially as needed to support his daughter, but she wasn't sure how she felt about accepting alimony. At first, she'd been terrified about the idea of starting over and doing it all on her own—her confidence had been shattered—but now she was starting to feel better, stronger, and she didn't want that taken away. Besides, she was enjoying the teaching position. "Honestly, I really don't care. At this point, I just want the papers signed."

"I guess I can understand that. But darling, the man was in bed with two Dallas Stars cheerleaders when you walked into the hotel room—on your anniversary—to surprise him. Try to keep that in mind when deciding how tight to squeeze the vice grips you've got on his balls."

An image of the green and gold cheerleader uniforms lying on the floor of the hotel room and the perfect, tanned, stretch-mark free bodies straddling her husband on the hotel bed flashed in her mind, and she felt ill. "Trust me, it's not an image I can easily forget."

"Good. Have you bought a new place yet?" she asked.

Her cheeks flushed at the mention of her soon to be new home. Jackson Westmore's house. If anyone had told her she'd be back in Glenwood Falls renting a home he owned, she would have laughed. "I found a place last night, actually. We can move in next week. It's just a rental for now, but I may decide to buy it once the divorce is finalized."

"How many mil?"

She smiled, shaking her head at her friend's lack of tact. "It's five hundred a month to rent, and I would think it will be worth about three hundred thousand."

Jocelyn was silent.

"Joce?"

"I'm sorry. I'm picturing you and Dani living in a dingy one-bedroom home in a bad neighborhood."

Jocelyn had never ventured beyond Beverly Hills; her father being the owner of the Kings, she'd grown up ridiculously rich. She'd never understand that outside of L.A., nice family homes could cost a lot less.

"It's two thousand square feet, three bedrooms, three baths, right on a lake, with a fantastic view of the mountains. We're doing fine, Jocelyn," she said with a smile, grateful and happy that it was the truth.

"Well, if you need anything…"

"Thanks, Jocelyn. Take care."

Disconnecting the call, Abigail smiled as she made her way back to the arena. Things were going to be okay, and word that she'd landed on her feet would reach her old "friends" in L.A. A new surge of hope flowed through her.

But her smile faded as she reached the bench near the glass where she'd left her purse and winter jacket and looked toward the game in time to see Dex body-check Dani into the side boards.

She dropped the coffee cup as she watched her daughter crumble to the ice.

Running to the door leading out onto the ice, she collided with Jackson, rushing toward it from the opposite direction. "I've got this," he said firmly, gripping her shoulders to steady her quickly before releasing her and skating away.

Her jaw clenched and her eyes filled with tears of worry as she turned to stare where her daughter lay motionless. The other players had stopped to gather around, and the high school–aged referee held them all away as Jackson lowered to his knees on the ice.

Her baby girl lay injured, and there was nothing she could do but stand there and watch. Her hands clutched at her chest, and she ignored a tear that escaped her eye and slid down her cheek.

Becky joined her a second later, placing a supportive arm around her shoulder. "I'm sure she's fine," she said, but Abigail only heard the worry in the other mother's voice, not the words that were meant to reassure and provide comfort.

On the ice, Jackson was speaking to Dani, but she'd yet to move. Abigail could see her eyes open and her lips moving, so at least her daughter was responsive. Then an excruciatingly long moment later, she saw Jackson help Dani to her feet.

Applause sounded around them from the stands and the other players on the ice, as Jackson led Dani toward them. Abigail's heart pounded loud in her ears and Jackson's reassuring nod almost buckled her knees.

As they approached, a million thoughts clouded her mind. This sport was too dangerous. Playing in the same league as the bigger, older boys was just asking for someone to get hurt. Would her daughter realize that now and reconsider?

A big part of her—like ninety-five percent—hoped so, but the small, almost insignificant part wondered what that would teach her daughter about life, if she quit after falling?

Damn it! If she could pay someone for the right answer right now, no price would be too high.

But as Jackson opened the door, her daughter was smiling as she left the ice.

Behind Dani, Jackson's gaze was the complete opposite—stone cold, anger blazing in his eyes as he looked toward the stands on the opposite end of the arena.

Letting her gaze lift momentarily from her daughter, Abigail turned to follow the direction of his stare. Kurt Miller sat on the top bleacher with several other hockey dads, a wide grin on his face. The others at least had the decency to appear concerned.

But the boy's father was smiling?

A second later he gave his son a thumbs-up sign, and Abigail's blood ran cold. He was encouraging this dangerous and aggressive behavior? Forgetting her daughter in her anger, she swung around to head for the stands, to smack that stupid grin off of the guy's face, but Jackson's hand caught her wrist before she could get far.

"Whoa. Hold up."

"Did you see…"

"Yes, I did. And I'm going to deal with it. Take Dani to the locker room, and I'll be in in a minute," he said.

"But Coach, I want to keep playing," Dani said, standing between them.

Jackson's expression softened as he tapped her helmet. "You're a champ, but safety first. There's always next practice."

Her face fell.

"Hey, chin up. You did great today. And besides, he may have checked you, but he didn't get the puck," he said with a wink.

Dani beamed at the praise.

Abigail's stomach did an involuntary lurch when the coach's prideful, concerned gaze met hers. Oh God. Jackson Westmore was stirring up more than his fair share of emotions in her these days.

She shook it off. It was just how awesome he was with Dani and the other kids that had her softening toward him, she told herself.

Dani and the other kids had been nowhere in sight the night before, a nagging voice reminded her.

Shit. Glancing away quickly, before he could successfully confuse the hell out of her even more, she said, "Let's go, honey." Leading her daughter toward the locker room, she asked, "Are you really okay?" She stared at Dani, looking for any sign of injury. Of course, concussions or internal bleeding couldn't be detected...Oh God, she had to stop thinking the worst, or else she would be the one needing medical attention for an anxiety attack.

"I'm fine, Mom. It was a good, clean hit," she said with a shrug and Abigail winced.

How often had she heard similar comments from Dean after getting injured during a game? Too many.

At first she'd gone to all of his games, finding an intense attraction in watching him play, but her pregnancy had changed her thoughts and feelings on her husband's chosen career. She'd become much more aware of Dean's risks every time he stepped onto the ice. Three concussions in ten years...she often wondered how much more he could take.

While part of her couldn't give a shit anymore—the hurt he'd inflicted hardening her heart—he was still Dani's father, and that meant he would always be an important part of their lives. Her life.

And it seemed her little girl was more like him than she'd

ever realized. The sigh that escaped her lips held far too many levels to count.

*   *   *

All he saw was red as he climbed the bleachers toward Kurt.

He forced a breath. Be professional and calm. Deal with this with a cool head. A good minor league coach didn't knock a parent out.

But boy was it tempting when he noticed the same stupid grin on the man's face. Maybe he *should* have let Abby deal with him.

"Hey, Kurt. A word?"

The man nodded as he stepped down onto the lower bleacher, away from the other fathers. "Don't tell me. I've got a future NHLer on my hands, right?"

Jackson's jaw tightened. "Actually you've got a suspended minor league player—two games—and Dex is sitting out the rest of practice."

Kurt's smile faded as his gaze turned steely.

Not as satisfying as a punch, but still quite satisfying... until Jackson glanced toward the players' bench, where Dex watched them nervously.

Shit. It wasn't the kid's fault his father was an asshole, pushing him in this direction. The poor boy was always so focused and disciplined, Jackson was fairly certain he'd lost the thrill of being on the ice a long time ago. It was sad. At this age, they should be playing for the love of the game, not any unreachable goals of an NHL career someday.

"It was a clean hit," Kurt argued.

"You know checking isn't allowed in this league." They'd disallowed any fighting or body-checking years ago, much to the relief of many parents.

But not all. He prepared himself for the argument he knew was coming next.

"So what is he supposed to do next year on the Peewee league and then the Bantam team with older kids who know how to check?"

"He will learn. Besides it looks like he has it nailed already." He took a breath before continuing. "Look, I'll spend some time with him this season teaching him how to defend against the check and how to set it up properly." He didn't want the kid going into the bigger league unprepared, either, and there was no doubt the kid was good enough to make the division the following season.

"Whatever," Kurt muttered.

Knowing he would get nowhere with the guy, Jackson turned to leave. Next was the hard part: telling the kid he was suspended. Disappointed looks from the kids he coached were his downfall. But he couldn't allow unsafe play on his team.

"Girls shouldn't be allowed to play hockey," he heard Kurt say behind him.

He turned. "I'm sorry?"

"I said, hockey is a men's sport. Little girls can expect to get hurt when they're playing with the boys."

His teeth clenched. "Look, I understand the changes to the league may not be what everyone wanted, but I think any kid who wants to play should have the opportunity."

He snorted. "I bet you'd see it differently if Taylor was a boy. The truth is, you know these minor leagues are the only chance your niece will get to play."

Jackson forced a deep breath. Getting into this with Kurt was not the right thing to do here. "I've got a team to coach," he said.

"Exactly. Your job is to coach, and we've made a lot of sacrifices so that Dex could play on this team."

"Well then he needs to play by my rules. No checking. If it happens again, he's off the team."

* * *

"Mom, quit waking me up. I'm fine," Dani grumbled rolling over to her side and pulling her covers up over her head.

Abigail gently touched the homemade quilt, made from her own baby blankets, and then quietly slipped out of the room, wishing her daughter had agreed to sleep in her bed with her that evening. Checking on her every couple of hours would be easier, and the tormenting, fearful what-if thoughts plaguing her might be a little less intense. She closed the door as quietly as possible.

"How is she?"

The sound of her father's voice behind her made her jump. She hadn't noticed her parents' bedroom door open across the hall. "She's okay." She pulled her cardigan tighter around her.

"Kids are tough. It's harder on us, believe me."

Abigail nodded. "I just keep thinking the worst."

"Come on. Tea will help," her father said, heading downstairs.

Abigail stifled a yawn. She was exhausted, but knowing she wouldn't catch a wink anyway, she followed him.

Seated at the table with a steaming cup of chamomile tea on the table in front of her moments later, she said, "You and Mom were lucky. I was never interested in sports. I didn't risk getting hurt like this." The most physical extracurricular activity she'd participated in was the cheer team, and the worst injury she could get was a sprained ankle. Twelve years ago, the teams weren't as into throwing one another into the air or building sky-high, dangerous-looking pyramids as they were now. Pompoms and dance routines had been the extent of it.

Her father laughed and shot her a look. "I wish physical injuries were the worst we had to endure with you."

"Huh?"

"Just wait. Once Dani starts getting her heart broken, you'll see what I mean."

Abigail gave a sad smile. "I was good at that." It seemed she still was. "Thanks for not saying 'I told you so,'" she said quietly, taking a sip of the tea. Her parents had expressed on more than one occasion the fact they didn't think Dean was the right one for her. Of course her head-over-heels teenage heart hadn't listened. She'd thought they were just worried about her settling down so young and committing to a hockey life, where she would potentially be alone in big cities a lot of the time. Her parents had been right, and admitting that was tough.

Her father reached across the table and touched her hand. "You can't help who you love, sweetheart, and besides, without Dean, there'd be no Dani."

She nodded. How many times over the last few months had that same thought been a source of strength for her. She could never regret her choices. She wouldn't change a thing about her life so far…except of course this part could be a little better.

An image of Jackson's enraged yet cool expression on the ice that evening flashed in her overactive mind. He'd gone immediately to Dani's side, and he'd somehow made her daughter feel like a superhero for taking the hit. Reassuring her that she'd acted like a pro out on the ice had made Dani beam, and the way his worried expression had checked for any injuries had almost had Abigail needing medical attention. Any man that dedicated to her daughter's well-being and feelings was more than a little fantastic.

How had she never noticed this side of Jackson before?

Feeling her father's intent, perceptive gaze, she stood.

"Going to try to get some sleep?"

"No, I'm going to check on her again," she said carrying her cup with her.

He nodded and hesitated before saying, "Your mom told me you found a place to rent and possibly buy?"

She stopped in the doorway. "Yeah, Jackson Westmore's house over on Oak Avenue." Trying to say his name without giving away the fact that she'd just been thinking about him was a challenge.

"The three-bedroom bungalow on the lake?"

"Yes. How did you know?"

"I was at the hardware store last month and heard him tell Reagan Chase, the paint expert, about the place. Said he got it for a steal because the previous owners had to vacate quickly."

Well, that explained the low rent he was planning to charge her. It was also good information to know if and when she decided to make an offer on the place.

Her father was frowning. "Odd that he decided to rent it to you."

"Yeah, no kidding. I guess we've decided to leave the past where it belongs and move on," she said with a shrug. In truth, she'd never fully understood his animosity toward her in the first place, except to assume it was her monopolization of Dean's time. But she was starting to wonder whether it had been Dean's time he'd actually wanted.

"That's not what I meant. I'm just surprised he decided to turn it into a rental property. I didn't even think he'd planned on selling this one. I thought he'd bought that house for himself. It certainly sounded that way. He was picking out some high-end finishing products for the renos…Not usually the case for a house you plan to flip quickly and hope to turn a profit on."

She frowned. "He didn't say anything." Though he had said he wasn't sure he wanted to sell it…and he'd skirted around her interest in owning it.

"Well, maybe I got it wrong. First time for everything, right?" he asked with a wink, getting up and placing his mug into the dishwasher.

"Yeah, maybe," she said distractedly as he kissed the top of her head, said goodnight, and left her to ponder what he'd said.

As she slowly climbed the stairs to the guest room where Dani was sleeping, she couldn't help but wonder if her father was right. Had Jackson bought the house with the intention of turning it into his own home?

If so, why was he willing to let her and Dani live there first?

CHAPTER 9

"So, tell me again why we're doing this tonight instead of watching *Monday Night Football*," Darryl asked, struggling under the weight of the marble countertop they carried from the truck into the house.

Jackson set his end in place. "Careful…easy. This thing cost a small fortune," he said, watching nervously as his buddy set his end in place. "And I told you—I need the house ready sooner than I thought."

Darryl studied him. "Did you decide to sell it?"

"No. Just decided to rent it out for a while." He shrugged, opening the new stainless steel fridge and removing two Coors Lights—the only thing in there—and tossing one to Darryl.

Darryl popped the top on the can and took a gulp before saying, "You wouldn't be renting the place to Abby Jansen, by any chance?"

The tone of his friend's voice annoyed him—as if he thought he knew something he possibly couldn't. "Yes, actually. So?" he asked despite his better judgment, leaning his hands against the new countertop.

"So…nothing. I just think you're doing an awful lot for a woman you claim to dislike. A woman who is in the middle of a nasty divorce from your best friend." He took another swig of the beer.

Jackson shrugged. "She needed a rental for a few months, and I wasn't quite ready to move yet." The last part was a lie. The lease on his place had been up two months ago, and he was going month to month, planning to move into the house once the renovations were complete, but his friend didn't need to know that. "Besides, it was Becky's idea. She cornered me in front of Abby at the bar the other night. How was I supposed to say no?"

Darryl laughed. "I'm just confused about this soft spot you've developed for her suddenly."

Hardly suddenly. Try a soft spot that had only grown softer and more longingly desperate over the last twenty years. "I don't know what you're talking about. Grab that other side. I don't think it's quite even," he said, pretending to study the piece of marble. He'd admired the black and gray swirl pattern for months before biting the expensive bullet and ordering the slab.

"It's perfect." Darryl tossed his empty can in the blue recycle bin near the door, opened the fridge, and retrieved another one. "And it's not just the house."

He folded his arms. "What are you talking about?"

"Dex's suspension—two games?" He raised an eyebrow.

"He checked Dani into the boards. Checking is illegal in this league. You know that." He swallowed hard. It was true. Yet, he knew his buddy had a right to be giving him this look. Since the day before, he'd replayed the event over and over in his mind, including how he'd handled the situation.

He may have been a little harsh with the kid's suspension, but the sight of Dani hitting the boards and Abigail's look of pure terror as she watched…

"Yes, but two games? Dani was fine."

He sighed. "I reacted in the moment. Maybe it was a little harsh, and I'm sure that smug asshole of a father didn't help matters. But you know safety is my main priority for these kids."

Darryl nodded. "Okay, but let me ask you something. You don't have to answer—just think about it—would your reaction and suspension have been the same had it been James who'd hit the boards?"

He wanted to think so, but his gut told him otherwise. The day before he hadn't been thinking with his head. Making decisions based on his tortured, useless heart wasn't the right way to deal with things. He sighed. "I'll talk to Dex."

*   *   *

Abigail collected the stack of papers she was grading and slid her feet back into her shoes the following afternoon after her first day of substitute teaching in a week. Admittedly, she wasn't being called in as often as she'd hoped. Luckily, she was staying plenty busy with the fundraising committee planning, whose meeting was scheduled to start in ten minutes in the staff room. Dani had gotten a ride home with Taylor that day, and Becky had invited her to stay for dinner. She'd pick her up after the meeting.

As she left the classroom, she nearly collided with one of her colleagues. "Oh, sorry, Beth," she said, readjusting her folders in her arms.

"No worries. My fault for hiding around corners," the

music teacher said, as she stuck a poster to the bulletin board outside the classroom door.

Abigail glanced at it. FATHER AND DAUGHTER FALL FORMAL. Crap. The school still had that? She bit her lip. Would Dani want to go? Dances and dresses weren't exactly her daughter's thing, and the chances of Dean being available to take her were slim.

Hopefully she wouldn't bring it up, and Abigail wasn't about to.

A few minutes later, she entered the staff room, where the other teachers were already waiting and the sports coaches chatted near the window, drinking coffee. Her gaze met Jackson's and she felt her cheeks redden. Since her conversation with her father the night before, she couldn't erase the nagging thought that maybe Jackson wasn't as anti-Abigail as he'd always appeared, and that idea was too confusing to even start to entertain.

She had enough to deal with, so she forced her own conflicting emotions aside.

Breaking the eye contact, she smiled at the other teachers, all of whom she'd met at the staff meeting she'd attended earlier that week. "Hi, everyone," she said, relieved to also see Kelli enter the room. The woman had offered to help her head her first fundraising meeting for a smoother transition. The previous meeting Abigail had mostly sat back and listened.

A series of greetings and small talk followed, until finally Kelli said, "As you all know, Abigail will be taking over heading the fundraising efforts this year in my absence…"

A series of nods and warm, friendly, if uncertain smiles met her around the table.

Their apprehension over her leadership didn't bother her.

Truth was, she was probably the most doubtful of her abilities as any of them, but she refused to show it.

Fake it. Make it. Wasn't that how the saying went? She could handle this responsibility and hopefully before long, they would all see that.

"I'll turn the meeting over to her now. They are all yours, Abigail," she said, and there was a note of reluctance in her voice.

"Thank you." She avoided Jackson as she summoned the courage to continue. "I've reviewed last year's fundraising ideas and efforts and after looking at the numbers, I think what we're doing as a team is working well." She paused. "But, I think there are other opportunities we could explore and places where we can expand the efforts as well."

A few looks were sent across the table, and she refused to let them destroy her confidence. She cleared her throat as she flipped through the fundraising file. "For example, the bottle drive…"

Mark Hanly sat straighter, pulling his sport coat together to hide the coffee stain that was perpetually on his dress shirt. The man must have a leaky chin, she mused. "That's usually my thing," the fourth grade teacher, soccer coach, and father of three said.

Abigail smiled. "And it looks like it's one of the more lucrative drives, so congratulations on your effort there," she said.

The man nodded and his shoulders relaxed. "We try."

"My only suggestion would be trying to get some of the local businesses on board with the efforts."

"How?" he asked.

"Well in L.A.…"

Several more looks and facial twitches threatened her confidence slightly, but Jackson's encouraging nod somehow made her feel better. The intensity in his eyes was another story, so she turned slightly to address the opposite side of the room.

"At Dani's former school, they invested in plastic recycling containers with the school's logo on the front. Local businesses agreed to place them in their establishments and donate the bottles and cans to the school's programs, divided equally between all of the sports, music, and theatre groups."

"Wouldn't the bins be expensive, though?" Ally Carter, the young kindergarten teacher, asked.

"There would be an initial investment for them…" Abigail flipped through her papers. "I got a quote from Southern Colorado Disposal. Fifty would cost the school one hundred eighty-nine dollars at their discounted price, and to keep costs down, we could attach our own house-made labels onto them."

"But the bottle drive only brought in a little over four hundred dollars last year. Isn't it a little counterproductive?" Mark asked.

She was prepared for this meeting. Taking out her photocopied stats of the money raised by Montessori Academy in Los Angeles, she passed them around the table. "As you can see, the K to six school raised a total of three thousand, four hundred fifty-six dollars in nine months by soliciting the help of the community." She smiled at the wide-eyed, positive expressions among the group as they reviewed the numbers.

"And you think we could get enough businesses on board?"

She nodded. "Absolutely." Glenwood Falls may be a small community, but its residents band together. "A lot of the business owners have kids or relatives in these programs, and I'm sure they will all be happy to help."

A collection of nods went around the table, and when her gaze settled on Jackson again, her breath caught in her throat at the look—was that admiration?—on his face. Somehow his approval felt like a small victory, and she refused to read too much into it. She'd yet to shake the strange, unfamiliar feelings she'd experienced the night he'd mentioned kissing her or the intense gratitude she had for his attention to Dani the day before at practice.

"I think it sounds like a great idea," Sam Fisher, a first grade teacher and choir director, said, breaking into her thoughts. "With funds like this, we could start traveling to some of the nearby music competitions."

Ally nodded. "And the theatre group could afford to bring in guest acting coaches…" Her excitement was evident.

"Let's not start spending money before we actually have it," Kelli interjected.

Abigail heard a note of insecurity in the woman's voice, so she was quick to agree. "Kelli is right. We have a lot of work to do first," she said with a laugh.

"Okay, well, how do we get started?" Mark asked, opening his notebook.

As she launched into her preplanned strategy of attack for the efforts, Abigail felt lighter, more confident, excited…happier than she had in a long time. She was making a difference, adding value, and it did wonders for her self-esteem.

An hour later, *her* excitement wasn't the only one felt in the room as everyone discussed several new fundraising ideas that in the past they thought might be too time-consuming or too costly. She was relieved that in each scenario, she was able to encourage the idea and provide valid advice on how to make the suggestion work, based on her previous involvement and experience.

Checking her watch, she couldn't believe that over an hour and a half had passed already. "I think this meeting went well. Let's call it an evening and meet again next week to discuss the progress we've made. Sound good?" she asked.

Everyone agreed.

"Great." She closed her folder and reached for her purse on the floor.

"Uh, there's one quick thing, if I could?" Jackson said and she stopped to glance at him.

"Of course. What's up?" she asked, hoping her voice sounded light and didn't give away the nerves she'd felt just being in the same room with him.

"This weekend is the team's first away game. It's in Allenville, about two hours away. It's an evening game, so the team will be staying overnight," he said.

"Do you require funding?" They would obviously need to arrange transportation and overnight accommodation for the players.

Jackson shook his head. "No. The school bus has already been reserved, and the motel rooms paid for from last year's funds." He hesitated.

"So what do you need?"

"Chaperones." His gaze locked on hers. "Specifically a female chaperone."

Right. Crap. Now that there were two little girls on the team, it wasn't good enough to have just Jackson and Darryl, the assistant coach, go on the trip. She scanned the room.

Everyone else busied themselves in collecting their belongings or chatting among themselves, avoiding her gaze.

Great, no volunteers.

She sighed as her surrendering gaze returned to Jackson. "I can do it." She'd have to go anyway. She'd never feel comfortable letting Dani go with the team two hours outside of Glenwood Falls without her.

A hint of a desire reflected in his expression as he obviously realized the same thing she did—they would be spending a lot of time together that weekend. In a hotel…With kids, she quickly reminded herself, before her thoughts wandered off to unsafe for work territory. "Gr…" He cleared his throat. "Great. That's settled then. Thank you."

"Great," she repeated, wondering how many more layers of her life would end up tangled with his.

And worse—why that thought wasn't as terrible as she'd like it to be.

* * *

"This is so exciting."

"We are totally going to kick some butt."

"Remember the goalie is weak on his left side, so always shoot to his left."

Abigail sighed as she listened to the girls in the back of her SUV chat excitedly about their first game of the season—also their first away game that Saturday evening. She wished she shared their excitement, but there was so much about the next twenty-four hours making her anxious, she could barely focus.

The school would only approve funding for three motel rooms and two adult chaperones, which meant the assistant coach would be driving to Allenville on his own and then driving back after the game. Which meant she was stuck on a school bus for two hours and then at a motel with Jackson.

Pulling into the school's parking lot, where the school bus waited and other parents migrated, saying goodbye to their kids as they rushed onto the bus, excited and without a care, the knot in her stomach drew even tighter. Jackson stood at the bus door, collecting the signed permission slips from the parents and checking off the attendance as each kid passed him, lugging their heavy hockey bags onto the bus.

Dressed in a pair of jeans and a denim-blue long-sleeve Henley that hugged his biceps and chest and tapered at his waist, he looked like the sexiest hometown hockey coach she'd ever seen. His hair was gelled in a spiked mess, and the five o'clock shadow on his jawline continued to tempt her. The desire to touch him returned—his face, his muscular chest, those thick thighs straining against the denim…Damn, this was going to be a long bus ride.

"Hey, guys," he greeted them as she and the girls approached moments later. "Ready for your first game?"

"Beyond ready," Taylor said.

"Yeah, we're going to crush them," Dani agreed.

Jackson laughed.

Had the deep, rich sound always made her tummy flutter like this?

"Love the positive attitudes and the enthusiasm, but remember: it's about having fun, okay?"

"Yes, Coach!" they said in unison as they passed him to board the bus.

"Do you think they heard any of that?" he asked her.

"Nope."

"Me neither." He tucked the clipboard under his arm. "So, are *you* ready for your first game?"

"I'll never be ready," she admitted. The last week, watching Dani practice, she started to feel a little better about things. There were no more injuries or rough play during practice, but a game against an opposing team could be a different story.

What if there were other parents like Kurt Miller teaching their children to win at all costs?

"She'll be fine," he said, squeezing her shoulder.

But would *she*—that was the question. Her eyes fell to his hand on her shoulder and she resisted the urge to move closer. Her skin tingled under the warmth of the touch and, just as it had the night in his house when he'd tended to her injured foot, her pulse raced. Where were these feelings coming from? Her body had never reacted to him this way. She had to get a grip. There were far too many reasons why getting involved with Jackson would be another life mistake. Though knowing that did nothing to help suppress the urge to crawl inside his strong arms and make him follow through on that kiss he'd threatened.

He dropped his hand a second later and wiped the palm on the leg of his jeans, as if touching her had been unintentional.

Awesome.

She readjusted her bag on her shoulder and moved past him. "See you on the bus," she said.

* * *

"See you on the bus."

Sixteen-year-old Jackson had sighed as he'd stared at the tenth grade class ski trip schedule in his hands. They'd each been partnered up for safety on the Copper Mountain slopes, and somehow he'd been paired with Abby. He scanned the list of other partners, and wished his name was anywhere else. The thought of the embarrassment he would face once they hit the ski slopes was making it hard to breathe. He wouldn't need to fake a stomachache to get out of participating, like he'd planned; he was pretty sure he was about to get sick for real as his gut twisted and turned.

The news about Abby's recent breakup with senior Roy Leger had gone through the school faster than chicken pox, and for a brief moment the day before, he'd thought maybe he'd ask her to the winter formal, seeing as how it was only a week away, and now that she wouldn't be going with Roy…maybe she just might consider him, seeing as how most everyone else had dates already.

He hadn't planned on going at all, but for about thirty seconds the day before, watching Abby twirl a strand of her long blonde hair around one finger while she finished their math exam, he'd envisioned what it might be like to go with her.

Of course his daydream had ended with the thought of her laughing at him when he tried to dance, and he'd immediately hated himself for even entertaining the stupid notion.

Abby Jansen dated guys like Roy Leger—older guys who had their driver's license, who were good at all sports, not just hockey, and who treated her like she was invisible. She deserved to be treated so much better…

She also deserved to have a good ski trip and not have his bailing affect her day on the slopes. For two weeks, all she'd talked about—not to him, but he'd overheard, of course—was how much she was looking forward to this trip. She'd taken ski lessons the winter before and claimed to have skied the black diamond runs and the extreme terrain runs—the tougher and more advanced trails at the resort.

He never should have agreed to this field trip, but the other option had been to stay behind and participate in the drama class's Christmas production—no thank you.

Though being forced into a pair of tights for their version

of *The Nutcracker* suddenly seemed less embarrassing than falling on his face in the snow with Abby watching.

"You okay, buddy?" Dean's voice behind him said.

"Oh, yeah, fine," he muttered. He glanced at the sheet. "Hey, who did you get paired with for this?" Albert Keeley's name was next to Dean's. The only other tenth grader who seemed to be more nervous about this trip than he was.

Albert was a genius, having skipped the second and third grade, putting him two years younger than the rest of the class, which made it even harder for him to make friends. He was maybe ninety pounds and the most uncoordinated kid Jackson had ever seen.

"Yep, this is going to suck. I seriously doubt Albert will want to leave the bunny slopes, so I need to figure out a way to sneak away to get some skiing done," Dean said. "Who'd you get?" He glanced at the list in Jackson's hand and then punched his shoulder.

"What was that for?"

"For getting the hottest girl in school as your partner."

His buddy had looked genuinely annoyed.

Jackson had scoffed. "Abby? No way," he said, but the words were too high pitched—the way his voice always went an octave higher when he was lying or nervous. He was both now.

"Switch partners with me," Dean said quietly, pulling him out of earshot of Mr. Hannigan, the teacher taking attendance at the door of the bus.

"Uh…" He hesitated for a brief second, before realizing his friend was offering him a way out of his embarrassment and a way out of skiing that day. "Okay." He'd nodded eagerly. "Do you think we need to tell Hannigan?"

"Nah, it's fine," Dean had said, reaching into his pocket for a fresh piece of gum. Spitting the old piece into the trash can on the school yard, he popped the new one in and ran a hand through his hair. "Wish me luck."

Jackson had frowned. "For what?" he asked, his stomach now a tornado of discomfort as he had a sinking suspicion he knew exactly what his buddy meant.

"I'm about to make Abby Jansen my girl in time for the winter formal."

And that's when he had thrown up a little bit in his mouth. His best friend was planning to make a play for Abby? He'd never even shown any interest in her before. And besides, Abby was the girl *he* wanted to date. Guys didn't do that to one another.

Of course Dean had no idea he had a thing for Abby. If he said something now, would his friend reconsider? He opened his mouth, but his confidence failed him at the final, crucial second. "What about Lily?" he croaked out instead—the ninth grader Dean had just started hanging out with. His friend refused to call anything "dating" or any girl his "girlfriend," but Jackson had been sure he and Lily were an item.

"Crap, you're right." Dean paused, then he smiled, slipping an arm around his shoulders. "Take one for the team will you, man?"

"You want me to take Lily to winter formal so you can ditch out on her for Abby?" Fantastic. Then he would not only not get to go with the girl of his dreams, but he'd have to watch Dean—his best friend—with her?

Teenage life sucked.

"Come on, you know if the roles were reversed, I'd do it for you."

The problem was, it was true. Reluctantly he nodded with a sigh. "Fine. Okay."

"Thanks, man. You're a good friend." He'd climbed onto

the bus then, and Jackson had dragged his feet as he followed.

As he boarded, Abby had looked past Dean and smiled at him, patting the seat next to her.

He'd looked away and scanned the rows for Albert, then avoiding her gaze, he took a seat next to the only other kid on the bus who felt about as sick as he did.

*   *   *

Abigail watched as the last kid climbed onto the bus, followed by Jackson. Sitting alone in the third seat from the back, as far away from Dani as possible to give her daughter space with her friends, she waited to see if he would join her. An odd sense of déjà vu washed over her as the familiar surroundings from her youth—the worn gray, high-backed bus seats covered in graffiti with kid's initials and hearts, the square windows that never went down all the way or refused to close—brought to mind her own school field trips.

One in particular had started exactly like this. Her sitting in a seat toward the back of the bus, waiting for Jackson to sit next to her as they headed to Copper Mountain for the ski trip. She had never understood how he'd ended up sitting with Albert instead, and suddenly her new partner had been Dean. At the time, she'd been thrilled to have Dean Underwood's undivided attention, especially since she'd just ended things with her boyfriend of six weeks, Roy Leger. But still, she'd been bothered by the fact Jackson had disliked her so much he'd preferred to have Albert as a partner that day instead of her.

She held her breath as her gaze met his and an odd look of indecision flashed across his face. He hesitated just long enough for her to notice the pause, then he averted his gaze, did a quick head count of the kids, sat in the empty seat at the front of the bus, and started a chat with the driver.

Okay then. Obviously their unspoken truce didn't extend all the way to sitting side by side for two hours.

* * *

The excitement level of the team as they reboarded the bus after that evening's game had him smiling with pride. They'd won their first game of the season, away from their home arena. The Allenville team had consisted of all boys, except for their goalie. She'd blocked so many impressive shots at the start of the game that he'd been preparing his we'll-get-'em-next-time speech. The score of 5–4 had meant the game had been nail-bitingly close for all three periods, but they'd pulled out the win.

Best of all, it had been Dani who'd scored the winning goal. The little girl's excitement had only been outdone by the support of her teammates. Jackson hadn't known he'd been so worried about the boys' acceptance of the new female additions until that moment when their pride had been a weight lifting from his chest.

And then there had been the look on Abby's face. The image of her beaming expression had made him want to take her in his arms and later blame an ill-timed kiss on the spontaneity of the moment. He had to hand it to her; she'd landed on her feet: within weeks of being back she'd secured a new job, earned the respect of her reluctant co-workers, and settled back into small-town life.

The truth was, he'd never pictured Abby fitting in with the pro-hockey/high-profile lifestyle. Not that she wasn't capable; it was just that the girl he'd known had preferred the outdoors—camping, fishing, hiking—to fancy dinner parties. She'd preferred her running shoes to heels. Maybe that was why all the guys liked her so much.

And looking at her now, she seemed to have fallen right back into the girl she used to be. From the back of the bus, she smiled at him as he took his seat next to Dex, and his heart echoed in his ears.

She had to feel the fire simmering just beneath the surface whenever they were together. The mutual attraction and sexual tension in the air around them couldn't be his imagination. Before, it had been his lack of confidence and fear of rejection that had him sitting back while another guy had stolen her affection. But he wasn't that same insecure kid anymore. He knew what he wanted. And he was pretty damn sure she wanted it, too.

Unfortunately a busload of preteens wasn't the best place to confirm his suspicions.

With an adrenaline-infused high coming off of the kids in waves, he suspected it was going to be a long night trying to monitor two rooms of boys, who'd just consumed liters of soda pop and gallons of ice cream at their victory dinner. But within forty minutes of arriving back at the motel, they were all out cold.

He grinned as he yawned and turned out the main lights in the adjoining hotel rooms, then slipped out onto the balcony into the crisp fall night air.

"The boys are out, too?"

Abby's voice on the balcony to his right made him turn. "Yeah. So much for 'partying all night.'" He laughed. "I'm not even sure they finished the leftover pizza we brought back."

She nodded, drawing a pale pink cardigan tighter around her body. The soft color was a stark contrast to her tanned skin, and his eyes were drawn to her chest visible above the fabric.

He wondered if her skin was as silky soft as it looked.

"I never thought they'd get any sleep tonight," she said.

Right. The kids. Stay focused on the kids. "It was a great first game," he said, forcing his eyes from her face, illuminated only by the moonlight.

"Dani is so proud of herself for that winning goal," she said leaning over the balcony rail.

His gaze flew involuntarily to her perfectly shaped curves. How his friend could let an ass as great as that one walk away was beyond comprehension.

In his silence, she glanced at him.

He raised his eyes, but it was too late. He was busted for staring at her ass. He cleared his throat, trying to remember what she'd said. Dani's winning goal, right. "She should be proud. It was perfectly executed, and that Allenville goalie was a superstar. If she can score on her, she'll be MVP of the team by the end of the season."

Abby nodded and an awkward, long silence followed.

"Yep, the kids did great." That's it, just keep repeating the same meaningless small talk until the uncomfortableness grows and one of them went back inside.

She nodded again.

Another excruciating silence. Damn. Would he ever not feel like an awkward, self-conscious teenager around her? If he could even just get to the point where he could spend time with her without feeling as though he had to be stand-offish or ignore her to prevent his real feelings from showing, he'd take it. Apparently, that wouldn't be tonight. "Well, goodnight."

"Jackson," she said as he turned to go back inside.

"Yeah?"

"I wanted to talk to you about the house."

"Oh right, of course." He'd meant to give her an update, but with the kids there hadn't been time. "I just finished the kitchen a few nights ago, so you can move in anytime."

"That's great. Thank you. I hope you didn't go through any trouble getting it ready early."

"No trouble at all." As long as paying five hundred dollars to put a rush on the laminate floor installation didn't count.

She hesitated, looking as though there was more she wasn't saying. "Okay, but actually, I was wondering…well, I heard that you bought the house for yourself. That you'd planned on moving in there. Is that true?"

He should have known she'd find out that had been his plan. Enough people around town knew he'd bought the place for that reason. Hell, he'd already ordered the mailbox for the end of the driveway with WESTMORE written on it. "I hadn't really decided yet." He shrugged. "But even if I do decide to keep it, it wouldn't be for a while. You and Dani can have the place as long as you need it."

She frowned. "But then what are the chances you'd consider selling it to me? The thing is, I'm just not sure moving in and getting settled is a good idea, if you decide you don't want to sell it after all."

He swallowed hard, but didn't think twice before saying, "It's yours if you want it."

A questioning look flickered in her eyes as a soft breeze blew a strand of her hair across her face. She tucked it back behind an ear. "But…"

Striding toward the edge of the balcony, he stopped, resting his hands against it. "Look, Abby, I…" He what? How did he tell her there was nothing he wouldn't give her? "The house…" And anything else that was his to give. "Is yours if you want it."

"I think I do," she said quietly. "But then I'll feel terrible for swiping your house out from under you."

"Don't." His eyes locked with hers and all of a sudden an urge to be honest with her, to tell her how he'd always felt about her, even if it was too late, was so overwhelming, he almost gave in. Luckily common sense and an unwillingness to make things even more awkward between them stopped him. She didn't feel that way about him. She was divorcing his best friend. And for those two big reasons, he couldn't tell her. It would only make things worse. "Dean is my best friend, and you and Dani are…important to me," he said instead, stumbling over the understatement.

Her expression clouded at the mention of Dean but she simply nodded.

He wondered how many different meanings, how many different intentions she could hide with a simple nod.

Too many. And he'd be an idiot to try to figure them out.

He offered a small smile as he added, "Besides, you and Dani will turn it into a much better home than I would have." He turned to leave, the desire to tell her how he felt about her nearly strangling him. The longer he said nothing, the more he felt the opportunity slipping away. "Goodnight. I'll see you in the morning."

"Why is that?" she blurted out quickly as he reached for the balcony door handle.

She wasn't making his usual avoidance and escape easy that evening. "What do you mean?"

"I just mean—Why don't you…um…Why aren't you…?"

"Married?" Was that where she was going with this?

Again the simple nod.

He sighed, placing his hands on his hips. His gaze fell on the dark mountains, which were shadows against the navy, starlit sky. "I guess I just haven't found the right one," he said. Impossible to do when she'd already married his best friend.

"Are you looking?" she asked with a laugh. "'Cause I've seen quite a few women sending you not-so-subtle hints— Linda, the basketball coach, for one."

"Linda?" She must have her signals mixed up. "No way. She's just a friend."

"Maybe to you, but I think she likes you."

There was more than friendly curiosity in her tone. Jealousy, maybe? He shook his head. "Well, either way, I'm not into Linda." The problem was, he hadn't found anyone in town he was into enough to consider a relationship with. He'd dated women over the years. He'd even gotten semiserious about one—Cameron Day, a young professional snowboarder, who'd lived twenty minutes outside of Glenwood Falls. She'd taught him how to ski finally, and they'd been really close, but unfortunately her skiing career was her priority, and he'd understood that.

Since her, he'd been on a few dates—mostly Becky's doing—but until he found someone who made his chest ache with longing to be near them, like Abby did, he'd rather be alone.

"What about me?" she asked, her eyes downcast on the railing between them. "How come you've never liked me?"

"Huh?" That's what she thought?

She gave a nervous laugh. "Jeez, listen to me. I sound like an eight-year-old. I just meant…well, exactly what I said." She stared at him, waiting for the answer to the million-dollar question.

One he didn't know. "I do like you." Too much. "I… well…it was…" Oh God, he felt like he was drowning. Just tell her the truth.

"It was because I stole your best friend away, right?"

No, it was because his best friend had stolen *her* away. Her answer seemed a lot less complicated, and he sensed non-complicated was what she needed right now, so he nodded. "I guess so, yeah. But if you hadn't, hockey would have eventually. The game first, friendship second," he said.

She looked away. "Don't I know it."

"Well, goodnight," he said again, hoping this time she'd let him go. He had a hard time looking at her sad, thoughtful, faraway expression without wanting to wrap his arms around her and tell her he'd never put her second, that her heart would be safe with him.

But unfortunately, he wasn't sure that sentiment went both ways.

CHAPTER 10

❧

$\mathcal{T}$he following weekend was moving day.

"You really don't have to be in a rush about this. You and Dani are welcome to stay as long as you need to," her mother said, blocking Abigail's path to the front door.

They'd had this discussion a million times since she'd told her parents the house was ready to move into. "This is getting heavy, Mom." Her grip started to slip, and she readjusted the box in her arms. Her forearms burned, and she suspected she would be feeling this the next morning. She didn't care, the thought of sleeping in their own place that evening fueling her strength.

Her mother sighed, moving aside. "Okay."

"Mom, it's just a few blocks. I'm not leaving Glenwood Falls again." She meant it. Moving home may have felt like admitting failure or defeat in the beginning, but now that she was back, creating a new life for herself and Dani, it seemed like the best place to be. She had a job, a new place, and best of all the support of her family and friends nearby.

Glenwood Falls may not be as exciting and fast paced as L.A., but that was a good thing. She'd never entirely fit in with that world anyway. She'd been happy there, but that was because of Dean and Dani, and she'd made the best of the lifestyle options she'd had. But this, this felt right. This felt like home.

She carried the box outside just as her father pulled into the driveway with the U-Haul loaded up with their furniture from the storage locker, where she'd stored the bigger items until she'd found a place. She'd been on her way over there to help him load everything. He must have gotten help from Mr. Kelsie, the owner. Abigail smiled. One less thing to worry about. "Perfect timing," she said, accepting the keys from him. "I just finished filling the car, and Mom is driving me crazy."

He laughed. "You have to be patient with her. This is the first time she's had you and Dani living so close. Neither of us want to lose that again. We've just missed having you home the last nine years."

"I know, Dad. And as I just told Mom, I'm not going anywhere. Just six blocks away." She shot a glance toward the house, where her mother stood, looking out the living room window, a tissue clutched in her hand, her eyes red and puffy. "Is she going to be okay?" she asked, suddenly feeling bad. One day, Dani would leave home, and she suspected she'd be the one standing in the window with tissues. She blew her a kiss and her mom smiled, returning it.

"She'll be fine. Just maybe invite her over to help you un-pack once you get settled," he said. "Are you sure you can handle this thing?" He nodded toward the U-Haul.

"I drove one all the way from L.A. Six blocks should be easy." Somehow driving her belongings to her new place made her feel more independent. "But thanks, Dad," she said, giving him a hug.

"Okay, I'll meet you at the house to help unload everything," he said, taking her car keys.

* * *

Jackson climbed out of his truck when he saw the U-Haul turn the corner onto the street. Abby was behind the wheel, and he did a quick glance around to make sure the neighborhood kids weren't playing anywhere near the street.

The woman he remembered couldn't park a Smart car, let alone a ten-ton cube van.

But as he watched her slowly, carefully back the van into the unpaved driveway, his this-should-be-good look changed to one of admiration.

Impressive.

Great, just something else to love about her.

Her SUV pulled up behind his truck and he waved to her father as the man got out.

"Gotta admit, I nearly had a heart attack just now watching Abby back that thing in," Jackson said.

"Me too. I wasn't sure there would be a house left to move into," he said with a laugh.

"I heard that," she said walking toward them.

His eyes did a once-over on her body and immediately he was both grateful and annoyed her father was standing right next to him. Dressed in a pair of tight black capri leggings and an oversized T-shirt that hung off one shoulder, exposing a pale blue bra strap, she looked amazing. Her long hair tied back in a high ponytail and her face free of makeup, she rivaled a Cover Girl model for best fresh face to the world.

"Hi," she said, stopping in front of him.

"Hey. That was impressive," he said.

"Odd how that comment strikes me as almost more offensive than the ones I just overheard," she said with one eyebrow raised.

"I just meant those trucks aren't easy to drive."

"For a girl?"

Oh shit. He wasn't getting out of this one. He'd learned quickly living with his sister to just apologize. "Sorry," he said. He reached into his pocket for his keys. Removing the only house key he had from his key ring, he handed it to her. "Here you go. Welcome to your new home."

She took it and smiled. "Thank you. And I appreciate you getting the renovations completed early."

He nodded. "No problem."

She turned to her father. "Dad, if you want to unlock the door, I'll start unloading the SUV."

"Where can I start?" Jackson asked.

She stopped and swung back in surprise. "Oh, that's okay. You don't need to help. We got it."

"Who do you think helped me load the stuff from the storage unit into the U-Haul?" her dad called out as he unlocked the front door.

Her eyes widened. "You helped?"

He shrugged. "Right place at the right time to be useful. I was at the bank across the street and saw your dad drive up with the U-Haul."

Her expression was unreadable. "Oh, well, thank you."

"So, I'll start unloading the truck?"

She hesitated.

"That bedframe of yours weighs about a thousand pounds," her father said.

She sighed. "I guess that's a yes, then."

* * *

The sight of Jackson Westmore moving her personal items into a house he currently owned and she was now renting was too much to wrap her mind around. However, it was far too amazing a sight to look away. He'd abandoned his sweatshirt somewhere between the bedframe and the couch. Now, his bulging biceps testing the confines of the sleeves of his white T-shirt and his forearm muscles straining under the weight of an oversized box nearly caused her to drool onto the counter, where she stretched to peer out the kitchen window. She was suddenly jealous of her moving boxes. What would it be like to have his arms holding her that way?

He shifted the weight of the box and wiped sweat from his forehead onto his shoulder as he walked up the front path toward the house. He glanced toward the window, caught her staring and smiled. Her knees nearly gave way beneath her as she stepped back out of sight.

Get it together. It's Jackson Westmore. Dean's best friend and a man she should not be having this insane attraction to. It had to be her recent dry spell in the sex department causing it. Though admittedly no one else was making her want to pounce on them.

Hearing the door open, she took a deep breath and squared her shoulders. . .lationship, even a casual one, was not in her plans right now.

Not even a hot, steamy, passionate one, she thought as he entered the kitchen and set the box on the counter. "Thank you," she said.

They'd barely spoken since the night she'd practically begged him to like her on the balcony at the motel, and she still felt embarrassed by her need for acceptance. It had never bothered her before that he didn't like her. Why was it suddenly so important?

Because he was her daughter's hockey coach and her new landlord didn't seem to be working as an answer.

"No problem," he said. "Were you enjoying the view?"

She willed her cheeks not to turn red. "I don't know what you're talking about. I wanted to make sure you didn't drop my good dishes," she said avoiding his eyes. Her gaze fell to a vase of flowers on the table. "Where did these come from?" she asked, approaching the vase and smelling the lilies—her favorite.

"Just a small housewarming gift," he said with a shrug.

Her eyes widened.

"Becky's idea," he said quickly, shoving his hands into his pockets.

A sense of disappointment overwhelmed her. "Oh."

"I just realized I don't have a key for the padlock on the shed door out back, so I'll cut the lock off and get a new one. The hardware store is closed now, but I'll swing by with one soon, if that's okay."

"Yeah, no rush. I don't know if you noticed, but I'm not really a puttering around out in the shed type."

He laughed and her breath caught. Where had those incredibly sexy dimples come from? Had he always had those? He'd never smiled this much at her before...and she longed to see it again. Which was more than a little stupid. She glanced away, turning her attention back to the flowers. "Thanks again for your help." She was eager to be alone to start unpacking, but mostly, she was eager to be away from those dimples and the dizzying effect they were having on her. Where had she packed her vibrator again?

"No problem." He headed toward the door and she followed. "And I'll stop by soon with the new lock and key."

"Great. Thank you."

He hesitated by the door.

"Everything okay?"

"I lied."

"Huh?"

"The flowers were my idea," he said, waving as he headed off toward his truck.

CHAPTER 11

❧

*W*ow. Are you sure you're only having one baby?" Abigail asked, sitting across from Becky the next day. Dani had spent the day with Taylor while she'd continued to unpack and get things organized. She stared behind her friend at the mound of baby clothes that was spilling off the couch.

Becky laughed. "I better be. Dani, your mom's here!" she called out as she picked up a tiny pink and white jumper to fold.

"Pink and white? So, you found out the sex of the baby?"

Becky shook her head, holding up an identical jumper in blue and gray. "Nope. Just covering all the bases."

"Isn't that getting kind of costly?" Abigail asked, before she could stop the comment. "Sorry, that was completely rude."

Becky shook her head as she yawned. "Not at all. Actually, it's pretty cheap since I made all of this." She shrugged. "Whatever I don't end up needing, I'll give to

Kelli, or Jackie, or one of the other million pregnant ladies in town. You know, I swear it's contagious. When one of us gets…"

"Wait a sec," Abigail interrupted. "You *made* all of this yourself?" Standing, she crossed the room and scanned the pile. She picked up the cutest little denim dress with purple flower embroidery on the front pockets. "Like made the entire thing? Even the embroidery?"

"Yep. The glamourous life of a military wife. I have to keep busy or I go crazy missing Neil." She sniffed and reached for a tissue. "Jeez. Hormones are the worst."

Abigail smiled. "I remember I used to watch old episodes of *Friends* when Dean was on the road during my pregnancy, and I'd end up crying my eyes out and be a blubbering idiot when he'd call. He was always so worried about leaving me…" She stopped, the brief glimpse into a better time, the memory of a loving Dean making her uncomfortable. "Anyway, these are amazing, Becky. Have you ever thought about selling them?"

She scoffed, blowing her nose. "No way! Not anymore anyway. Now I just do it for fun, and it really is a lot cheaper than BabyGap."

"And much better quality. That's why I'm serious. Expectant moms would much rather spend money on these handmade items, and they're so much cuter than what's in stores. You could make a fortune."

She frowned, examining a pale green knitted sweater with alligator-shaped buttons. "You think so?"

"I know so." She continued her search through the pile of clothing. "I mean, look at this jacket." She clutched the tiny hooded khaki jacket with safari animal buttons and patches to her chest. "This seriously makes my ovaries hurt."

Becky laughed. "Now you're crazy."

"Okay, so maybe it doesn't make me want to rush out and get pregnant, but if I already was pregnant you would be my baby designer. I'd buy anything Becky's Baby Boutique sold." She folded the jacket and added it to the pile.

Becky picked up another dress—yellow with a white lace trim and daisies on it. "How much would you pay for this?" she asked.

"At least fifty dollars."

Becky's eyes widened. "Okay, Miss Desperate House-wife. You are crazy. This cost me three dollars in fabric and…a dollar fifty in lace."

"Exactly. You'd make a fortune!" she said, ignoring the desperate housewife comment. She knew her friend must think her life in L.A. had been one big episode of the popular drama series, but it wasn't as fantastic as she probably imagined.

"I wouldn't even know how to start selling this stuff." She bit her lip. "The Sunday morning flea market?"

She nodded. "That would be good, but also kinda time-consuming." Her friend was far too busy to sit at a flea market table all day, every Sunday, and the cost of the table would cut into her profits. "But why not start an online business? Less overhead and add shipping costs into the price…" Her excitement rose as she talked, but she sensed she was losing Becky.

"I don't know. That seems complicated, and I'm still not convinced anyone would buy this stuff."

Abigail sighed. Becky was sitting on a gold mine—quite literally—and she didn't even know it. "I have a friend in L.A. who owns a baby boutique store in Beverly Hills, Baby Couture. She needs to see this stuff."

"Help me up, I have to pee…again," she said, changing

the subject. "I swear this kid is training to be an Olympic gymnast someday."

"Better than another hockey player," she said, teasing, letting it go. For now.

"You're right about that."

As she left the living room, Abigail studied the pile of clothes. If Becky didn't believe her, maybe her friend Jocelyn could convince her. She quickly selected the khaki jacket and the daisy sundress from the pile and stashed them in her purse, brushing aside a small pang of guilt.

If these items were the hit she suspected they would be, Becky would forgive her for stealing her baby clothes.

* * *

"Abigail, these are incredible," Jocelyn said two days later, after Abigail had couriered the items to her in L.A.

"I know, right?"

"I mean the stitching is perfect, and the little details—those buttons are the cutest things I've ever seen."

Abigail beamed. "I knew you'd love them," she said refilling her coffee cup and carrying it outside onto the back deck. She sat in the rocking chair she'd bought from a local woodworker and enjoyed the early October breeze over the lake. She was a little worried that she hadn't been getting a lot of substituting hours in the last two weeks, but she did appreciate the extra time to get the house in order and the opportunity to enjoy perfect, crisp fall mountain mornings like this one.

"So, who is this designer?" Jocelyn asked. "Is there a website I can order from?"

Abigail did a silent squeal and seated happy dance before saying calmly, "It's a work in progress, still a fairly new company. You're lucky to be getting a sneak peek at the fabulous product line."

"So you're teasing me with product I can't have." Jocelyn didn't even realize her tone was bitchy—that was just her style, so Abigail took no offense. Instead, she used it to her advantage.

"Well, I could—I mean, *the designer* could put an order together for you and send it next week, along with an invoice." In her mind, she was already designing Becky's nonexistent new company logo.

"You want me to buy items I've never seen and agree to an open invoice?"

Sure, when she worded it like that, it sounded a little risky, but she knew Jocelyn well enough to know she was interested in the product…and she also knew Jon, Jocelyn's husband, had just signed a five-year contract with the Kings worth $56 million. If anyone could afford to sign an open invoice, she could. "Ten more sample items for four hundred dollars." Forty dollars apiece, when she knew Jocelyn would attach a sticker price of a hundred dollars or more, was a great incentive, and if Becky really did only spend three or four dollars to make the items, then she'd have one hell of a profit as well.

Jocelyn hesitated just a second before saying, "Send boy clothing. I'm overstocked on girl items right now."

"Will do," Abigail said, desperately trying and most likely failing to keep her excitement out of her voice. She rocked happily in the chair and sipped her coffee, feeling rather productive and pleased with herself.

"You really should consider moving back here. We could do great business together," Jocelyn said.

She smiled. "Thanks, but I'm not a businessperson. I'm just a substitute teacher."

"Ha! Darling, you just sold me product unseen. Ditch the brats and come work for me."

Abigail laughed. "I'll send you that invoice."

* * *

"Is right here okay?" Jackson asked Paul Samson, the owner of the Taco Hut on Main Street, as he placed the bottle recycle bin in the corner near the door the next day.

"That's great," Paul said, coming out from behind the counter to turn the OPEN sign on.

"Thanks again for allowing us to place one in here." The Taco Hut was five minutes from the high school and saw a lot of lunch traffic during the week. He'd been surprised when Abby had announced them as one of the participating businesses in their bottle drive efforts, as he knew they made decent money from the recyclables. To be donating that to the school was impressive, especially when Paul was one of the only business owners on the list who didn't have children participating in the programs the school offered. At thirty-five, the man was still the town's most eligible bachelor.

"Well, it took a little convincing, I won't lie, but Abby Jansen can be quite persuasive."

Something in his voice wiped the smile from Jackson's face. "Yeah, she's been great on the fundraising committee," he said, putting a clear plastic bag inside the bin.

"It doesn't hurt that she's still sexy as hell. She could have asked me for just about anything the other day when she came in here, and I probably would have been too busy checking out that body to even realize what I was agreeing to."

Jackson's jaw tightened. "She's a smart woman, and the school will definitely benefit from having her on board."

"I'm sure it's not too hard having her around…or maybe it is hard, if you know what I mean," Paul said with a wink.

Locker room banter had never bothered Jackson when he was young and stupid, but at twenty-nine he'd come a long way from disrespecting women, and he'd have hoped Paul would have grown up as well. Apparently not.

"Here's the number to call when it's full. We'll stop by and replace the bag."

Paul took the card with the school's number on it. "I'd rather just call Abby."

That's it. Swiping the card back, Jackson turned and grabbed the recycle bin. "You know what? Thank you, but Glenwood Falls Elementary won't be needing your support this year," he said, pushing through the door and heading straight toward the truck, ignoring Paul's look of surprise. "Asshole," he muttered, throwing the truck in reverse.

Paul's words had nearly gained him a black eye, and he hated the jealousy that coursed through him. Until that moment he hadn't really considered that there were probably more men than just him in the town who were head over heels for the woman. Men who didn't have the deterrent of being her ex-husband's best friend. Men who wouldn't hesitate to approach her.

He hit the steering wheel. Damn it! What would the impact of watching her fall in love with someone else be on him? Once had been tough enough. A second time would be the death of him.

He had to tell her how he felt and let whatever happened happen. Friendships and loyalties aside, he had to at least go after what he wanted this time. If she didn't want him, he'd somehow learn to live with that. But something in the way she'd watched him work the day before—the desire he'd seen in her eyes—made him think that maybe she just didn't

CHAPTER 12

❧

*D*on't be mad."

"Every time Taylor starts a conversation like that, I end up baking until three a.m.," Becky said, reaching into the washing machine and tossing the wet clothes into the dryer above it.

"I promise I don't need you to bake. Though that does remind me—the school's having another bake sale fundraiser next week."

Becky shot her a look, eyebrow raised as she shut the dryer door and picked up a basket of dry clothes. "Once this new baby arrives, I'm using him or her as an excuse to get out of everything—no more baking, no more cooking, no more chauffeur. I hope you all are prepared for that."

Abigail suddenly felt the tiny pang of nervousness about the news she was about to give. Taking care of a baby was hard work, and Becky had so much on her plate already. Maybe going behind her back and launching a baby clothing company hadn't been the right thing to do. She bit her lip, hesitating as she followed her down the hall, where she carried the laundry basket into the nursery.

But a second later, her uncertainty vanished as she saw yet another full inventory of baby clothes in the basket. Her friend wouldn't have to make anything new after the baby was born; she already had enough items to fill two stores for a year. Feeling confident again, Abigail said, "Okay, remember that friend I told you about in L.A. who owns the baby boutique on Rodeo Drive?"

"Yes. In fact, I Googled the store after you left, and oh my God! The stuff she sells is so beautiful, but crazy expensive. Fifteen hundred dollars for a crystal butterfly mobile for above the baby's crib?" Her eyes widened and she shook her head. "Who's crazy enough to pay that much for something like that?"

Abigail glanced at her feet. She had. Or Dean had. It had been her push present—the gift from her husband after she delivered Dani. She'd thought the whole concept of getting jewelry or an expensive gift just for going through labor was ridiculous, no doubt another occasion dreamed up by diamond manufacturers, but all the other hockey wives had gotten one, and Dean wasn't about to let anyone outdo him. "Anyway," she said. "I sent her a few of your items."

Becky's eyes widened.

"And she loved them," she said, continuing quickly.

"She did?"

"Yes. And she placed an order for more." She smiled, and waited for Becky's to appear.

Instead she frowned. "What?"

"Boys' clothes specifically," Abigail said.

Becky shook her head. "Abby, you're crazy. I appreciate your support in this, but I'm not ready to sell my stuff. I've seen the clothing she carries and the price tags that go with it. My items are not worth two hundred and fifty dollars apiece."

Crap. Two hundred and fifty? She'd undersold Becky's items. She'd be better prepared for the next call to Jocelyn. Abigail reached into her purse for the check she'd received that morning for the first two sample items she'd sent. "Jocelyn's customers felt otherwise." She handed over the $80 check. "Sorry, I think I underpriced them."

Becky's mouth dropped and she slowly lowered herself into her chair. "Someone bought my items?"

"Yes. The khaki jacket and the yellow sundress."

She narrowed her eyes. "I was wondering what happened to them."

Abigail pointed to the check. "This."

Becky sighed. "This is a lot of money for two items."

"Right. So I think a smile, a high five, perhaps even a woohoo, would be appropriate," she said with a laugh.

Becky finally smiled. "Okay. Woohoo!"

"That's better. Now, let's see about the items for the first order." She sat on the floor and started looking through the items in the basket. "This stuff is so fantastic," she said, holding up a navy hoodie with a front pocket pouch. The dinosaur on the front was wearing sunglasses and offering a peace sign. "Jocelyn is going to freak."

"*I'm* going to freak." Becky looked worried again as she stared at the check in her hand.

"Look, just take a breath and tell me which ten pieces you can part with—boys' stuff."

"I made this stuff for my own child. I'm not sure I want to part with any of them."

"You may not even be having a boy. Besides, there's enough clothes here for three boys. Pick ten things." Tough love would be the only way to get this done. She held up the dinosaur hoodie again. "This one?"

Becky sighed. "Fine. I have another one of those decals so I can make another one."

"Awesome. What else?"

Twenty minutes and a lot of coaxing later, they finally had ten items.

"Are you sure about this, Abby? I mean, she's not just buying this stuff as a favor to you, is she?" Becky asked, looking worried.

The woman had no idea how talented she was. "Are you kidding? Jocelyn was named one of the top entrepreneurs under thirty in L.A. last year."

"Exactly. I'm not sure my stuff is good enough."

"She was also listed second on *Cosmo*'s Bitchiest Women in Business. Believe me, she isn't doing this as a favor to me. She isn't as successful as she is by following her heart."

"Okay." Becky looked at the check again. "We *could* use the money, and I had been contemplating whether or not I should go back to work, so Neil wouldn't have to take the tours overseas so much, be home more…"

Abigail smiled. "Then this is perfect. You can still be home with the kids and have your own business bringing in money, a lot of money." She stood and, taking the items, added, "Follow me into the kitchen. I have something else to show you."

Set up on the table were the brochures and company letterhead she'd designed to send to Jocelyn after their phone call a few days before.

"Oh my God, Abby, these are gorgeous," Becky said, picking up the trifold brochure with the logo BABY CHIC in blue and pink lettering across the front. Inside were the pictures of the jacket and the dress she'd already sold.

"If you want to change the name or the design or…"

Becky cut her words short with a big hug. "I can't believe you did all of this. It's beautiful," she said, moving away and reaching for a tissue. "Stupid hormones," she said with a laugh. "Really, though, thank you."

Abigail smiled. "You're welcome. So, you're okay with all of this? This is exciting, right?"

Becky nodded slowly. "Excited, definitely. Sure? Not entirely."

"That's okay. I'll be sure about it *for* you, until you are."

* * *

"Mom!"

Dani's shrill voice made her jump and nearly spill her coffee on the fundraising brochures she was checking for the bottle drive—pamphlets to hand out to the business owners in the community to garner more support. They'd already had ten companies sign up, but one of their biggest, Taco Hut, had unexpectedly changed their mind, so they needed to make up the difference.

"In the living room," she said, setting the coffee aside, far away from the pamphlets she'd picked up from FedEx that afternoon. She knew some of the fundraising committee members were still reluctant to believe investing money in the project could yield bigger results, so she'd paid for the brochures herself, not wanting to add to the initial investment cost. Small price to pay to show everyone she knew what she was talking about.

"You will never believe it."

She smiled as her daughter vibrated in front of her. "Whatever it is, it must be pretty awesome."

"Taylor is going to the NHL game tonight with Jacks… Coach Westmore in Denver!"

Her smile faded slightly. "That sounds awesome, for Taylor," she said, waiting for what she knew was coming next.

"And they invited me to go with them!"

Abigail plugged one ear and winced at the high-pitched squeal that nearly drowned out the words.

"Can I go? Can I? Please?" She clutched her hands in front of her and bent slightly at the knees, a desperate pleading look in her dark eyes.

"Oh, sweetheart, it's a school night, and Denver is an hour away." She bit her lip, feeling like the world's worst mother as her daughter's excitement deflated like a day old helium-filled balloon.

"But Taylor's allowed to go," she said, a new whining to her voice.

"Yes, but it's Taylor's uncles who are playing tonight." Becky had mentioned something about the first game of the season where her brothers would play one another—Ben on the home team, and Asher playing for New Jersey.

"So when the Kings play against the Avalanche I can go to the games to see Dad play?" she challenged, crossing her little arms across her chest.

How had she foolishly thought she'd escape the preteen attitude for a few more years at least? "Well, we would have to talk about that when the time came."

"Right. The answer would be no then, too. You hate Dad."

Knife expertly to the heart. Wow, kids were good at that. "I don't hate your dad." Just because she'd carefully selected photos without him in them to display in the new house didn't mean anything.

"This sucks," Dani said, slumping onto the couch.

Abigail sighed. "We could go to Slope and Hatch for dinner and see a movie?"

Dani glared at her.

The sound of a vehicle pulling onto the gravel driveway made Abby glance outside in time to see Jackson's truck park and Taylor jump out, wearing her Avalanche jersey.

Great. Her daughter had called in reinforcements. "What are they doing here?" she asked, her mouth going dry as she saw Jackson climb out of the truck. Even in jeans and his own jersey, all she could envision was the rock-hard body she knew was underneath, an image of his straining back muscles as he'd carried in her furniture, and the odd rush of color to her cheeks whenever she passed the lilies on the table.

"They assumed you'd say yes. We all thought you were cool," her daughter grumbled.

"Nice, Dani," she said, running a hand quickly through her hair as the front door opened and Taylor burst into the living room.

"Are you ready? Where's your jersey?" she asked, glancing at Dani.

"I'm not allowed to go," Dani mumbled, still glaring at Abigail.

Taylor added her own daggers to the attack.

"It's a school night…"

"My mom's letting *me* go," Taylor said.

She sighed. Being tag-teamed by preteens was not her idea of a good time.

"You two ready?" Jackson asked appearing in the doorway. His question was directed at the girls but his gaze was locked on her.

Her pulse raced and she told herself to get a grip. It was just flowers. And intense, long-lasting eye contact that seemed to hold a lot of unsaid words…

"Dani can't go," Taylor said.

"It's a school night," Dani said, rolling her eyes.

"Becky said Taylor could go," Jackson said, looking confused.

Seriously? She expected it from the kids, but he could help her out a little. She shot him a look.

"Oh, I mean…If your mom says no, then it's a no, girls."

All three of them stared at her.

She wasn't sure which expression was worse, but she couldn't stand the pressure. "Fine! Go." This was one battle where she had to wave the white flag. Giving in to her daughter's bad attitude wasn't something she felt good about, though. Now more than ever, she had to be the enforcer of rules and not let her single mom status and the guilt Dani could inflict on her weaken her in her daughter's eyes, otherwise the teen years would be hell. "*But*—because of the eye rolling and not-so-nice comments—you're staying in this weekend."

Dani either didn't hear or didn't care as she jumped up to hug her quickly. "Thanks, Mom! You're the best!" she said, rushing off to get her jersey.

Taylor ran off to join her.

"Wow, I go from worst to best in the matter of seconds lately," she said, sitting back down with the brochures.

Jackson laughed. "Becky can tell you all about it. Preteen girls," he said with a shudder. "Kinda makes me glad Neil is in the military and carries a gun."

"Yeah, I may have to hire him," she said.

He came closer and glanced at the brochures. "These look great. You design them?"

She nodded, feeling her hand shake slightly at his closeness. She could smell the same cologne she'd noticed lingering in the house after he'd been there a few days before, a smell she'd been hoping would linger just a little longer and feeling stupid about it.

He picked one up and turned it over. "I should get you to design some for my real estate business."

"Thank you, but they're not that good." She took the brochure back. "Just hopefully good enough to convince the local businesses to support the school programs."

"I'm sure they will."

"It's so odd that Taco Hut backed out. Paul seemed so eager to help when I met with him." Of course he'd also made her want to take a shower, the way he'd sized her up making her feel uncomfortable. She'd made a note not to be the one delivering the recycling bin or picking up the bottles. Which was why she'd sent Jackson.

"Yeah, it's weird," he said.

"And you're sure he didn't say why?" She eyed him suspiciously.

"Nope."

His phone chimed with a text message and he looked relieved to escape the conversation. "Excuse me," he said, reading it quickly and then tucking the phone away as the girls reappeared.

"Ready!" Dani said, dressed in her own Avalanche jersey and baseball cap.

"Let's go, Uncle Jackson. The first five hundred people get a free foam finger."

"We certainly wouldn't want to miss out on that," Jackson said with a wink.

Her stomach flip flopped. "Well, have fun," she said quickly, standing and kissing the top of Dani's head. "Wish I was going to a game instead of grading papers all night."

"You can," Jackson said, beside her. "That was Darryl who just texted. He had to bail on us, so we have an extra ticket."

Dani's eyes lit up. "That's great. Come with us!"

Shit. No, she hadn't really meant it. The idea of going with them made her stomach hurt for too many reasons. She hadn't gone to a game in over a year. She would have to drive an hour and back trying to make small talk with a man whose sexy body kept resurfacing in her mind, and sit through an entire game in those close-quarters seats? Nope. No thank you. "I can't. I said I'd like to, but I have work to do." She gestured to the cluttered coffee table. "And still lots of unpacking to do," she added for good measure, motioning to all of the yet to be unpacked boxes in the corner of the living room.

"Please, Mom," Dani said, surprising her with her genuine want of including her that evening.

Which made it so hard to say no. "Maybe next time," she said.

Dani's face fell. "All right," she mumbled.

Damn it! Over the last few weeks, things had gotten so much better between them. Dani seemed to be adjusting well and their relationship was getting stronger. She hated the thought of disappointing her. "You know what? Screw it. I can pull an all-nighter grading the papers when I get back. Who needs sleep, right? Just give me a second to freshen up."

"You look beautiful," Jackson said.

All three females stared at him.

He swallowed hard, and clearing his throat, he shrugged and said, "What? We're going to be late."

The girls seemed to accept the reason for the compliment as they hurried out to the truck, but Abigail continued to stare at him.

"Was that a compliment?" she asked.

"Yes, well, you're going to have to try to look a lot less

beautiful if you expect me to keep those things from slipping out."

She cocked her head to the side. "You managed so successfully for years. What's changed?"

"Nothing. Or maybe everything." He took a step toward her, and the look in his eyes reminded her of the one he'd had in the kitchen the night he'd tended to her foot, the night she'd been certain he'd been about to kiss her.

Her mouth went dry as she stood frozen in place, a million thoughts running through her mind. What was he doing? What was *she* doing? And why was she just standing there waiting for something to happen? What did she want to happen? Her eyes searched his for any clue of how he was feeling. To see if he too was suddenly struck with this odd churning in his stomach or tightness in his chest.

The hallway felt as though it were closing in around her as he came closer. Her breath caught and held in her throat, and her eyes were unblinking as she continued to stare at the crystal blue eyes staring right back at her, giving nothing away…and saying so much at the same time.

He stopped inches from her, his warm breath against her forehead, his gaze still locked with hers. Then taking her by the shoulders, he gently turned her around in the direction of her bedroom.

Huh?

He gave her a little shove and she stumbled forward, glancing back at him with a confused frown.

"Hurry. We don't want to miss out on the foam fingers."

Right. The foam fingers. Wouldn't want to miss out on those.

* * *

The stadium in Denver was a buzz of excitement as fans flowed in, had their tickets checked, and received their foam finger. Abby repressed a sigh as she accepted hers—how many of these things had she gotten rid of before the move? At least this one said Avalanche and not Kings. The girls waved theirs proudly as they rushed on ahead, and Jackson shook his head, refusing one from the cheerleader dressed in the team's colors of blue and burgundy.

Abigail frowned. "I didn't know saying no was an option."

Jackson laughed. "I have a million of those things already."

She shot him a wary look, and he took hers and jogged back toward the cheerleader. As he handed it back, he leaned closer to her and said something that made her giggle, and a crazy, irrational sense of jealousy made Abigail's cheeks grow hot. She turned away, keeping an eye on the girls as they headed toward their seats, desperate to push the feeling aside. Hockey players and cheerleaders—not her favorite visual.

"There," Jackson said rejoining her.

"She was bubbly," she said, hating the note of jealousy in her voice.

He grinned at her. "I'm pretty sure they're getting paid to be. Trust me, it didn't go to my head."

Strangely enough, his words had a reassuring effect on her, and she was embarrassed for having let the sight bother her in the first place. Being with him that evening had an odd, relaxing vibe to it. One she hadn't expected. After their awkward, tension-charged exchange in her hallway, she thought the hour-long drive to Denver would be filled with long silences as they both contemplated what had just happened.

Instead, he'd hooked up Taylor's iPod to his stereo system and they'd all rocked out to the G-rated version of all the latest hip-hop songs.

"You know the words to Lady Gaga?" she'd asked in disbelief as he'd belted out the chorus of "Applause."

He'd grinned, turned the music louder, and removed his hands momentarily from the wheel to perform a crazy chair dance that had the girls giggling so hard in the back, Dani had sprayed soda out of her nose.

Nope. The ride to Denver hadn't been weird at all, and around the girls, the sensually charged electricity between them seemed to fade to a manageable spark. Now, as long as the girls were around whenever they were together, they might be able to keep their undeniable attraction under wraps. Where it belonged.

* * *

As they followed Taylor and Dani to their front row seats behind the home team players' box, Abigail asked the obvious question. The one everyone always asked their family. "Is it tough having Asher and Ben on opposite teams?"

He smiled as he took her drink from her while she removed her coat and sat. "It's fun, actually."

"Really? Thanks," she said, accepting her drink and setting it between her knees.

He sat next to her and nodded. "Really. I mean, we love teasing Asher that he's a traitor, playing for an opposing team, but the guys know we support both of them equally."

She raised an eyebrow, calling his bullshit.

"Okay, maybe Ben's our favorite, but I'll deny saying that."

She laughed as she nodded and the sight and sound

created a warm feeling in his chest. He was happy she'd agreed to join them that evening for the local game. The drive from Glenwood Falls had been much more fun with her in the truck with them. He hadn't even minded acting like a fool, singing and dancing. It was worth it just to see her laugh.

Unlike their usual tension, the evening felt comfortable… As comfortable as it could be with her sitting so close that their legs and arms brushed, and the smell of her soft perfume made him want to bury his nose in her neck and kiss the hollow there to see if she tasted as good as she smelled. No doubt their two smaller companions were helping to keep his thoughts on the PG side.

"How often do their teams play one another?" Abby asked.

"Twice a season, and they are the two games of the year that we never miss." He always took Taylor to see her uncles battle it out on the ice. Their coaches liked to play them—Asher, a defenseman, and Ben, a left wing—on the same shifts, knowing their blood ties meant nothing to either of them when they were on the ice. If anything, their sibling rivalry drove them even harder to be the best player in the Westmore family and in the league.

"Which brother is the better player?" she whispered, as the lights in the arena dimmed and the opposing team skated out onto the ice from an entrance covered for protection from irate fans.

"Me," he said with a teasing grin. He saw Asher skate out onto the ice, and he and Taylor cheered loudly, earning them looks from other fans seated nearby. It didn't bother him. These games were always intense: he and Taylor cheered when their team scored and they cheered when the opposing team scored. The regular season ticket holders seated around them, consisting of mainly other players' family and friends, knew their situation and thought their spilt loyalty was humorous. And once the rest of the fans realized the situation on the ice, Ash received some love from them for a good play as well.

"That's a given," Abby said next to him.

"Seriously, though, it would be impossible to compare the two. I mean their players' cards would suggest Ben's scoring this year so far makes him the better player, but Ash's defensive skills have been credited for a lot of wins this season." He remembered the many years he'd spent with his younger brother, who was determined to play offense, teaching him his skills and natural abilities were better suited for the defensive line.

It wasn't until Asher didn't make the A-list Bantam team when he tried out that he decided to listen to Jackson and become a defenseman.

The home team's music started and the strobe lighting in the stadium started to spiral through the stands, the red and blue lights flashing and the scoreboard overhead playing highlights of the team's historic moments. As the players skated onto the ice, the board lit up with their pictures and profiles.

The same involuntary pang in his core hit him as it always did when he saw the Westmore name light up the screen next to the picture of his brother.

Just once he'd like to see his own picture up there.

"Uncle Ash looks like he's favoring his right side," Taylor said, leaning toward him and speaking above the cheering crowd.

His eyes landed on his younger brother, stretching and warming up with his team at their end of the rink, and he immediately noticed what his niece was referring to. Asher did seem to be in some sort of discomfort as he leaned to the left. "Probably just an injury. I'm sure he'll work through it," he said.

Neither of his brothers had ever willingly sat out a game. Their father's "suck it up" motto ran deep in the family bloodline.

As the game started, he sat back in his seat, then leaned forward again, his gaze glued to the play. His knees bounced and his hands clasped and unclasped on his lap.

"Are you always like this, or just when both of your brothers are playing?" Abby asked, and her voice almost made him jump. He'd momentarily forgotten she was there. Hockey did that to him, stole his focus and concentration. A lot of women had sat on the dejected side of his passion for the sport, part of the reason he was still single.

He forced a sigh and sat back. "I take my hockey pretty seriously."

"Understandable." She looked about to say something more, but her lips clamped together.

"Go ahead and ask," he said.

"Ask what?"

"How I feel about being the Westmore brother not in the NHL."

"Oh, that's not really any of my business." She glanced toward the ice.

"It sucks." No sense lying about it. It did. It sucked every time he played a game of local league hockey with his buddies and they won effortlessly because they had him on the team. It sucked whenever he came to a game like this one, when the memories of the three of them playing together plagued him and he felt like the odd man out. And it really sucked when he remembered the woman sitting next to him had married an NHL player and would never settle for a mere minor league coach. "It sucks," he repeated, as the first penalty was called against Asher's team.

He felt her hand on his and suddenly it sucked a little less. His gaze flew to her hand and then back up to her eyes. His heart pounded and it took every ounce of strength not to turn his hand and link fingers with her.

"You're a fantastic coach…and player," she said.

He barely heard the words. All he could focus on was the look in her eyes that told him so much, yet revealed nothing at the same time. A look that could mean they'd finally reached some sort of truce or a look that could mean she just might be feeling some of the things he always had. Reading too much into it could potentially break his heart, but reading not enough put him back into the stalemate with his feelings where he'd always been.

"Thank you," he said after a long pause, as the crowd erupted around them.

"Woohoo, Uncle Ben!" Taylor said, jumping to her feet to bang on the glass next to him.

His gaze never left Abby's face.

"I think Ben just scored," she said, her eyes never leaving his.

For the first time, maybe ever, he had something more important holding his attention. Abby Jansen was looking at him. Touching him. And even if there wasn't a damn thing he could do about it right now, he would enjoy the moment. Turning his hand, he linked fingers with hers and squeezed tight. "Good for Ben."

CHAPTER 13

✎

$\mathcal{H}$e was favoring the right side again, wasn't he?" Ben asked as he handed over the mashed potatoes the following evening. They had all taken their usual places around the dining room table for what was a true rare occurrence—a family meal together before Asher flew back to New Jersey with his team.

"You know I don't play favorites," Jackson said, dishing a large scoop onto his plate before handing it to Becky at the end of the table.

"He was though, right?" His older brother insisted as Asher joined them at the table, carrying the roast for their mother.

She followed him with the gravy boat.

Ben eyed Asher as he sat. "You injured little brother?"

"Wouldn't you love to know?" Asher reached for a roll, tearing it apart before taking his seat across from them.

"Hat off at the table," their mother, Beverly, said. "And enough hockey talk. Let's eat."

The boys knew better than to go against their mother, and by the end of dinner, the conversation had turned to his business. "So, have you sold the house over on Oak Avenue yet?" Ben asked, pushing his licked-clean plate away.

"No. I decided to rent it out for a while."

"I thought you were planning to move into that one yourself," his mother said, looking at him in surprise. "It's such a beautiful place and right on the lake. It would be perfect for you."

Only Becky knew that Abigail and Dani were living in the house, and he'd been hoping to keep it that way for a while. "I don't know yet," he said with a shrug, sending a silencing look at Becky the blabbermouth.

"He can't move in there. Dani and Ms. Jansen are living there now," Taylor spoke up.

Oh, right, the shorter blabbermouth.

Becky grinned and shrugged as if to say, *There're no secrets around kids,* as she stood and started collecting the plates. "Taylor, help me clear the table for dessert," she said. "Before your uncle murders you," she whispered to the little girl sitting next to him as she passed.

Taylor stood to help.

"Abigail Jansen?" his mother asked.

"That's right, I heard Abby was back home." Ben studied him.

Don't give anything away, or they will pounce like vultures on prey, he thought, avoiding his brother's gaze as he handed his empty plate to Becky. "Yes, she is back, and yes, I'm renting her the house. She was looking for a place for her and Dani…" He shrugged. "Besides, don't all of you look at me like you know something you don't. This was Becky's fault. She and Abby are best friends these days." An image of her fingers entwined with his at the hockey game the night before, and the way she'd looked at him before climbing out of the truck, told him maybe they were friends now, too…more than friends?

Damn if he could figure it out.

"My fault?" his sister asked, looking innocent as she passed dessert forks around the table.

"Yes, your fault. You were the one who suggested she move in, remember?"

"Hey! I'm not the one who asked her to the hockey game last night."

All heads swung in his direction. Hyenas, a pack of them, ready to attack.

His mother looked ready to start planning a wedding, and even Ash, the quieter, less overbearing brother, was looking at him with a smirk.

Quick—divert attention. "Yeah, well, I'm not the one going into business with her," he said, shooting a pointed look at Becky.

His sister's eyes narrowed into thin slits, and luckily there was a table between them. The knife she held to cut the ice cream cake looked really sharp.

The heads swung toward her.

"What business?" his mother asked.

"I think I hear the football game. Boys, shall we leave the ladies to talk?" Jackson said, standing quickly and grabbing his plate of dessert.

His brothers were quick to do the same.

"Jerks!" Becky called as they left her with their mom, who no doubt would have a million and three questions for her about her new venture with Abby.

Better her than him in the hot seat, he mused. Though he knew he'd get an earful from her later.

Sitting on the sofa, sandwiched between his two brothers, Jackson turned the volume up on the game.

Ben turned it back down. "Don't think you're off the hook that easy."

"What?" he asked, a mouth full of cold ice cream giving him a brain freeze.

"Correct me if I'm wrong, but isn't Abby Jansen divorcing your best friend?" Ben said.

"Not that he doesn't deserve it," Asher said, his attention glued to the television, but obviously listening. "I saw him at a club after we played in L.A. last year, some redhead clinging to him like he was a life preserver."

Yeah, Jackson had to admit maybe Team Dean wasn't the right team to have always supported in the past. Though he wondered how much of his new feelings toward his best friend were a result of attempting to reduce some of his own guilt for the ever-growing attraction he felt for Abby. "She was looking for a place and I wasn't ready to move yet, so it worked out. Besides, as you said, Dean's my friend. I thought it was the right thing to do for his family."

"I don't know about that, but I'm glad you didn't move in there yet. There might be an opportunity for you to check out," Ben said, glancing at his cell as it chimed with a message.

"No."

"No? Just like that? Not even going to hear me out?" he asked, reading the text on his screen next to a picture of some hot brunette.

While Ben was busy replying, Jackson turned to Asher. "Do you know what this is about?"

His brother nodded, checking hockey stats on his own phone. "The Eagles, they're looking for three new flex players for when the boys get called up."

His old team. Jackson turned to Ben. "Like I said, no."
He'd tried that path to an NHL career before without success. He was older now and in less than ideal shape. He
couldn't compete with the young nineteen-year-olds anymore. His brother should understand that. At thirty-one, Ben
had five or six good years left before he'd be forced out by
the younger, faster, better players. He'd be retired by forty.

"Try out. What's the harm in that? If you don't make it, I
won't bug you about it anymore." His phone chimed again.
This time it was a picture of a blonde next to the message.

He shook his head. "Forget it."

"You know you still want to play, man," Ben said, typing
furiously, as another text came in.

Did he? There was no denying the twist in his gut when
he watched his brothers play or the feeling of remorse he felt
whenever he watched replays of his own time on the ice, but
did he truly still have the burning desire to play?

Luckily Ben's cell rang, saving him from having to answer. His brother grinned. "I have to answer this." He turned
the phone toward him and an image of a cute redhead flashed
on the screen.

A brunette, a blonde, and now a redhead—his brother always covered the bases. He shook his head. "How many of
these women do you have on the go, man?"

"Enough to stay busy, but not too many to keep them
all straight," he said with a wink, answering the call. "Hey,
baby. I was just thinking about you…"

Jackson shook his head as he turned up the volume on the
football game. Ben's playboy lifestyle was going to come
back to bite him in the ass someday. It just hadn't happened
yet.

* * *

Abigail's arms ached as she moved the last box of her items into the middle of the living room and surveyed the mess of stuff she'd just unpacked. The unexpected outing last week had put her behind schedule getting things organized, and she was determined to get everything done that evening. She hated clutter and living out of boxes.

Why had she packed so much from the house in L.A.? Looking at the stacks of old books, CDs and DVDs yet to organize, she wished she'd had a backyard bonfire with all of it instead. She yawned.

Where on earth did she begin?

A glass of wine sounded like as good a place as any.

After pouring a glass of pinot grigio, she picked up the divorce papers she'd received from Olivia Davis that afternoon and carried them into the living room. She sat on the floor near the fireplace and read the documents.

She was a free woman again. Dean had finally conceded to the settlement her lawyer had been fighting for and she had full custody of Dani. She should be celebrating. But with Dani spending the night at Taylor's, the extent of her celebration was a bottle of wine and unpacking. The symbolism wasn't lost on her. In her hand, she held the end of her past and all around her was her new future waiting to start.

"Knock knock…"

Jackson's voice in the hallway made her jump. What was he doing there? She quickly stashed the divorce papers under the couch and stood, knocking over the wine glass. Luckily the cheap plastic goblet was empty, and she bent to right it as Jackson entered the living room.

"Hi…Hey…" She stammered, tucking her hands into the back pockets of her jeans. "What are you doing here?" She hadn't seen him in a few days, though it would be a lie to say he hadn't crossed her mind—too often for comfort, in fact.

And now he was standing in her living room—*his* living room, technically—looking amazing in a pair of jeans that hugged his thighs, a tear in the right knee, and a black collared shirt, opened at the neck beneath a black leather jacket. His hair was gelled in a purposeful mess, and the five o'clock shadow along his jawline—as always—tempted her touch.

What the hell was it about that stubble?

Shoving her hands even deeper into her pockets, she commanded her body to stay firmly where she was.

"I came to drop off the new lock and set of keys to the shed in the backyard. Sorry, it took longer than I'd planned…" He looked around the cluttered space. "Wow, I wasn't expecting you to have so much stuff."

She shrugged. "I'm hoping to be unpacked and organized by Christmas." She forced a laugh.

He studied her for a moment, then shook his head as though shaking a thought away. "Anyway, here are the keys." He started toward her with his hand extended, and she was nodding, though not really hearing his words.

Her mind had taken an unwanted detour to the look in his eyes when she'd touched his hand at the hockey game. Such a simple gesture…a stupid simple gesture that had served to complicate things between them, blur some imaginary line. She took the keys and played with the key ring, trying to summon the courage to say something about the other night. To explain that whatever that was wasn't something that could turn into something more.

He cleared his throat and spoke before she could. "The other night at the game…"

Her head whipped up. "Yeah?"

"That was…"

"Nothing?" she said weakly, hoping to fill in the blank correctly. Or partly hoping at least.

"I wouldn't say nothing," he said. "I mean, there's something happening…" He coughed. "Between us."

She was shaking her head furiously, but an argument refused to verbalize.

No doubt because it would be bullshit.

Jackson took a step closer. "So you're saying you didn't feel a connection?"

"I didn't feel any connection," she said quickly, backing up slightly. The heat from the fireplace now toasting the back of her legs. "That would be crazy…weird, right?"

Another step closer. "Crazy weird because?"

"Because of Dean," she said emphatically.

"Right. Dean," he said as his gaze fell to the floor and landed on the divorce papers under the couch. "But it looks like there is no Dean anymore…at least not for you." He moved even closer and now was just inches away.

Oh God, it was hot in here, and it wasn't just the fireplace. She swallowed hard, the urge to close the gap between them overwhelming. But…"There's still a Dean for you though, right?" Damn. She had no idea which answer she wanted from him. Her mind was hoping his friendship with her ex-husband would be enough to make him retreat. But her body was screaming *Dean who?!*

His gaze locked on hers, and he reached out and tucked her hair behind her ears, cupping her face with his hands. "What if it doesn't matter anymore? What if all that matters is what I want?"

"What do you…"

Her words were silenced by his mouth crushing hers a second later. Her arms fell limp to her sides and she blinked several times, not moving, not breathing…too in shock to kiss him back. She just stood there motionless as his lips finally realized they weren't getting any response from hers.

He backed away a fraction of an inch, still touching her face. "I have no idea where that came from," he said.

"No shit," she whispered, still in shock.

He released her and took a big step back. "I'm sorry," he said, running a hand through his hair. "I'm going to go." He started to walk toward the door, then stopped and turned. "No, you know what? I'm not going to go."

"You're not?" She'd somehow found her voice again.

"No." He paced the living room between the stacks of boxes, head down, muttering to himself as though trying to make sense of what had just happened.

Had he forgotten she was standing there? "Jackson, do you want to let me in on what's happening right now?"

He glanced up at her and stopped pacing. His Adam's apple bobbed twice as he seemed to weigh his words. "Abby, the thing is…" He stopped.

"The thing is…" she coaxed.

"Remember second grade?"

Her eyes widened. The *thing* started that far back? Wow, this was obviously not a short story. "No."

He sighed. "Of course not. The truth is…" He stopped again.

Oh for the love of God! "Jackson, why did you kiss me?" Should be an easy enough question, but he looked confused, pained…tortured.

He stared at the ceiling for what seemed like forever, before lowering his gaze to hers. "Because I have feelings for you."

Feelings? "Like *good* feelings?" she asked, lowering

herself back down to sit on one of the unopened boxes. She couldn't trust her legs for this conversation.

"No, terrible, unwanted, unreciprocated, completely wrong feelings…but they've always been there, and now it seems they have a mind of their own," he said, his shoulders slumping as though a weight had lifted from them.

Only to be placed on hers. What the hell did she do with that information? "But you…"

"I know."

"I mean you treated me…"

"I know." He sighed, sitting on a different box in front of her. The cardboard gave way and he ended up half stuck between the folds. "I know this is terrible timing." He looked frustrated as he tried to reposition himself in the box.

At any other moment, the sight might be hilarious.

"And it's been killing me trying to decide if I should tell you any of this. I've held it in so long, I thought I could continue to keep it hidden, but the truth is, since you've been back, it's been harder and harder to keep this to myself. Being around you and not touching you, not kissing you, not holding you is torture, and I think you've felt it, too." He paused.

His words were an arrow straight to her heart, but she had no idea what to do with them. Her own feelings for him had come on so sudden, yet so strong, and now he was telling her that he'd always felt something for her? She bit her lip as she nodded. "Things have definitely felt…different lately."

"Different." He looked disappointed as he nodded. "Okay."

A long silence fell between them.

"So, that's why you always…"

"Yes."

"And you never…"

"Yes."

Realization was a long time coming, but now the effect of it hit her like a freight train. Becky had been right. Abigail's ex-husband's best friend had always been in love with her. Was *still* in love with her.

Oh shit. Shit, shit, shit. She stood and now it was her turn to pace. "But…Oh, but…"

He struggled to crawl out of the nearly flattened box. "Abby, don't freak out."

Too late.

"I didn't tell you because I didn't expect you to ever feel the same way, and that one-sided kiss just now pretty much confirmed it," he said.

She stopped and stared at him. "It did?"

"Yeah. I mean I've always known you'd never…"

"I'd never what?"

"Go for someone like me. Go for…me."

And why the hell not? "How do you know that?"

"Because you dated guys that were…*not* me," he said, placing his hands on his hips, a look of frustration etched on his handsome face.

"You never showed the least bit of interest. How could I possibly have known how you felt?"

"You're right. And now it's too late."

Too late. She nodded slowly, wondering why that idea made her stomach turn. She didn't return his feelings…did she? She had some feelings—definitely attraction—but real, sincere feelings?

Her mouth went dry.

Oh God. One thing was certain, she didn't *not* share his feelings.

"Now that I've made things even more awkward between us than they've ever been, I think I'll go." He headed toward the door. "Let's try to forget about all of this, okay?" he asked, his expression desperate as he lingered, a hand on the door.

Forget about it. Yes. Definitely the best thing to do. The *only* thing to do.

Then why was she walking straight toward him, her eyes locked on his? *Stop, Abigail. Do not do something you'll regret.*

Too late. Her arms reached up around his neck as she stood on tiptoes to place her lips gently against his. Not the desperate, longing, full crushing attack he'd placed on hers, but a soft, inviting gesture she had no right to offer.

"Abby," he moaned against her mouth placing his hands on her hips. "This is not forgetting about it."

"I know, but the way I see it, if we're going to forget about it, why not add more things to the list?" she whispered, licking her bottom lip.

* * *

Impossible. The only word to describe this moment right now. This sight before him of Abby Jansen's beautiful face just inches from his. The feel of her body so close, pressed against his, would be impossible to forget. And impossible to recover from. Their lips had touched twice, and already the dull aching in his heart had magnified. His untimely kiss, then hers, sent his common sense packing. He'd fantasized about this moment so often, he wasn't sure the reality of it would ever compare.

Not that he could find out.

He shook his head, desperate to free himself from the fog clouding his judgment as he broke away from her kiss. "Abby, you know this is not a good idea," he said, not knowing where he found the strength to remove her arms from around his neck and hold her away. His seventeen-year-old self would be kicking his ass right now.

Her lips formed a pout that would buckle the strongest of resolves. "Well, it certainly can't be any worse than any of my previous decisions," she countered.

He wasn't so sure about that. "Believe me, there is nothing I want more than to take advantage of your bad judgment right now, but wherever this is coming from is not from a clear head, and I don't want to hurt you." He also didn't want to hurt himself by giving her any more control over his heart than she already had and had always held.

She frowned as she folded her arms across her chest. "So, you didn't mean any of what you said—you don't have feelings for me?"

"Don't do that, Abby. If I didn't, I'd pick you up right now, carry you into that bedroom I'd hoped would be mine, and make love to you until I was the only man you could remember."

She let her arms fall, allowing her sweater to fall open and reveal the tight lace of her tank top across her breasts, as she stepped toward him. "Maybe that's exactly what I need."

Maybe tonight. But then what?

She reached up with both hands and cupped his face, her eyes locked with his. "Make me forget, Jackson. Forget everyone else but you."

* * *

When his lips met hers, there was still a brief hesitation in his eyes, but as her fingers crept up the back of his neck and tangled in his hair, she felt all resistance melt from his body. His grip tightened on her waist as his mouth crushed hers.

She felt his tongue along her bottom lip and a soft moan escaped her as her lips parted. His fingers dug into her flesh as he held her in place.

He didn't need to. She wasn't going anywhere. Jackson's kiss was leaving her breathless, full of desire, and with an aching need she hadn't known existed. And damn, what a kiss. She pressed her body even closer, desperate to feel every inch of him against every inch of her as she deepened the connection even further.

A second later, they were both gasping for air when he reluctantly broke away.

"Better than that first one?" she whispered against his lips.

"Much." The sweeping motion was so quick, she barely saw him move, but a second later, she was in Jackson's arms and he was headed down the hallway toward the master bedroom.

Her arm gripped him tightly around the neck, and she snuggled closer. He was the first man in a long time to make her feel anything. The fact he was making her feel *so much* was the terrifying part. Her body ached to feel his hands on her. Her lips were dying to get another taste of his. And her heart pounded with excitement as he reached the bedroom door.

"Are you sure about this?" he asked, the sound coming from deep in his chest.

She nodded. "No."

He gave a small, frustrated laugh. "Which one do I listen to—your words or your body?"

Oh shit, she didn't know. "I'm sure," she said, sounding anything but.

"Abby…"

She reached for the knob on the door and pushed it open.

"I'm sure," she said, hoping this time she sounded at least less *unsure*.

It must have sounded good enough because Jackson carried her inside and laid her gently on the queen-size, four-poster bed. He hesitated, staring down at her. "You're sure?"

"Stop asking me that," she said, reaching out for him.

"Okay, but for the record, this is not a good idea."

"Shut up and kiss me again."

He didn't hesitate, lowering himself down on top of her, supporting himself on his right elbow as he touched her face, brushing her hair away. "You are so beautiful. Even more so than I remembered…"

She swallowed hard. There would be no mistaking this for an impulsive, lust-filled bad decision. At least not from his side of the bed, and suddenly it seemed as though she were making a much bigger decision than just offering her body to him.

His smile was soft as he brought his lips to hers once more.

They were both all in, mouths hungrily searching for a stronger connection.

Her hands slid down his back and slipped beneath his shirt, her nails dragging softly upward over the muscles as she eased it off.

God, he felt good…Too good. It had been so long since she'd wanted someone—needed someone—as badly as she did him in that moment. His body felt incredible, and she couldn't wait to get the rest of his clothes off of him. The realization that in moments, Jackson Westmore would be completely naked in front of her made her pulse go wild.

His hand trailed down her cheek, across her chest, and down the front of her body, tickling her even through the fabric of the tank top. God, his touch was even better than his kiss. Gentle, yet full of desire. She could barely breathe for anticipation. He reached for the edge of her top, then stopped, breaking away slightly.

No! Don't stop! "What's wrong?" she asked.

"Just having a hard time turning my brain off, that's all," he said, his breath labored, his expression full of pure wanting.

Slowly, she reached for the edge of her shirt and, moving even slower, peeled it off over her head, shaking her hair free of the fabric as she tossed it aside. "Does this help?" she asked, saying a silent thank-you to her diligent workout routine with her former trainer.

His gaze left hers to scan her body—her breasts, her stomach, then back again. "A little bit, yeah," he said moving closer and lowering his mouth to her neck. Leaving a soft trail of hungry kisses along her collarbone and downward over the swell of her breasts exposed at the top of the plain white satin bra, Jackson reached behind her to the clasp.

"This needs to come off. Now."

* * *

A second later, his breath caught at the sight of her exposed chest and stomach, the perfectly shaped, full breasts better than he could have imagined. He buried his face between them, his hands cupping and massaging until she moaned in delight. The mere sound of her enjoying his touch almost finished him off. God, he didn't stand a chance at lasting long. Not when he'd been thinking about, dreaming about, fantasizing about this moment since he was fifteen.

"Oh my God, Jackson, don't stop…" she whispered, tossing her head back and taking quick shallow breaths.

Based on the sounds she was making, he felt safe in his prediction that neither would she. Which was good, because he'd hate to disappoint her. Taking her fast, rough, and hard was so tempting, but he forced air into his lungs and made himself slow down. Years of pent-up sexual attraction for this woman was driving him crazy, but now that she was lying here almost naked in front of him, he longed to make it last.

He kissed her flesh along her cleavage, leaving a trail all the way to her nipple, which he licked softly at first, then roughly sucked and flicked his tongue across it. She tasted so good. Like honey—smooth and sweet—and he wasn't sure he'd ever get enough of her. His body ached and he longed to savor every inch of her. Take all night to explore each part of her.

Sliding his tongue along her skin, he moved to her other nipple, and now she was almost whimpering below him. "I knew these breasts would knock me on my ass, but damn it, Abigail, I had no idea," he murmured against her skin.

"You like them?" she asked, her voice pure seduction, running her hands through his hair, pressing his lips against her.

His cock spasmed as a rush of blood left every other extremity weak with desire. "They're perfection."

She pushed his head away, and for a second he thought she might ask him to stop, but instead she reached for the button on her jeans and then quickly tugged them off of her hips, exposing just a thin silk thong underneath.

"Fuck me," he growled under his breath. He should have been prepared for the sight of her but sweet Jesus, her body, completely exposed except for the tiny strip of silk, took away his ability to think clearly. Every reason why this was not a good idea left him as he watched the slow movement of her long legs as she moved back farther onto the bed.

"Come here," she whispered, reaching for him.

He moved toward her, sliding his fingers into the waistband of her thong and slowly, as she lifted her hips, removing them and tossing it aside.

His mouth went dry as he stared at her naked body in front of him. Fuck. He was screwed. Any hope of stopping what was happening right now had disappeared the moment he flung the panties across the room.

He pressed his lips to her stomach, kissing a circle around her belly button, as his hands slid up the length of her long legs. Putting a hand on the inside of her muscular thighs, he pushed them open to slide a hand on her soft mound between her legs as his mouth continued to move south on her body. "You're so wet," he whispered against her skin as he slid a finger inside her.

"I'm almost coming already," she said, as his tongue flicked her clit, before it slid the length of her swollen, wet folds.

"No way, not so fast." He slowed the pace slightly. He'd been ready to explode the moment her soft hands had stroked his back, but knowing they were both so close to the edge, he was desperate to make this much anticipated, fantasized about moment last as long as he possibly could.

Which would never be long enough.

Removing his jeans and tight boxer briefs, he stroked the length of his erect cock, his palm skimming over the straining and throbbing flesh. It took every ounce of strength to hold back his orgasm and he wanted to come inside her body, not at her feet like an overeager teenage boy.

Her eyes fell to his crotch, and the wide-eyed appreciation

he saw in them made him even harder. He knew he was up to the challenge of meeting her every desire, to cherishing her body the way she deserved and making her forget the pain and disappointment of her past, even if only for that night.

He lay back down between her legs, and lifted them, wrapping them around his body. Her wetness met the tip of his cock and he almost exploded. And when her soft hands wrapped around him and started stroking, it took his breath away.

"You have to stop that or it's game over," he said, reaching for her hands, and holding them away from his body. He stared down at her, her expression pure desire, but the brief look of hesitation in her eyes made him pause. "We don't have to do this," he whispered hoarsely, though it would take every ounce of his strength to stop.

She swallowed hard. "I want you, Jackson."

He lowered his mouth to hers, kissing her gently. "A condom?" he whispered against her lips.

Her eyes flew open and she frowned. "You don't have one?"

His mind did a quick inventory of his wallet. When was the last time he'd needed a condom? Leaving her, he picked up his discarded jeans and retrieved his wallet from the back pocket. Opening it quickly, he was relieved to find one. He stopped and scanned the package for the expiration date.

Abigail propped herself up on her elbows and raised an eyebrow. "Are you serious right now?"

"What? It's been a while."

She smiled and the look of desire in her eyes only deepened.

Good to know his recent lack of action was working to his benefit. Ripping the package open, he handed it to her and she slid it over him. Slowly, painfully awakening every inch of him as her hands closed over him once more. He was far from inexperienced, but he felt like his eager seventeen-year-old self being touched for the first time as he waited for the protection to be firmly in place before picking her up, raising her body, and sliding her down over him.

A shocked little cry escaped her lips and she clutched his thighs, her nails biting into his flesh. For a second, he paused, thinking he might have hurt her, but when she closed her eyes and moaned, he plunged even deeper. "Oh my God, Jackson."

Hearing his name on her lips as their bodies rocked together in perfect rhythm was absolute torture as he tried to hold off as long as possible. He'd loved this woman for so long, and now here she was in his arms. "Abigail," he groaned as her hips moved up and down in a slow rhythm, teasing, killing him. Her hands in his hair, she kissed his neck and bit his earlobe, her mouth causing an intense mix of pleasure and pain he wanted to last forever.

Gripping her ass, he slid in and out of her body as she panted and moaned.

Frantically she clutched at him. "I'm going to come…I'm going to come…fuck me, Jackson…"

He thrust deeper one last time and she cried out, falling into him, her body shaking slightly.

"Jackson," she whispered.

Years of longing, wanting, and waiting took over. He exploded within her and a loud groan escaped him as his head collapsed against her chest and he held her tight.

When he lifted his head to look at her, he held his breath, expecting to see remorse or guilt in her eyes now that the heat of the moment had left them both spent. But all he saw there was an unexpected flicker of emotion that made his heart beat even faster.

CHAPTER 14

◦~◦

*T*he sun pouring through the curtainless window early the next morning woke her from the best sleep she'd had since moving home. For the first time in months, she felt rested, relaxed…Jackson Westmore's bare chest beneath her hand.

Scrambling to a sitting position, Abigail clutched her bedsheet to her body.

He was by far the sexiest sleeping man she'd ever seen. His hair was messed up in the best possible way and a memory of her running her hands through it while he made love to her flashed in her mind. She'd loved the feel of the thick locks, soft and silky between her fingers. The five o'clock shadow that had tickled her skin as he'd kissed her body was now a slightly longer scruffy beard that only enhanced his morning-after appeal.

The night before had been unexpectedly one of the most freeing nights of her life. His touch, his kiss, his words had made her feel sexy and desirable. She hadn't felt that way in a long time.

Lying back down next to him, she snuggled closer. She still couldn't believe that all those years he'd had feelings for her. That he still had those feelings. She wondered how things—how life—might have been different had she known. Their relationship probably would have been awkward and strained in a different way.

Better not to have known.

But she knew now. And here he was in her bed. Where he would be waking up any minute. A slight panic took hold.

Jackson moaned as he rolled to his side and she froze, praying he wouldn't wake up just yet. She needed a minute—make that a lifetime—to figure out what to say to him. After all, he'd had a lifetime to figure out how he'd deal with a morning after with her.

Closing her eyes and holding her breath, she edged to the side of the bed, dragging the sheet with her. Quietly, slowly, she tossed her legs over and stood, careful not to move the bed. Thank God she'd invested in that expensive memory foam. Forget bowling balls and wine glasses; if the company wanted to sell more mattresses, they should use a sleeping man and a confused, panicked woman to illustrate their usefulness.

Checking to make sure he was still asleep before she dropped the sheet, Abigail reached for the tank top and jeans she'd discarded the night before and quickly got dressed. Then she stood there staring at him, resisting every urge to say screw it and crawl back into bed with him, wake him up, and demand a repeat performance.

The sex had been nothing short of amazing. Amazing and without a doubt going to complicate things on a whole new level.

Where did they go from here? He was still Dean's best friend and Dani's hockey coach…and the only man to make her feel tipsy from a single touch.

She shook her head. She had no idea what he would be expecting from her when he woke up, and she had no answers.

Maybe she could let him sleep, sneak out of the house before he woke and not have to say anything at all.

Sure, except she was living in his house and teaching at the same school where he coached the team her daughter played on, and her closest friend in town just so happened to be…

Her eyes widened. Becky! She suppressed a groan. She hoped this newest development in their complicated-as-hell relationship wouldn't hurt her friendship with the other woman.

Either way, she needed coffee before she could deal with any of this with any kind of finesse. Tiptoeing toward the door, she grabbed her sweater from the floor and quietly opened it.

Jackson continued to sleep. Good, keep sleeping until she had time to work through her spiraling emotions. A few months should do it, she thought with a conflicted sigh as she crept out into the hallway.

Then the sound of the front door opening made her heart pound so loud, she was amazed it didn't wake him.

"Mom!" Dani called out.

Abigail dove back into the room, shutting the door quickly and lunging at Jackson. "Wake up, wake up," she hissed.

He looked confused and—damn it—cute as hell as he opened one eye. "So it wasn't a dream? I've had the same one for so many years, it was hard to tell…"

"Nope. Not a dream. Now get up and crawl out the window," she said, collecting his discarded jeans, shoes, and T-shirt from the heap on the floor and going to the window. She opened it and threw everything outside.

He frowned as he sat up. "Okay, I get that you're probably regretting last night…"

Not exactly. Well, not completely, anyway.

"But this is a little extreme, don't you think?" He moved back the sheets and she turned to avoid seeing the lower half of his perfect body, a body she'd now seen and touched every inch of. "Come back to bed and let's talk about it."

"Dani's home," she hissed, seeing his boxers poking out from under the bed.

He was out of the bed in record time, tripping over himself as he struggled to put the underwear back on. "Shit. I thought she spent the night at Becky's. What time is it?"

Abigail glanced at the clock on the side table. "Ten thirty? How is that possible?" She hadn't slept that late… ever.

"Mom! Where are you?" Dani's voice made her heart race again.

"Get out—go!" she said, forcing Jackson toward the window.

"Good thing it's a bungalow," he muttered.

"Wouldn't matter," she said, as he climbed out.

He shot her a look. "Don't think you're getting out of talking about what happened last night," he said, collecting his clothes from the ground.

Dani's footsteps outside the bedroom at that moment would have made her agree to anything. "Fine. Just go!" she said, closing the window as the door opened.

"Who were you talking to?" Dani asked, coming in.

Abigail's heart was lodged so thick in her throat, she

wasn't sure she could utter the lie, so she avoided the question. "You're home early." She bent to pick up the bedsheet from the floor and quickly tossed it onto the messy bed. Her cheeks reddened at the sight of the tangled sheets; it looked like ten people had been sleeping in it.

"Taylor and her mom had to go shopping to buy stuff for her stepdad's homecoming party."

That's right. Neil was coming home in a couple weeks from overseas. "Taylor must be excited."

Dani shrugged. "I guess."

A pang of sympathy replaced any other emotion she was feeling as she looked at her daughter's disappointed-and-desperately-trying-to-hide-it face. She knew Dani missed Dean. It wasn't easy on her to feel as though her father didn't want to see her or fight for time with her. She hadn't told Dani that Dean hadn't signed the visitation schedule, but Dani was a smart girl. "Are you okay?"

Dani went to sit on the bed and Abigail quickly reached out to stop her. "Let's go out in the kitchen," she said. Those sheets needed to be washed right away. She was surprised her daughter couldn't smell the lingering scent of Jackson's cologne in the room. It was the *only* scent filling her senses and conjuring up flashbacks that really weren't appropriate while talking to her daughter.

She sighed. Maybe washing the sheets could wait a little longer…

Once she'd set the coffee maker and popped two waffles into the toaster, she sat at the table. "Okay, what's going on?"

"The father-daughter dance is in two weeks…"

Right, the one she'd been too nervous to talk to Dani about. The one she'd been hoping they could bypass. She'd emailed Dean the week before about it, but the email had come back undelivered. Obviously he wasn't interested in any contact from her, which would suit her just fine if they didn't have a nine-year-old to think about. Her annoyance rose, but she forced it back down as she said, "Honey, I did email your dad…"

Dani's eyes lit up. "What did he say? Can he make it? I know the Kings are playing the Rangers the night before, but if he comes straight from New York, he could be here for the dance, then be here for the next evening's game against Denver."

Damn. She'd obviously put a lot of thought into this. How did she tell her the email had bounced back? She stood as the coffee maker beeped, giving her a moment to think about what to say. "Um…well, he's not sure, but he's going to try," she lied finally, unable to break her daughter's heart that morning. She'd find a way to get the information to Dean and try to explain to him how important it was to Dani.

Maybe Jackson could call him.

Sure, and he could let him know he'd slept with his ex-wife at the same time. She wondered if Jackson would have any guilt over it. Oddly enough, she had none.

"Great. I know he's busy, so it's not a big deal if he can't," Dani said, breaking into her thoughts. She took the waffles out of the toaster and opened the fridge. "Where's the maple syrup?"

"Sorry, sweetie. I haven't gone shopping yet." She gestured around the messy kitchen, where spices cluttered the counters and pots and pans still hadn't found a home. "As you can see, I haven't really gotten far with the unpacking. I was lucky to get my room set up…" She stopped. Lucky? Maybe if her bed hadn't been so accommodating, they'd have come to their senses the night before.

An image of Jackson's sexy-as-hell body flashed in her

mind, followed by the memory of his gentle, yet passionate touch. He'd always had feelings for her. He'd always wanted her.

She covered her smile with her coffee cup.

Then again, probably not.

*   *   *

Parked on the side of the road several blocks from the house and pulling on his jeans, Jackson almost laughed. He'd had his share of awkward mornings after, but this was admittedly the first time the woman had thrown his clothes out the window and made him crawl out in only his underwear, which he'd discovered he'd put on inside out.

It didn't matter. The night before had been worth it.

Grinning like an idiot, he pulled his shirt on over his head. He'd spent the night with Abby. The sex had been everything he'd imagined it would be. Her body was like silk, and the lingering effects of the L.A. sun still kissed her skin, giving her a beautiful glow. Soft in all the right places, curves that left him defenseless, and a passion he'd never expected had made every one of his fantasies come to life.

She'd wanted him. That was the biggest surprise. And while he suspected she was struggling with conflicting emotions that morning, she couldn't deny that there had been a connection far beyond the physical between them the night before.

A second later, his cell phone rang, interrupting the old country song on the radio. A glance at the display on the dash revealed Dean's number. His gut twisted. Shit. The only person who could bring him down from the high he was on. He let the call go to voicemail.

So he'd chickened out. There was no way he could talk to his buddy that morning.

He was surprised Dean was even calling him at all. The last time they'd spoken, his friend had been abrupt and distant.

He pulled away from the curb and drove down the quiet neighborhood streets, allowing his thoughts to return to the night before.

He'd had sex with Abby Jansen.

She was even more fantastic than he'd ever imagined. Her touch was magnetic, her kiss was intoxicating, and the way she'd whispered his name had been enough to silence any doubt or reservation he may have had about being with her.

Now he had to make her realize they were right for one another.

More to forget about…she'd said.

Nope. Just more to crave, more to long for…more at stake.

Damn.

His cell phone rang again as he turned the truck into his own driveway moments later. The generic ringtone and unfamiliar number lighting up the screen made him ignore it.

But the phone chimed with a new voicemail as he unlocked his apartment door. Tossing his keys onto the table in the entryway, he dialed the voicemail service.

"Jackson, this is Coach Turner from the Colorado Eagles. I'm calling to let you know about a closed tryout we're holding for several flex positions on the team. Too many guys are getting injured and getting called up. Anyway, it's not an open tryout. Invite only. Call me."

Jackson saved the message as he headed into the bathroom and turned on the shower. An invite to try out for his old team with a possibility of getting called up. He stared into the mirror, thinking about his brother's words the week before. Did he still want to play professional hockey?

If he did, now was his chance to try again. A private try-out meant his odds of securing a spot on the team again were much higher than at an open tryout. And with guys getting called up, his experience might just put him on top of that list. He may not have played professionally for several years, but he was on the ice almost every day. And he'd been the team's MVP player every year. He was still in decent shape, and with a few weeks of intense training…

But did he really want that chance anymore? Or was he finally ready to go after something else he'd always wanted?

An image of Abby sleeping next to him flashed in his mind, making his chest ache. Two dreams, always out of reach, were moving closer to reality. Which one did he work toward?

The problem was, he knew there was no way he could have both.

CHAPTER 15

S o when you asked me to come over to help you put the crib together, what you actually meant was…"

"To watch *you* put the crib together," Becky finished from her relaxed position in the rocking chair.

"Right. That's what I thought. Do you think you could just hold this side in place while I use that tiny, impossible to use metal thing to fasten it together?"

"I guess so," Becky said, struggling to get up from the chair.

Abigail secured the side and then stood back to examine her handiwork. Putting furniture together by herself was just one of the many things she'd gotten really great at doing with Dean on the road so much. "Not bad." She shook it. Sturdy. Perfect.

"Thanks, Abby. I swear I wasn't this big with Taylor, and I don't remember that pregnancy being so draining, either."

Abigail shot her a look. "Well, you are a little older this time," she teased.

"Tell me about it." She lowered her head. "Look at the gray hair. I swear they weren't there last week, and of course I can't dye my hair until after the baby is born."

Abigail smiled, loving her friend's dedication to doing everything by the book. In L.A. her hockey mom friends would never let a gray hair survive.

"Okay, what else did you need help with?" she asked, checking her watch. She needed to pick Dani up at school.

"If you could help me move the dresser over just a little to make space for the new change table, that would be great," she said.

"No problem." Grabbing one end, she helped her friend slide it a fraction to the right.

"That's great, thank you. I just really wanted the nursery to be set up before Neil comes home."

Abigail nodded, though she would have thought Neil would want to help with the preparations for the new baby. Then again, Dean had always been okay leaving everything up to her. Noticing a small wooden jewelry box on the corner of the dresser, she picked it up. "Hey, I have one just like this." The pine box was stained a light golden color with Becky's initials and a flower carved in the top. "Only mine has my initials on it."

"Ah, so that's where the third one went," Becky said with a grin.

Abigail frowned. "Third one? What do you mean?"

"Jackson made three in woodworking class senior year. He gave one to Mom and another to me for Christmas, but I never knew what he did with the third one."

Abigail felt a rush of heat flow through her at the mention of Jackson, and she looked away quickly, hoping her friend—*his sister*—didn't notice. "Mine was from Dean," she said. "They must have all had the same projects."

Becky shook her head. "These had to be their own unique design," she insisted. "In fact, I remember Dean made hockey sticks. He gave them to Jackson, Ash, and Ben as Christmas presents the same year."

Abigail started to shake her head, but then she remembered Becky was right. He *had* made wooden hockey sticks with the Colorado Avalanche logo on them. She examined the jewelry box again. "But maybe he made one of these as well." Her confidence in that was quickly fading.

Becky took it and turned it over, revealing a tiny *j* in a circle in the bottom left-hand corner. "Does yours have one of these?"

Realization dawned and her eyes widened. Jackson had made her the jewelry box. So why had he not given it to her himself? She'd just assumed it was a present from Dean under the tree Christmas morning, and he'd never said otherwise.

Becky touched her shoulder as she set the jewelry box back down. "He sure was loyal to Dean," she said.

He sure was. Was he still? A knot formed in the pit of her stomach. Was he regretting their night together? Or was he finally ready to go after what he'd always wanted. She stared at the jewelry box, her heart echoing in her ears. Something she was quickly realizing she just may want, too.

* * *

"Abigail, I'm glad I caught you before you headed out. Do you have a minute?" Principal Breen asked as Abigail walked past her office the next day.

After a day with two sets of kindergarten children, she was exhausted and all she could think about was the Jacuzzi tub and the bottle of wine chilling in her fridge. Dani was at Taylor's working on a science fair project that evening, and she was looking forward to a few hours alone to get her thoughts about Jackson sorted out before she came face-to-face with him again.

She forced a smile as she said, "Of course." Going into the office, she took a seat. "Everything okay?"

"Everything's great. In fact, I just met with some of the other staff, and they all had nothing but good things to say about you."

"That's great." Some of that day's exhaustion melted away. Her peers liked and respected her, and she fit in here at Glenwood Elementary. She waited for the woman to continue.

"Your involvement and fresh new ideas in the fundraising efforts have been a huge success and the kids love you…"

Then why did she feel a *but* coming? She held her breath as she waited.

"So I'd love to offer you the full-time maternity leave position starting next month, if you're still interested," Principal Breen said.

Abigail's shoulders relaxed. She had the job. All of her hard work on the fundraising committee and with the children had paid off. She smiled as she nodded. "Yes, of course. Thank you, Principal Breen."

"Thank *you*. Since you've been here, there's a renewed excitement among the staff. They are motivated again with the fundraising efforts, and several other teachers have expressed interest in getting involved, so I couldn't be more pleased to have you on board. I'm just sorry that it's not a permanent position."

She was, too. A maternity fill-in position for the rest of the year wasn't the best situation if Kelli decided to return to teaching after her leave, but at least it was a step in the right direction. Suddenly, the day seemed a lot less exhausting. And the good news was, she'd be teaching the fourth grade class—Dani's class—every day. No more five-year-olds, thank God. "I'm sure things will work out. Thank you again. I appreciate this opportunity," she said as they stood.

Smiling, Abigail left the office, the bottle of wine and Jacuzzi tub now serving a new celebratory purpose instead. As she lowered her head to button her jacket, she collided right into...

Jackson.

"Whoa, steady..." he said, grabbing her shoulders.

Her mouth went dry as she glanced up at him. Damn. She'd been hoping for a little more time—and him to look a lot less hot—before they had to do this. "Hi, sorry, excuse me," she said, trying to move around him. She didn't expect the escape attempt to work, but it was worth a shot.

He grabbed her wrist. "Not so fast."

She sighed as she turned. "Do we have to do this here?" She nodded toward the principal's office door, which was still open. Several teachers passed them in the hall, throwing curious looks their way. She felt her cheeks grow hot as she shifted uncomfortably from one foot to the other.

"You're right. Let's talk over dinner," he said, taking her hand in his and heading toward the door.

How about no? "I don't think that's a good idea, either." A restaurant full of people who might overhear their talk? Uh-uh.

"I do. After all, you should celebrate your new full-time position," he said with a grin.

Her eyes narrowed. "You were eavesdropping?"

He grinned. "I may have been listening a little, but I already knew. I was one of the staff who couldn't say enough good things about you."

"You? The man who acted like he hated me our entire lives?"

He wrapped an arm around her shoulder and whispered, "That was before I saw you naked."

She hit him, but a slow smile betrayed her. "You're still a jerk."

"Maybe, but I'm a jerk who's taking you to dinner."

* * *

The Emerald City Restaurant was quiet that evening, which he was grateful for. He wanted time alone with Abby to talk about what had happened between them and how she was feeling about it, and he knew he couldn't trust himself to have the conversation in the privacy of her home. Yet he wasn't eager to have to deal with the uneasiness of too many onlookers, either. Therefore he made a note to tip the waiter well when he led them to one of the more secluded booths in the far end of the restaurant. "Thank you," he said, as he waited for Abby to climb in before climbing in on the same side.

She shot him a warning look. "There is another side," she said.

"I like this side," he said, turning in the booth to face her. "Look, we both know the other night was…"

"Incredible."

She sighed. "Okay, yes, incredible, but also…"

"Passionate."

"Can you let me finish?"

He smiled. "Fine, but first…" Taking her face in his hands he lowered his lips to hers. The surprise look in her eyes should have given him cause to reconsider, but the hell with it. It didn't matter that he knew he'd crossed a line and he'd broken some sort of bro code; for the first time in his life, he was ready to go after what he wanted. And after the night they shared, he knew she wanted him to.

She closed her eyes and fell into him, and he deepened the kiss, savoring the taste of her peppermint lip gloss and sliding his fingers through her soft hair. Her hands were pressed against his chest, but she wasn't pushing him away. Instead, they clutched the fabric of his T-shirt, drawing him even closer.

When he reluctantly broke away a moment later, he was happy to see Abby was as out of breath as he was. "Okay, now you can talk."

"I don't remember what I was going to say." She sighed, resting her forehead against his chest. "What are we doing?"

He leaned back and, placing a finger under her chin, forced her gaze to his. "I'm doing what I should have done a long time ago. Abby, I know I should keep holding back how I feel for you because of Dean, but the truth is, that friendship isn't worth giving up this chance with you. I'm not even sure I know my friend anymore, after how he treated you and Dani."

"Jackson, I just got divorced. I'm not ready for…this. Whatever this is. I'm sorry my kissing you and…other things have been misleading, but I'm not sure I can do a relationship right now. Dani and I are starting over and rebuilding a life here."

He nodded. "I'm not asking for anything except a chance. I know you've been through a lot. I know you may still…have feelings for Dean," he said through clenched teeth. The idea that he might always have to compete for her full affections made him even more determined to prove that he was the right one for her. Had always been the right one.

She shook her head and started to say something, but he placed a finger to her lips.

"And that's okay. I just want a chance to prove to you I would never hurt you the way he did. I don't care how long it takes. Take your time. I'm not going anywhere, Abby. My love is not going anywhere."

She swallowed hard and her eyes widened at his words. "I can't promise I'll ever be ready," she whispered.

"I'll keep waiting," he said firmly. Then he smiled. "On one condition."

She frowned. "Which is?"

"You and Dani come to the fall fair this weekend with Taylor and me."

"No."

"It won't be a date," he said quickly. "Just two friends hanging out."

She sighed again. "I think we skipped over 'friends,' don't you?" she asked.

"Well, then *friends* shouldn't be that difficult," he countered. He wasn't about to let her push him away. Not when he was finally ready to show her how much he cared about her.

"Fine. But I don't think friends sit on the same side of the table, so get over there," she said, trying to nudge him out of the booth.

He stayed exactly where he was. "This friend does."

CHAPTER 16

❧

"The last time I was here was…Jeez, it had to be senior year," Abigail said, as they entered the fall fair grounds a few days later and headed toward the ticket booth. The park was lit up with amusement rides, carnival games, and craft tables. Loud rock music played on overhead speakers, and the sounds of laughter and squeals of self-induced terrified fun could be heard all around them.

"It's been a while for me, too," Jackson said.

She frowned. "Really?"

He shot her a puzzled look. "Overpriced, cheapo carnival toys and pee-in-my-pants rides aren't exactly my thing."

She laughed at the too-accurate description of the event. "Actually, now that I think about it, you really weren't impressed when we came here years ago." She shrugged. "But I just thought you were annoyed to be around me again, as usual."

As they reached the booth, he pulled out his wallet and handed Taylor forty dollars. "Here, get enough for you and

Dani," he said before turning back to her. "I *was* annoyed to be around you, but only because you were there with Dean."

She handed Dani her own money and said, "Well, I'm sure it didn't help that I forced you to get on every ride with me twice because of Dean's weak stomach, and then I remember you spent the money you were saving for new hockey equipment trying to win the oversized six-foot teddy bear at the ball toss game for Becky." A teddy bear that had sat in the corner of her bedroom until she left L.A. Dean had tossed one ball and won it for her, after Jackson had spent a small fortune trying.

"As I remember, you got the bear," he said grumpily.

She laughed. "The truth is, I didn't want the bear! You guys were so determined to see who could win it, I didn't have the heart to say anything, but the thing was awkward and heavy and kinda ugly."

He laughed, too. "Well, for the record, I wasn't trying to win it for Becky."

"You were trying to win it for me?"

"I would never have admitted to it, but yeah. Seventeen-year-old boys would do anything to make a pretty girl smile," he said, turning to look at her. "Including getting on rides that terrified the shit out of them."

"You were scared?" He hadn't seemed scared. In fact, *she'd* been the terrified one, burying her face into his chest and clinging to his shirt as they'd rode the creaky, ominous-sounding roller coaster. Then feeling super awkward for getting so close to a guy who hated her, once they'd gotten off the ride.

"The ride freaked me out, but what I was really afraid of was that you'd notice the problem I was having in my jeans," he whispered.

She shook her head. She still couldn't believe he'd liked

her back then. And he'd never said a word. He'd sat back and let Dean date her, take her to prom, marry her…She stole a quick glance downward toward his crotch and raised an eyebrow.

"What? I was seventeen and you were crazy hot. You're still crazy hot, but I've learned to control myself these days."

"Really?" The passionate sex the previous weekend seemed to indicate otherwise. Not that she'd been a voice of reason, either. She still wasn't convinced their "let's be friends and see how things go" plan was going to work. Not when her pulse raced at the sight of him and when the smell of his cologne made her want to cuddle closer to him. Nope, definitely not "friendly" feelings she was experiencing.

"Well, you could help a guy out a little by not wearing those skin-tight jeans that hug your hips and ass so perfectly…" He moved closer and put his hands on her hips. She swallowed hard, her breath caught in her chest. His touch made her dizzy. She only managed to resist the temptation to lean into him and pull his arms around her waist because there were far too many people around.

"Or these V-neck sweaters, teasing the life out of me with the hint of lace peeking over the top." His gaze left hers to drop to her chest and goose bumps surfaced on her exposed skin as a shiver of anticipation ran through her. "Those beautiful, sexy…"

"We got the tickets!" Dani said, approaching suddenly.

Jackson quickly dropped his hands and Abigail stumbled away from him lightning fast.

"Great!" she croaked. "Let's go spin until we puke." She released a slow breath, ignoring Jackson's gaze still on her as she fought to control her thundering heart. He may have hidden his attraction to her ten years ago, but he certainly was making up for lost time now.

* * *

Jackson watched from the safety of the ground as Abby, Taylor, and Dani climbed into the front seat of the roller coaster. This friendship plan of theirs was already getting derailed. How did he expect to spend time with her and keep his hands and lips to himself when all he wanted to do was hold her, kiss her, make up for the years he'd been too afraid to act on his feelings?

"Why the front? Can't we move back a few rows?" Abby asked, sounding nervous. Yet, she was doing it. She got points for bravery at least.

"The front is the best row. You can see everything better," Taylor said.

"Great. So we can see falling to our death better. Just what I wanted," she said, moving over to allow the two girls to climb in.

"You sure you don't want to get on with them?" she asked Jackson, her tone pleading.

"Not a chance in hell. Have fun," he said, as the kid operating the ride lowered the bar over their knees.

The lock snapped shut and Abby's face paled.

"This is going to be epic," Dani squealed.

Jackson laughed and waved as the ride started and the rickety train car struggled to make the slow, torturous climb to the top of the first drop. His stomach turned just watching the thing.

He still had no idea how Abby had talked him into getting on it with her. Sure, he'd had a crush on her, but his feelings must have run deeper even back then, because there was no way he would have gotten on otherwise.

Thank God the seats could only hold three, otherwise he may have abandoned common sense once again and done it.

If for no other reason than to have her body pressed against his, and have a valid excuse to hold her for three and a half minutes in front of the girls.

Years ago, holding his best friend's girlfriend while his buddy watched from below had made him feel guilty as shit. But it had been Dean's fault, refusing to get on the ride with her. His buddy had missed the opportunity, and he'd gotten a chance to be the guy Abby smiled at, clung to, laughed and screamed with…And now it seemed once again, Dean's loss was his gain.

And this time they weren't teenagers. This time she knew how he felt about her. This time things were different. And he refused to feel guilty about any of it. He deserved to be happy, and so did Abby. After what Dean had put her through, it was a lot less difficult to put this new relationship with Abby ahead of his former friendship.

New relationship? Maybe not yet. But he had every intention of waiting until she was ready to take a chance on love again. Though he hoped he could help her get there and fast. The idea of waiting too long for the chance to make love to her again was tortuous.

His cell phone rang in his pocket and he reached for it, checking the call display. Coach Turner. He hadn't returned the man's first call. Mostly because he hadn't made a decision yet. A month ago, he would probably have taken the chance, but now things were different. He let the call go to voicemail and tucked the phone away. He'd have to get back to him. And he'd have to tell him no, he thought, an unexpected disappointment creeping into his chest at the thought. Then his gaze met Abby's and the disappointment faded entirely.

He watched as the roller coaster stopped at the top and hovered, the front car dangling precipitously over the steep plunge. All of a sudden the roller coaster in front of him seemed a lot less threatening than the emotional ride he was on within himself.

* * *

"No one wants to go on the Ferris wheel?"

All three shook their heads.

"After I braved all of those insane rides and lost my Ray-Bans on the Twister?"

Dani sighed. "Forget it, Mom. It's boring. It just goes around in a big, slow circle." She turned to Taylor. "In L.A. we had one with cages that rolled and rocked and it went a lot faster. That one was fun."

"For you! I had to get the fairgrounds security to come unwrap my hair from around the metal on the cage." Most terrifying moment of her life, being rattled around inside a cage, with her hair stuck, and Dani thinking it was hilarious.

"I warned you to put your hair in a bun," Dani said, as though the embarrassing incident, resulting in the shortest hairstyle she'd ever sported, had been her fault.

"Fine. I'll go on it by myself," she said, tearing three tickets from the sheet and heading off toward the Ferris wheel.

A second later, she smiled as she heard Jackson say, "Wait up! I'll get on with you."

"Great!" she said.

Though a minute later, sitting in the gently swaying chair, her shoulder touching his, her thigh brushing his, and the soft scent of his cologne filling her senses, she wasn't sure she'd be able to relax and enjoy the ride. Her pulse was racing faster now than it had on the roller coaster.

Spending time with him when they had to keep things casual in front of Dani and Taylor and the rest of Glenwood

Falls was proving impossible. They hadn't kissed since the dinner date that wasn't a date, and she was dying for it. His scent had disappeared from her bed pillows and she longed for its return, too. She forced a steadying breath. They couldn't rush things. She'd meant what she'd said in the restaurant—she wasn't quite ready yet. There was no doubt that she was attracted to him, and she knew she liked him a lot more than was safe, but another failed attempt at a relationship was not what she needed right now. So she had to be sure…of him, of herself, of everything before she allowed things to go further.

"You okay?" Jackson asked.

"If by okay, you mean completely tormented, then yeah," she said.

"Good to know the feeling's mutual," he said with a smile.

"Stop that. Those dimples don't help," she said, forcing her gaze away at the sound of his laugh.

"I'll try to be less irresistible." The ride started and the chair went higher, and Jackson turned to look at the mountains against the dark sky in the distance. "Great view from up here…as long as I don't look down," he said, clutching the side of the chair.

She nodded. "This was always my favorite ride. If you look that way, you can just barely make out the top of the houses in the neighborhood where we grew up," she said, pointing to the left.

He leaned closer and nodded. "You're right." He turned his face toward her and an odd expression flickered across his features.

"What?"

He shook his head. "Nothing."

"No, really what?" He couldn't look at her like he was

seeing her for the first time without explaining the meaning behind it.

"It's just…" He stopped. "It's going to sound like a dumb line."

"Give it a shot anyway," she said with a smirk, enjoying the slight look of embarrassment on his face. He reminded her of the young boy she used to think hated her, and the smirk faded. For the first time her heart ached for that boy. She'd always fought for his approval, but he'd had to deal with seeing her with someone else. He'd had it much worse.

"You just look so beautiful—the flush of color in your cheeks from the adrenaline from all the rides, your hair all messy, the way the lights reflect against the color of your eyes—it's…breathtaking."

Well, her breath had certainly been taken away.

He trailed the back of his hand along her cheek. "You would think that ten years would be enough to erase these childhood feelings, but since you've been back here, they've only grown. And the other night…"

"Something happened," she whispered.

"Something amazing happened," he agreed. He traced a finger along her lips, and she swallowed hard.

"But now that I know how great we are…or could be together, we both have to suffer," she said softly, laying a hand on his leg in an attempt to steady herself from the intoxicating dizziness she was feeling that had nothing to do with the ride.

He studied her. "Are you suffering, too, Abby?" he asked, his lips just inches from hers, his hand covering hers on his thigh. Her body ached with desire. She slid her palm farther up his leg and his eyes widened. He cupped her face and the need in his eyes matched the reaction happening beneath her hand. "Damn, I want you so bad," he grumbled.

She couldn't think straight. She couldn't breathe. All she wanted to do was kiss him. Actually she wanted to do far more than that. "Glad the feeling's mutual," she murmured, feeling a dull, throbbing ache between her own legs.

His lips met hers and a second later, her other arm went around his neck and she pressed her body into his. She didn't care if everyone in town saw them. Right now all she wanted was the kiss he'd resisted taking the first time they rode this Ferris wheel together.

Unlike their previous kisses, this one was torturously slow. He took his time, grazing his lips over hers, the feel of his breath against them causing her palms to sweat in anticipation.

She needed more. Craved more. She moved closer, pressing her mouth to his, her tongue separating his lips. The kiss was long, hot, and wet, and she was struggling with the need for air and the urgent need for more of him as the ride went around and around.

His hands cupped the back of her head and she clung tighter to him, all hopes of taking things slow, being "just friends" slipping further and further away. They'd been fooling themselves to think they could take a step back after the night they'd shared. Her common sense and ability to think clearly vanished when he was so close, so real, and so incredibly tempting.

"Mom!"

The sound of Dani's voice above the music and the fairground crowd made her eyes snap open, and she pushed Jackson away. Damn.

The ride had stopped and the chair had reached the bottom. The ride attendant rolled his eyes as he opened the door to let them out. Dani's expression was a mix of confusion, hurt, and anger as she turned and ran toward the restrooms.

Shit. Moving past Jackson, Abigail ran after her daughter. "Dani, wait…just hold up…" She stopped short as her daughter disappeared into one of the porta-potties and slammed the door. She struggled to catch her breath, more from the effect of Jackson's kiss than the dash across the fairgrounds. "Dani, please come out."

"Go away!"

"Dani, we should talk about what you just saw." Though what she would tell her daughter, she had no idea. She could barely comprehend the emotions spiraling through her, let alone explain it to her nine-year-old.

"No."

"You can't stay in there all night. Come out, let's talk." She wiggled the handle on the door. This was a disaster. The last thing she wanted her daughter to have to deal with right now was the idea of her mother and her hockey coach together.

"Dani, please come out."

"I don't want to talk to you."

Jackson and Taylor stopped next to her. "She won't come out."

"Let me try," Jackson said, tapping on the door. "Dani, how can you stand it in there? Isn't it stinky?"

Abigail punched his arm. "Seriously?"

"I'm not laughing," Dani called out, but the slightest edge had been removed from her voice.

Abigail clung to it as she tried again. "Please just come out…" She glanced at Jackson. "Where it's less…stinky and we'll talk about what you saw."

"No."

She sighed. Fine. She'd have to try to explain it through the porta-potty door…with other people nearby, listening. Though, half the park had probably witnessed the kiss anyway. "Look, sweetheart, that was…" Incredible. Mind-blowing. Probably going to happen again. "…nothing. I know it *looked* like something." It certainly felt like something. "But it wasn't. Nothing is happening between Coach Westmore and me," she said. Not yet anyway…Oh God, who was she kidding? There was so much happening between them.

Now Jackson punched her in the arm. "Seriously?"

"Can we deal with *us* later? I'm trying to get my daughter out of a porta-potty," she hissed.

Taylor rolled her eyes as she pushed them both aside. "You two suck at this." She knocked on the door. "Dani, it's me."

"Why aren't you locked in one of these, too?" Dani called out, sounding betrayed that her friend hadn't joined the porta-potty revolt.

"Because, as gross as it was, seeing them trying to eat each other's face…"

Thanks, Taylor.

"It's also kinda awesome," she said, surprising her. "I mean, think about it. We are best friends, which is cool, but wouldn't it be even cooler if we were cousins?" The excitement in her voice rose.

Abigail's mouth fell open. Cousins? Taylor had witnessed one ill-timed kiss between them and already she was marrying them off? She was more like Becky than anyone realized. She shook her head and went to say something, but Jackson touched her arm, nodding toward the door.

The red latch signifying *occupied* switched to green.

Oh thank God.

The door opened and Dani came out slowly. She still glared at her, but she hugged her friend. "Cousins would be pretty cool," she mumbled.

Fantastic.

When she turned to Jackson, he was grinning.

She narrowed her eyes as she shook her head. "Do not get any ideas," she hissed as she followed the girls back to the fairgrounds.

"Far too late for that, pretty girl."

* * *

"Thank you so much, Dad. Dani will be so thrilled," Abigail said two days later as she gathered her things to head home after class. She still hadn't heard from Dean about whether or not he could take Dani to the Father and Daughter Fall Formal that weekend, so she'd decided to ask her own dad.

Going to the dance with her grandfather may not be what Dani wanted most, but Abigail was desperate. Her daughter was at least speaking to her now; there had been a two-day silent treatment after the kiss incident, and she knew Dani still wasn't crazy about the idea of her with Jackson. And she wasn't sure if her reassurance that a repeat of the kiss wasn't going to happen anytime soon had made anyone feel better.

But right now, it was probably for the best. She was still getting her new life on track, and despite the intensity of her feelings for Jackson, she couldn't ignore the fact that her divorce had been finalized less than two weeks ago. She couldn't possibly move on that fast. Right?

"What time should I pick up my date?" her dad asked, breaking into her thoughts.

"Oh, um, six fifteen..." Her cell phone beeped with an incoming call. "Dad, hold on just a sec." She glanced at the call coming in and her heart stopped. Dean. "Actually, I'll have to call you back."

"Okay, sweetheart."

Clicking over she cleared her throat. "Hello?"

"It's me."

No shit. "Yes, caller ID is a fairly accurate psychic." It was the *reason* for his sudden call that remained the mystery. He'd blocked her incoming emails, and the one time she'd tried to call, it had gone straight to voicemail.

"I'm just calling to find out the details of this dance on Friday," he said tightly.

He actually planned to attend? The man who gave away all of his custody and visitation rights was suddenly interested in a school dance? The same guy who hadn't called to see how his daughter was in over a month? She wanted to tell him to screw off, that they didn't need him, but she knew how much him being there would mean to Dani.

Therefore, it was the first time in many months she didn't want to punch him in the face. At least not as hard. But she was still pissed at the lack of contact with his daughter. "How did you know about it?" Had he somehow still seen her email, though it had bounced back?

"Dani called me yesterday," he said.

She did? Abigail had told her she could call her father anytime she wanted, she just hadn't known Dani had done it. "The dance is at six thirty at the elementary school gym."

"I'll pick her up at your place. You're still staying at your parents', right?" His tone held an unconcealed note of condescension.

And she'd never felt as smug in all her life as she said, "Actually, no. We have our own place now."

He was silent for just a second too long, letting her know she'd hit her mark. She felt like doing a happy dance on the teacher's desk.

"Fine. Just text me the address."

"Sure."

"And I'd like to have her overnight."

Her mouth fell, and any victory or relief she might have been feeling vanished. "What do you mean?"

"I mean, at the hotel in Denver. I'll be playing there Saturday night."

Dani had mentioned that, but she'd been doing her best to forget. She'd foolishly been hoping Dani would as well. She clenched her jaw. "We didn't negotiate any visitation schedule," she said, forcing her voice to remain calm and confident.

"Abigail, don't start that shit. I didn't fight you for custody because I travel too much and I never would have won, and I wasn't able to commit to a visitation schedule for the same reason. But I expected that we would be adults about all of this and when I had time to see Dani, you wouldn't have a problem with it." His voice was hard and cold, and she almost shivered.

She swallowed hard. Damn it. She knew he was right. Despite everything, he was Dani's father. More importantly, Dani loved him and she'd never forgive her if she refused visitation requests.

The truth was, she had no reason to. Dean may have been an asshole to her, but as far as Dani was concerned, he'd never hurt his daughter. Never *would* hurt her.

"Abigail?"

"Yes, I'm here. She can stay overnight with you in Denver," she said, feeling sick about it already.

"See you Friday."

She disconnected the call and sat staring at the phone. See her on Friday…As if life wasn't complicated enough.

*   *   *

Did she let him in or make him wait out on the step?

Abigail glanced at the phone in her hand. Dean's text was two words.

I'm here.

She wouldn't get any answers from that. What *was* the protocol for divorced parents? Too bad the divorce papers hadn't come with a *How to Deal with an Ex* instruction manual. She sighed, standing on tiptoes to peek through the small frosted-glass window in the door. If he was still sitting in the rental car, she'd just let Dani go to him once she was ready.

Damn it. He was pacing the driveway.

Her heart nearly stopped at the blurry image of her ex-husband in a dark gray suit and light blue dress shirt standing near the car. He never wore a tie, and that evening was no exception. Despite the distance and the frosted glass, she could make out the tanned, muscular chest beneath his open-collared shirt. His dark, wavy hair was longer, reaching the collar of his jacket, and he'd started to grow his beard, as he did at the beginning of every season. Unlike a lot of the other hockey wives, Abigail had always liked the beard; it made him look stronger, tougher, sexier somehow…and still did.

She sighed. Did he have to be so good-looking? Divorcing an unattractive man had to be easier, she thought as she reluctantly opened the front door.

He glanced up and her breath caught. For a brief second, she almost forgot this was the man who'd cheated on her and broken her heart. For just an instant, he looked like the same man who would stand in her driveway, waiting to pick her up for dates on Friday night.

But he wasn't that man anymore.

The silence hung heavy on the cool breeze blowing the leaves from the deck into the porch and finally, he held up a hand in greeting. "Hey."

"She's almost ready. You can come in and wait. If you want."

He looked hesitant as he checked his Rolex. "Sure," he said.

A second later, the awkward, strained silence moved into her entryway.

"Nice place," he muttered.

Yeah, the hallway is pretty great, she thought. "Feel free to come in," she said, leading the way into the living room. She wondered if he knew this house was Jackson's. She wasn't sure how often the two men spoke these days…or what they spoke about. The idea that her ex may have been giving Jackson information or insights into their dissolving marriage made her stomach sick.

Dean followed behind her, scanning the room. "The furniture actually looks better in this smaller space," he said.

She nodded. He'd never been a fan of the light tan and blue checkered pattern sofa and chair anyway. She'd picked it out when they'd first moved into the house in L.A. He'd been busy with training camp and hadn't been available for consultation. Over the years, she'd learned not to wait for him to make decisions.

"Does the fireplace work?"

She nodded again. Small talk with a complete stranger was easier than this.

His gaze landed on the photos on the mantel and he moved closer, taking in each one.

She was silent, waiting to see if he'd notice or comment on the fact that he wasn't in any of them. She'd purposely sorted through their family photos, selecting only shots of her and Dani. There were several of him in Dani's room, but not on her mantel.

"Was this from the trip we took to Maui?" he asked, picking up her favorite: one of her and five-year-old Dani in snorkel gear on the beach. Dani held up a starfish, and the smile on the little girl's face reflected the happiness they'd all felt on that trip. They'd spent days lying in the sun and nights sitting on the deck watching the sun set over the ocean.

It was the last vacation they'd taken where she could honestly believe they were a real family unit. Dean had still been committed to their relationship, and his mind hadn't been on someone else while he was making love to her. She pushed the thoughts aside as she answered. "Yes."

"That was a great trip," he said quietly, setting the photo back down.

She remained silent.

He picked up another shot of them from the year before, about a month before she'd caught him cheating. It was taken at the birthday party they'd held for Dani in their backyard. They were standing in front of the rented bouncy castle. "I'm pretty sure I was in this one."

"I'm pretty sure I cut you out," she said, taking the photo from him and setting it back where it was. She didn't like him touching her stuff.

He cleared his throat as he turned away. "You seem to have settled in nicely. This house must back onto the lake, right?" he asked, glancing out through the window that faced the backyard.

She was back to nodding again.

"And Dani's settled in at school?"

Again the nod. Jeez, she looked like a moron bobbing her head up and down. Say something. The problem was, without the tense arguing they often did when they spoke, she had little to say. Things really were over between them, and small talk with a man who'd hurt her wasn't coming easy. "Dani's doing really great, adjusting and making new friends," she said.

"That's great." His eyes trailed the length of her and he paused before saying, "You look really great, too, Abigail."

Her teeth clenched. Not as great as the two cheerleaders she'd walked in on him with. She forced the image and the thought away as she took a deep breath, choosing to ignore the compliment. "Dani!" she called down the hall instead. "Your dad's here. Are you almost ready, sweetheart?"

"Just a second," came her excited reply.

"She's a little nervous about wearing a dress and heels," Abigail said quietly. They'd gone shopping the day before, and seeing her little girl try on the semi-formal dresses had brought tears to her eyes.

Dean smiled. "I'm sure she's going to look as beautiful as you do."

The second attempt at a compliment irritated her even more than the first. "If you'll excuse me, I have to finish getting ready myself." She was already set to go, but suddenly him being in her new home, in her new space was making her feel stifled, and she needed to regroup.

"Hot date?" he asked behind her, his tone a mixture of annoyance and jealousy that he attempted to mask behind a joke.

She stopped, almost wishing that were the case. "I'm actually chaperoning tonight."

"I'll admit that makes me feel a lot better," he said.

"Well, as long as *you* feel better," she said sarcastically, as Dani's bedroom door opened.

All trace of annoyance at Dean disappeared as she saw

Dani. Her hand flew to her mouth and embarrassing tears sprang to her eyes. Her hockey jersey–wearing daughter was almost unrecognizable in the lavender dress and white one-inch heels. Her dark hair was pinned back in a high ponytail and the pale lipstick she'd given her looked so sophisticated.

"Do not cry and embarrass me in front of Dad," she hissed.

Ah, there was her daughter. She smiled, as she quickly wiped her eyes. "Sorry, I'm good," she said, moving back to let Dani pass her in the hallway.

"Dad!" she said happily.

Dean smiled and accepted her hug. "Hey, princess. Wow, you look amazing," he said, letting out a low whistle.

Dani beamed. "I'm ready. Let's go."

"Okay, sweetie. I'll see you there."

"Do you want a ride?" Dean asked. "We're going to the same place."

Maybe, but not together. From now on they would probably be attending a lot of Dani's important life events separately. And that was okay. "No, thank you. I'll meet you both there."

CHAPTER 17

❧

$\mathcal{T}$his is stupid."

Agreed, Jackson thought tugging at the tie his sister had insisted he wear. He looked around—hardly any dad at the dance was wearing a tie. "It's not that bad," he lied.

"You don't want to be here any more than I do," Taylor said, calling his bluff and folding her arms across the front of the light blue dress he knew she'd had no input on. "You're a fill-in for a stepdad. Have I mentioned this is stupid?" She pulled on the curls around her shoulders, tying them back into a messy ponytail with the elastic band she always wore around her wrist.

"Stop fidgeting. You look pretty." True, he'd barely recognized his niece as she'd come out of her bedroom under duress, Becky threatening not to buy her the snowboard she wanted for Christmas otherwise. But, it was true; she looked like a little lady that evening and nothing like his star player, which put his protective uncle senses on high alert.

"I look like a girl," she said, distress etched on her tiny features.

"Newsflash."

She sighed. "Uncle Jackson, do we really have to stay?"

He hesitated. Becky thought this was important, and he really wasn't in any position to contradict his sister's parenting. She wanted Taylor to explore both sides of her personality, though he personally thought his sister was dreaming if she believed her daughter possessed even one feminine bone in her body. "Unfortunately, yes," he said, taking in the decorated school gym. Green and gold helium-filled balloons covered the ceiling. Tables covered with gold paper tablecloths and balloon centerpieces were placed along the walls, framing a dance floor area. The DJ was set up on a stage in the corner, and the sound of hip-hop dance music filled the air. Strobe lighting and an aluminum foil–covered papier mâché disco ball completed the tacky setup. It brought back too many memories of his own school dances, where he'd felt just as uncomfortable and out of place.

"At least Dani's here," Taylor said, looking past him a second later.

He turned to see Dean enter the auditorium as well. So his buddy had made it. Good. He knew how important this was for Dani, even if Taylor had trouble with the idea.

"Let's go talk to them," he said. At least he'd be able to catch up with Dean, if nothing else. Though, he may not be able to get through a conversation with his friend without asking him if he'd lost his mind letting Abby go. And of course, he'd probably keep his own recent endeavors to himself. He wondered if Dean had been inside the house when he'd picked up Dani, if he and Abby had spoken...He couldn't help but wonder how their first face-to-face as divorced parents had gone, or if she'd told Dean anything about them.

Probably not.

Then she appeared in the doorway, looking stunning in a dark blue, knee-length dress that clung to her hips and accentuated her tiny waist. Hips and waist he'd kissed every inch of. Hips and waist he couldn't wait to get his lips on again. Unfortunately, after their on-display kiss at the fair, she was more adamant than ever to take things slow. He understood but didn't love it. And how the hell was he supposed to be at this dance with her without being able to dance with her, hold her, kiss her? Yet another sense of déjà vu washed over him. "Actually, you know what? This *is* stupid."

Taylor's eyes lit up.

"Look, your mom wanted photos." He grabbed his cell phone and dragged her in the opposite direction, over to the balloon archway in the corner. "Smile," he said, leaning closer and barely giving her time to before he snapped the selfie and headed toward the empty dance floor. He took her hand in his and held the camera out. "Say cheese." Snap.

By the time they reached the dessert and punch table, Taylor's laughter was actually genuine. "You're crazy, Uncle Jackson."

"Do you want to get out of here or not?"

"More than I want to breathe," she said, suddenly serious. "What's next?"

"Pick up a cupcake," he instructed.

She reached for a vanilla one with blue frosting, but he shook his head. "Not that one. One of the cherry chip ones with the red frosting your mom made." His sister had instructed him to take at least one picture of her hard work in the kitchen before the kids got to them.

"Hey, buddy."

Shit. So close.

Taylor stopped mid-bite and looked past him, her eyes wide. Pieces of cupcake fell from her mouth as she gaped. "Oh my God—Dean Underwood…" She pointed.

Dean laughed as Jackson turned to face him. "Hey! Look who made it," he said, his eyes searching the auditorium for Abby.

"Hi there," Dean said with a wave at Taylor, who was still frozen, staring at one of her hockey idols. "She okay?" he asked him.

Jackson wrapped an arm around her shoulder, drawing her forward. "Dean, this is Becky's daughter, Taylor," he said.

"My friend I've been telling you about," Dani said, linking her hand in Dean's. The look of pride on her face to be there with him made him glad that Dean had finally shown up for her. For his own sake that evening, not so much. Dean being there would no doubt have Abby on edge, and she certainly wouldn't allow herself to be dragged into the equipment room for a quick kiss.

"Right, Taylor, the best left defenseman on the team."

His niece blushed. Actually full-on blushed. He'd never thought it possible. "Th-thank you, Mr. Underwood…I'm a huge fan," she said, finally finding her voice.

Dean smiled. "Call me Dean. Any friend of Dani's is a friend of mine."

"Dean," his niece whispered, still in a fangirl trance.

Jackson shoved her shoulder. "Why don't you take my phone and go get some shots of you and Dani doing stuff so we can get out of here," he said, handing her his cell.

She frowned. "What's the rush, Uncle Jackson? The dance just started."

Wow.

"Come on, let's go take a picture in the wacky photo booth," Dani said.

Taylor hesitated.

"I'll be right here," Dean reassured with a wink.

Taylor looked ready to faint as she nodded and allowed Dani to drag her toward the rented photo booth, where dozens of kids were lined up waiting for their turn to put on crazy hats and glasses and get their photos taken.

So much for getting out of there.

"So, buddy, how's things?" Dean asked, sliding his hands into his pockets.

"Good." His friend's ex-wife was driving him to distraction, but other than that…

"The business? Still doing well?"

"Yeah. Just bought a place over on…" He stopped. Dean obviously had been to the house to get Dani. Did Abby tell him she was renting and possibly buying his house? He wasn't about to say anything. He knew Dean thought he despised Abby. Admitting that they'd gotten friendly—understatement—wouldn't be a good idea. "It's going well."

"Good to hear. I tried calling you about the Colorado Eagles tryouts. Did you hear about them?"

"Yeah, I got a call from Coach Turner last week." He shrugged. He'd yet to return the man's calls, and tryouts were coming up fast. He just wasn't sure going back was the right move. Especially not now with things progressing—painfully slow—with Abby. Being two hours away in Loveland wouldn't help, with a training and game schedule keeping him so busy.

"That's great. These are closed tryouts, man. I know a bunch of guys who were hoping to get that call. You're going to try out, right?"

At first, he'd been tempted, but the more he'd thought about his odds, the less the idea appealed to him. Making a fool out of himself by not making a team he'd once been a part of was the last thing his ego needed. "Ben's been harassing me every other day about it, but I don't think I will," he said with a shrug.

Dean stared at him as though he'd lost his mind. "Why the hell not?"

"I'm almost thirty, man. The minors are full of nineteen-year-old kids. They're younger, faster, more skilled...I'd look pathetic trying out for a team I quit three years ago."

"Look, I'm telling you, these kids may be quick, but they aren't more skilled. And with all of the players getting injured this season, all the teams are bringing guys up from the farm teams."

"Ben said they brought four guys up last game." He'd never seen a season where so many new players were getting their shot.

"Exactly my point. Guys are getting called up, leaving the minor teams scrambling for players. The thing is, if they bring in a few other men like yourself, they can keep their nineteen-year-olds, so the kids don't have to feel the pressure of going up and down. You have to go for this, man."

"I appreciate your confidence, I really do. I just think that part of my life is over." And he hoped a new chapter was beginning. His gaze landed on Abby pouring glasses of punch behind the drinks table and his heart raced. Definitely hoping life was taking a new, better direction.

"It doesn't have to be," Dean was saying, "Six months on the minor team, and I guarantee, you'll get called up and get a chance to play this time."

Jackson shrugged. "I don't know. I'm not sure it's what I want anymore," he said, but he had to admit talking about the opportunity with his buddy had gotten him slightly hopeful. Maybe he could succeed this time. Either way he knew he had to make a decision soon. If he decided to go for it, every waking minute of the next week would be spent on the ice. And if he made the team, he'd be living in Loveland…He glanced at Abby again. But damn, even twenty feet away was proving too much. "I'll think about it."

Dean slapped his back. "Good. I wouldn't want to have called in my favor to Coach Turner for nothing."

What? His buddy had gotten him the invite to the tryouts? He'd thought his past playing record had secured the spot. It was good enough. "You talked to Coach Turner?"

"I just got you the invite. The rest is up to you, and I know you'll kick ass."

His friend was still trying to help him with a hockey career, still believing in him…and he'd slept with his wife. He felt like a complete asshole, but he couldn't bring himself to regret his actions. And he hadn't asked Dean for the favor.

Dean's gaze fell across the room. "Abigail looks like she's doing well. New house, new job…" he said.

Jackson shifted uncomfortably at the mention of her. Time and distance must have weakened his bond with his friend because he couldn't detect the underlying meaning in the words. Was he happy for her? It was hard to tell. "Um…yeah." He nodded, staring at her and hoping the truth about his feelings wasn't written all over his face.

"She looks amazing."

Yes, she did.

"I think I fucked up."

Think? But it was too late now, wasn't it?

"I've been doing a lot of soul-searching lately, especially since signing those divorce papers. I made some mistakes, you know. It's the game. It's being away so much." He ran a hand through his beard. "And then seeing her tonight. She looks amazing," he said.

"Yes, you said that." Jackson's voice was hard as he turned to face him. Was Dean for real? He'd put Abby through hell and now, because she looked amazing and was doing fine without him, he wanted her back? "Dean, you're not serious, right? I mean, you hurt her a lot."

Dean's eyes narrowed, then he pat him on the shoulder. "Don't sweat it, buddy. It's not your problem."

Damn right it was his problem. He wasn't sitting on the sidelines while Dean tried to take what he wanted—in that moment—only to hurt her again when another set of long legs walked past. "Well, actually…"

"Dad, come on, let's get our picture taken under the balloons," Dani said, running up to them.

"Okay…Hey, why don't we ask your mom to join us," he said, his gaze locked on Jackson.

A brief flash of disappointment registered on the little girl's face but Dean didn't notice.

"Okay," she said.

"See you later, man," Dean said as they headed off toward Abby.

There's no way Abby will agree to it. He watched as they spoke, saw the look of terror in her eyes come and go before finally nodding and following them to the balloon arch.

Damn. This was bullshit.

Unfortunately, they looked like the perfect, beautiful family smiling for the camera and his heart fell into his stomach. *Was* his buddy too late realizing his mistake? Or was the history they shared and the fact they had Dani enough for them to try again? Did Abigail want that? He stared at her, trying to determine what might be going through her mind—and her heart—at that moment, but he couldn't tell. All he did know for sure was this familiar scene in front of him wasn't something he could continue to put himself through.

"Can we go now?" Taylor asked at his side, as though reading his mind.

"Yep."

*   *   *

As she watched Dean and Dani dancing to a hip-hop song among the other father and daughter couples, Abigail smiled. Her daughter looked happier than she'd seen her in a long time. Maybe they would all be okay. Dean could swoop onto the scene when he would, and between those times, she and Dani would make a new future together.

And hopefully someday she'd be ready to include someone else in their lives. A certain someone in particular. Her gaze scanned the gym for Jackson. She'd seen him earlier with Taylor, and he'd looked so amazing in his suit, filling in for Neil, that her heart had melted. She'd also seen him talking to Dean, but now he was nowhere in sight.

So much for a sneaked kiss in the equipment room.

Despite telling him that they needed to go slow, the urge to go fast—very fast—hadn't faded. In fact, in the few days she hadn't seen him, he'd been constantly on her mind. She'd missed him.

"Hey, sweetheart, would you mind if I danced with your mom for this one?" she heard Dean ask Dani as they approached, and her heart stopped.

"Oh, no…" She shook her head as she glanced at her daughter. How could he not see how disappointed Dani looked right now? How could he not realize how much she missed him the last few months or how excited she was that he was there? And why on earth was he acting as though they were all still some big happy family? The ink on the divorce papers was certainly dry by now. She was moving on. And her growing feelings for Jackson had a lot to do with her healing heart.

"Come on, Abby. For old times' sake," he said.

Old times' sake? The man had to be crazy.

"Go ahead, Mom. My feet hurt anyway," Dani said.

"No," she said firmly, staring at Dean. Then turning to Dani, she added, "I still have to finish up here before I can leave. I'm sure your feet can make it through one more dance," she said with a wink, ignoring Dean as she continued to toss empty paper plates and cups from the tables into the garbage bag she held.

She released a breath as the two headed back onto the dance floor. What was going on with Dean? For months he'd ignored her, dealing only through the lawyers, and when they did talk, they hadn't exactly been friendly. Now he wanted family photos and a dance with her? She'd caught him staring at her so often that she'd actually been uncomfortable. Whatever his new motive was, she didn't like it. And she hoped Dani wouldn't get caught in the middle of any more tension between them. *Just get through a few more minutes.*

She finished cleaning, fighting the knot in the pit of her stomach, and twenty minutes later, she hugged Dani in the school parking lot before her daughter set off to spend the night with Dean at his hotel.

"You're hurting me," Dani croaked.

"Sorry…Okay…" She reluctantly let her go. It was just one night. No different than when she slept over at Taylor's.

Who was she trying to kid? This was so much more stressful. An hour away in Denver, with Dean. Why had she said yes? The court document clearly stated she had all the say in the custody arrangement, but she couldn't deny her daughter this time with her father. Even if she would be up all night worrying and thinking the worst.

"You have everything?" she asked.

"Yes, Mom," Dani said, wiping her lipstick off of her cheek.

Still she held on.

"Mom, let go," Dani said, peeling her fingers from her arm.

"Okay, sorry. You'll have a great time." While she lay awake worrying sick about her. She forced a smile as Dani climbed into the rental car.

Dean closed the passenger side door and walked toward her. "She'll be fine."

She nodded.

"I'll have her back tomorrow by noon."

She nodded.

"You know you're welcome to join us," he said.

Her eyes narrowed. Suddenly she was seeing this visit with Dani, the perfect father act, for what it was. "You came here to spend time with Dani, remember?"

He frowned. "I just thought all of us together again might…"

"Might what, Dean?" she hissed, lowering her voice so Dani wouldn't hear. Lord knows the little girl had already heard and witnessed enough of their fighting.

"Look, I realize I messed up. After signing the papers, I'll admit, I panicked a little. I miss you…and Dani." He touched her arm.

She backed away. He couldn't be serious right now.

"I really think I want my family back."

Really *thought* he wanted his family back? Not *definitely* wanted his family back, but *maybe*? Well, she was completely certain that she didn't want *him* back. Her hands clenched at her sides. "That's not up to you."

He stepped forward. "Don't be so angry at me that you refuse to even think about it. Look how happy Dani was tonight, the three of us together," he said, handing her the photo of them under the balloon arch.

She took it and tucked it under her arm. Allowing the picture to happen had been a mistake. One she wouldn't be repeating. "Have a good night. Don't let her stay up too late, and have her home by noon, please."

"I know about the kiss with Jackson," he said, his expression suddenly unreadable.

She gulped. Fantastic. She felt her higher ground start to cave beneath her feet, but dug in her heels. She had no reason to feel guilty or make excuses. She was a free woman, and she'd do as she pleased. "Dani told you?"

"Yes. And I forgive you."

Her eyes widened. "You forgive me? For kissing a man after we were divorced? How big of you."

"I forgive you for kissing my best friend in an attempt to get back at me," he said.

That's what he thought? She was tempted to let him think it since it was none of his business anyway, and it was a much easier explanation. But she shook her head as she moved closer. "I didn't kiss Jackson to get back at you." She hadn't had sex with him for that reason, either. "I kissed him because I wanted to. You never even crossed my mind. In fact, you never cross my mind anymore, Dean."

He stared at her a second longer, as though weighing her words, before turning and getting into the car.

Forcing a smile despite her fuming anger at Dean, she

waved at Dani as they pulled out of the lot. She couldn't believe the way the evening had turned out. He thought he wanted them back. He thought they should give it another try. He must be insane. There was only one man she wanted. And it wasn't her ex-husband.

CHAPTER 18

～⌒～

$\mathcal{H}$e should have gone home.

Instead, he walked into the Grumpy Stump and straight toward the bar.

"Hey, Jackson, what can I get you?" Alan, the bartender, asked, stacking glasses behind the bar.

"Whatever she's been drinking seems like a good time," he said, leaning one elbow on the bar and nodding toward Abby. In the middle of the dance floor—alone—she seemed completely oblivious to anyone else in the bar as she belted out the lyrics of a current hip-hop song about being fancy he'd never heard before. And never wanted to again. "And what's with the music?" They usually played a mix of rock and country, not this crap.

Alan shrugged. "She requested it."

Jackson sighed as he looked at the fruity-looking drink Alan placed on a napkin in front of him. The lime-green liquid was in a martini glass that he wasn't even sure how to hold without spilling the contents, let alone drink with the excessive sugar rim along the top. "What is that?"

"An apple-lime-tini," he said.

"I'll have a beer—whatever's on tap," he said, tossing enough cash onto the bar for both drinks before turning to watch Abby again.

She didn't notice him, busy in her own little rock concert, long hair flying out around her as she danced, her hips swaying tantalizingly to the beat, unaware of the hard-on inducing effect she was having on every man in the place, including him.

"How many of these has she had?"

"Four."

Wow. "How long has she been here?" He'd left the school, dropped Taylor off at home, then went home to change and here he was…She'd been chaperoning the event that evening, and it was only nine thirty. She must have arrived fairly recently herself.

"About forty minutes ago."

Four drinks in forty minutes; that explained things. No doubt she'd skipped buzzed and went straight to drunk.

He should mind his own business. Drink his beer and leave. Better yet, forget the beer, resist the urge to find out why she was partying like a college girl on spring break, and just get the hell out of there while he still could. After seeing her with Dean that evening, he had his own feelings to sort out, and that wouldn't be happening if he stayed.

Damn.

He grabbed the beer, guzzled a mouthful, then headed toward her.

She didn't even look at him as she said, "No, thank you. I just want to be left alone."

"Well, maybe you should have gone home," he said.

Her head snapped toward him, and at first she smiled, but it faded as fast as it had appeared. "You," she said, pointing a finger at him.

Well, this should be interesting.

"This is all your fault," she said, moving closer. The smell of apple-rini-mini-tin-whatever lingering on the air between them.

"I just got here."

Her eyes narrowed. "Don't pa…pat…patro…" She paused. "Is the word pronounced pay…tronize or pa…tronize?" she asked, mumbling the words again both ways.

He reached for her arm. "I don't know. Why don't we go sit and get you some coffee and Google it?"

She yanked her arm away. "No. I'm dancing."

"How about sitting the next one out and talking?"

She shook her head. "You're the last person I want to talk to. I told you—I'm pissed at you."

Actually, no, they hadn't gotten that far. Her fascination about pronunciation had distracted her. "Okay, what did I do?"

"As if you don't know."

He sighed. He'd rather not play mind reader with drunk Abby. He reached for her waist as the DJ finally switched back to the regular country music and a slower ballad started. "Okay, we'll dance and talk."

She looked ready to argue, but then leaned against him, resting her head against his chest. "I do like this song…and you do smell good…"

He swallowed hard as her arms went around his neck. All evening, he'd wanted nothing more than to have her in his arms, and now that she was there, he held on tighter. But before his lips could take what they'd been craving, he had to know what was bothering her. He had no idea what had happened at the dance after he'd left, but obviously it hadn't been great. "So, why are you here?" he asked as they started to sway to the music.

"I didn't want to go home. Dani's with Dean tonight."

An empty house and all night ahead of them. His body reacted to the thought, and he shifted slightly away from her, afraid she'd slap him for the effect she was causing in his jeans.

She's drunk, his voice of reason reminded him.

Damn, he wished he'd arrived four drinks ago.

"I'm sure it's a normal parenting thing to be worried, but you know she's fine." His friend may in fact be the womanizer, cheater, and heartbreaker the media had splashed all over their front pages, but he'd shown up that evening for his daughter. Or at least that was part of the reason. His jaw clenched again thinking about what Dean had said about wanting Abby back. He'd have to pry her from his cold, dead arms.

"I'm not worried about her—she's fine. It's me I'm concerned about," she said, burying her face into his chest. "And what are you wearing that smells so good?"

"Soap," he said. "Look, why don't we get out of here? I'll drive you home."

She pulled away and wagged a finger at him. "Oh no. Just because I'm stupid drunk and crazy vulnerable right now doesn't mean I'm going to sleep with you again," she said, just a little too loud.

"Shhhh," he said, taking her hand and leading her away from the couples who were dancing far too close to them.

"What? Don't tell me you're afraid of small-town gossip?"

"No. *You* should be. I'm not the one who just got divorced. Besides, remember who your husband was."

She nodded. "Exactly. Thank you for reminding me. I'm pissed at you, and I'm not going anywhere with you. I'll call a cab."

"Let me drive you home and you can tell me what I did wrong. I promise I won't come inside." He held up a scouts' honor sign, hoping she didn't remember he'd never actually been a Boy Scout.

"Fine," she mumbled.

Two minutes later, he waited for her to climb into his truck, trying to keep his eyes off of her ass and failing miserably. What was he thinking promising to behave himself? Looking this good, she was asking to be kissed even more senseless.

He sighed. But he *had* promised, and while talking to her when she was drunk may not be the most productive, they needed to talk.

He climbed into the driver's seat and started the truck. "Okay. Now, do you want to tell me why you're mad at me?"

She folded her arms across her chest and stared out the window. "It doesn't matter."

He sighed. "It does to me." Reaching across, he touched her shoulder, and she turned to look at him. "Look, if it's still because of Dani seeing the kiss, I'm sorry."

She shook her head. "That's not it."

"Well, what is it?"

She rested her head against the seat. "I just wish you'd told me before, how you felt."

"Before when?" She'd been in love with his best friend since high school. When was he supposed to have told her?

"Before I fell for Dean…before I married him and had my heart broken…This is all your fault," she mumbled, her eyes drifting closed.

He touched her cheek softly before turning his attention

to the road. "Maybe it was all my fault." He just hoped going forward he could make things better.

Pulling into her driveway minutes later, he cut the engine, then going to the passenger side, he opened the door.

She was out cold. Great.

He climbed up into the truck and unbuckled her seatbelt, carefully lifting her out. At the door, he rummaged around in her purse for the keys, his arms aching as she grew heavier the longer he held her.

Finally, he unlocked the door, went inside, and carried her straight to her bedroom. He placed her on top of the covers and reached for the quilt draped over a chair in her room. But as he went to cover her up, her eyes opened.

"You're awake."

She grinned. "I just wanted you to carry me in," she said.

"Well, you're home safe and sound, so I'm going to go." He headed toward the door, and she followed him out into the hallway.

"Will you stay for a while?"

No. Definitely not a good idea. He sighed. "Sure."

She smiled. "I'll get changed. I'll be out in a minute."

Going into the living room, he sat on the edge of her couch. He really should go. He could tell himself he could stay and nothing would happen between them, but he knew that was a lie.

He ran a hand through his hair, the conflicting emotions inside of him making him crazy. He wanted Abby. He knew he could make her happy. He stood. He had to figure things out with sober Abby before this thing between them went any further, got even more complicated. "Abby, I'm going to go," he called down the hall.

"No! Wait…"

"We'll talk tomorrow, okay?"

"No, wait, please, I need your help," she said through the bedroom door that was slightly ajar. "The zipper…on…this…stupid dress—aghhh."

Jackson closed his eyes. No way. There was no way he could help her out of that dress and still stick to the man-code rules of not taking advantage of a drunk woman.

He hesitated, listening to her swear under her breath as she continued to struggle, hoping she'd solve her own zipper problem without his help.

"Oh, great, now I'm really stuck," she said a moment later, her voice muffled.

Shit. "What is the deal with the dress?" he asked, moving closer but still standing outside the door.

"It fit a few months ago, now just barely, and I tried pulling it off without unzipping it…" Her voice trailed. "You're going to have to help."

Damn it. He should leave her stuck. Maybe she'd learn a lesson about wearing such tight fabrics that clung in all the right places, making it impossible for a man who was desperately trying to do the right thing by suppressing his feelings—once again—a little easier.

Pushing open the door, he almost laughed at the embarrassed, pathetic expression of hopelessness on her face.

"I'm stuck," she said.

"Yes, you are." The dress was pulled up around her waist, barely covering the thin white seamless underwear she wore underneath, and the majority of the fabric gathered around her shoulders and neck. Her arms were poking through the top of the dress, her head sandwiched between them in an uncomfortable tangled mess.

Well, as tempting as it was, he couldn't leave her like that. "Let's try pulling it back down," he said, walking toward her.

"Okay," she mumbled. "Be careful, this dress cost a small fortune."

"Do you want to get out of it or not?"

"Yes," she said with a sigh.

"Fine. Stay still." He reached for the edge of the dress that was plastered against her upper thighs, and as his fingers brushed against the soft, satiny smooth texture of her skin, his mouth went dry. Stuck in a heap of fabric, Abby still had an intoxicating effect on him.

Trying to focus on the task at hand, he tugged on the fabric. It slid part of the way back down, then stopped. He frowned. "What happened?" He tugged harder.

"You've reached the part of the dress that cinches in at the waist. Trying to get it down over my ribs will be the hard part."

"How were you able to get it up *over* your ribs?" he asked.

She huffed. "Just tug really hard."

"I'm warning you, it might rip." Oh God, his fantasies about tearing her clothes off had never started like this, ever. Ironically enough, this was still turning him on.

"I don't care anymore," she said through a yawn. "I just want this off so I can go to sleep. I've had enough of this day."

"Okay, ready?"

"Jackson!"

He tugged as hard as he could and the dress moved. One more tug and it fell back into place.

"Oh thank God," she said, sliding her arms back into the holes. "Okay, let's try the zipper."

"You really are a pain in the ass when you're drunk. You know that, right?" he grumbled.

She turned and lifted her long hair. "Please."

He'd given up his dream home to the woman, he'd given up his heart—what was one more favor, he thought. Reaching for the zipper, he fumbled with the persistent metal for a few seconds, before it gave way. He quickly zipped it halfway down her back, just until the top of her bra clasp appeared, then let go and stepped away. "There. Do you think you can manage from here?" He had to get out of the room.

She nodded. "Yes, thank you."

"Sure. Okay, then. Sleep tight."

"I thought you were going to stay," she said, a look of disappointment in her eyes.

She was going to be the death of him. "I can't."

"I have an idea."

"No."

"You haven't heard it yet."

He sighed. "What's the idea," he asked, terrified he wouldn't be able to say no to any request.

"Stay and let's order pizza."

He smiled, as he shook his head. She was impossible.

"See, good idea, right?"

He was hungry, but not for pizza. But it wouldn't be the first time he'd settled. "Yes, it's a good idea."

* * *

"I uh…wanted to thank you for what you're doing for Becky," Jackson said a little while later. The fireplace flames served as the only source of light as well as providing a warm, comfortable feel as they sat on the floor around the coffee table, eating pizza.

The crust was thankfully soaking up the alcohol in her body, and Abigail was at least able to speak without having to focus really hard on her words. She still hadn't reached the sober point where she was feeling embarrassed by the drunken state he'd seen her in or the dress mishap, but she knew she would get there…for sure by morning.

For now, she felt…good. Having him there with her made her feel much better about Dani being with Dean. "I'm not doing anything. All I did was place a call. Her designs sell themselves," she said through a mouthful of cheese and pepperoni.

"It's funny. I remember telling her years ago she should do something like this, but she just laughed."

"You're too close. Sometimes it takes someone on the outside to tell you the same thing you've heard from family for it to really sink in."

He nodded, tossing his crust onto his plate. "Well, thank you. She's been really excited about the opportunity."

Abigail stared at his collection of crust. "What's going on there?"

He shrugged. "I don't eat the crust."

"It's the best part!"

"No way. There's no sauce on it, or cheese, or meat. I'm not wasting space in my stomach for just dough."

"I will," she said, reaching for one. Again, probably not something she would have done if she were just a little bit more sober.

He looked surprised, but then laughed. "You haven't changed at all, you know."

"What are you talking about? Sure, I have." She felt as though she'd aged a lot more in the last ten years than she actually had. The last year in particular had been a lot of growing, changing, and maturing.

"Not at your core. You are still smart and ambitious…"

She swallowed the pizza. "I just got my first real job two months ago."

"But you were active in charities and stuff in L.A."

That was true.

"And you're still funny."

"No, I'm not. I can't tell a joke to save my life." She'd always envied people who were naturally funny. The ones who could entertain a room full of people without even trying.

"Give it a shot," he said, popping the last of his pizza into his mouth and sitting up onto the couch.

She hesitated, chewing slowly. She had to have one good joke she could deliver. She nodded, swallowing the dough and sitting next to him, folding one leg beneath her. She turned to face him. "Okay, I got one."

He smiled. "Hit me."

"What does a walrus and Tupperware have in common?" she asked.

"What?"

"They both like a tight penguin," she said with a grin. "No, wait…Seal—they both like a tight seal!" Damn it. So close.

He stared at her, an amused look on his face, but not laughing.

"Well?"

"You're right. You're not funny."

She picked up a throw cushion from the couch and hit him with it.

He grabbed it, tossed it aside, and holding her hands together, he tickled her. "I wonder if you're also still as ticklish as I remember."

She laughed so hard she couldn't speak as she wiggled and fought to escape his hold. "Stop…please…" Putting her feet against his chest, she was finally able to kick free. She tried to scurry away, but his arms were around her in a flash. "What are you doing?"

He pulled her onto his lap, and gently moved her long hair away from her neck. He placed a soft kiss at the edge of her collarbone and suddenly the heat from the fireplace was too much. She was suffocating.

"Now that you aren't fall-on-your-face drunk anymore, I'm giving in to the urge I've been fighting all night," he murmured against her skin. His hands traveled the length of her thighs, gently massaging.

"Jackson…"

"Abby, I've never gone after the things I want because there was always an excuse—someone else was in the way or the timing wasn't right. But for the first time, I don't care that you were married to my best friend or that you might need some time after the divorce. I'm done making excuses that let me sleep at night, okay with my own inability to go after what I want." He turned her face to look at him.

She gulped. What he wanted was clearly written on his face, and she couldn't find her voice to argue. She didn't want to argue. And she couldn't blame it on the alcohol. The look in his eyes, his words, and his touch had an amazing sobering effect.

They also made her hot as hell.

They really should move away from the fireplace, she thought, as his lips moved toward hers.

Her cell phone rang on the coffee table, hidden beneath the lid of the pizza box, and she jumped up, startled. "That's Dani's ringtone," she said, all traces of their exchange seconds before melting away to panic. It was after midnight.

Handing the cell to her, Jackson ran a hand through his hair and started to clean up their plates and napkins.

"Hello? Dani?" she answered.

"Mom…" Her daughter's voice was quiet, but she was clearly crying.

Abigail's heart raced faster than it had sitting on Jackson's lap. "What's wrong?"

"I…I woke up…and I don't know…Dad's not in the room."

Anger was the only emotion coursing through her as her left fist clenched at her side. That asshole. "How long has he been gone, sweetheart?" She'd give him the benefit of a doubt—a tiny one. He might just be at the soda machine.

"I'm not sure. I've been awake now for about ten minutes waiting. There's a lot of noise coming from the rooms next door…"

The hockey team was staying in the hotel that evening. Dean couldn't even have gotten a room away from them and their partying?

"I'm scared…I want to come home," Dani said.

She was already in the hallway, reaching for her coat, when Jackson appeared from the kitchen.

"What's wrong?" he asked.

She ignored the question, instead saying into the phone, "Don't worry, sweetheart. I'm on my way. I'll be there as soon as I can. We can keep talking, okay?" She checked her battery life. Full charge. She'd put the call on speaker as she drove.

"Abby, where are you going? What's wrong?" Jackson asked, taking her keys from her.

"Is that Coach Westmore?" Dani asked, hearing him in the background.

Shit. "Yes, sweetheart." She covered the mouthpiece. "Give me the keys, I have to go get her," she hissed at Jackson.

He shook his head. "You've been drinking. I'll drive. Let's go," he said, out the door without stopping for his jacket.

Abigail felt a small sense of relief to not have to drive the hour to Denver alone. She hadn't even stopped to consider the fact she shouldn't drive. Gratitude for Jackson helped to numb some of the anger she felt for Dean and worry over Dani, but just a little bit. "We will be there really soon, just stay on the phone with me," she said, closing the door, and jogging toward the truck, where Jackson was already behind the wheel.

*　　*　　*

They made it to Denver in less than fifty minutes.

"She's in room 406," Abby said, disconnecting the call with her daughter as they rushed into the hotel lobby.

"Okay, you go get her, and I'll go find Dean." It wouldn't be hard. The noise coming from the hotel's lounge made it a safe bet. He clenched his teeth and willed himself to stay calm. His irritation with Dean at the dance paled in comparison to the anger he felt now. Dani was a child. In a strange city. In a hotel full of drunk, partying hockey players. Dean should have known better than to leave her alone.

"Thank you," Abby said, shooting him a look of gratitude as she took off down the tiled hallway toward the elevators.

He headed toward the lounge.

Damn it. So many familiar faces—players he'd once played with, others he'd idolized, all laughing and having a good time. The hotel lounge, which was normally quiet and laid-back, was full of women falling over the hockey stars.

He shook his head. This right here was his brother Ben's idea of a perk of the job. He knew Asher tended to avoid the partying and drinking and late-night womanizing, but Ben enjoyed every minute of it.

So did Dean, by the look of things.

His buddy was sitting in a far corner booth with another right wing from the team and three women. The table was covered in empty glasses, and Dean had an arm draped casually over the shoulders of the blonde sitting next to him.

His friend obviously still had a type.

Unfortunately he was too stupid to realize he'd had the most fantastic one on the planet and he'd messed it up, thrown it all away, and for what? A different body in his bed every night?

Feeling his annoyance start to climb to an unhealthy level, Jackson forced a breath as he approached.

"Hey, man. What are you doing here?" Dean asked, looking not as surprised as he should.

"Can we talk for a sec?" he asked, nodding away from the group of adoring admirers.

"Sure. Have a seat," Dean said, gesturing to the other side of the booth.

"In private."

Dean's stare was hard. "I'm with friends, Jackson. You're welcome to join us."

Friends. Right. The people who were here today, gone tomorrow. The ones who only cared about his MVP status on the team and the money in his wallet. One day hockey wouldn't be there for his "friend," and neither would these people.

And neither would he anymore.

But, if that's the way Dean wanted it—Fine. He sat in the booth and leaned across the table. "I'm here with Abby."

Dean's expression turned steely. "What?"

"Abby, your ex-wife," he said pointedly, shooting a glance toward the blonde who looked annoyed at the sudden mention of another woman.

"I know who Abby is. Why the hell are you two here?"

he asked, removing his arm from the woman and leaning on his elbows.

The smell of beer on his breath made Jackson even more determined to set him in his place. What had his plan been? To get completely wasted and then drag this woman back to his room, where his daughter slept?

He didn't know this guy anymore. Any loyalty or guilt he may have been struggling with over his feelings and intentions with Abby disappeared. Any question in his mind about who the better man for her was vanished. "We came to pick up Dani. She called, said you'd left her in the hotel room alone."

Dean's eyes narrowed.

The blonde looked confused. "Dani? Isn't that your daughter?"

Well, fangirl had done her research at least. And to her credit, she moved away from him, looking disgusted.

"Yes. My daughter is staying with me tonight, which is why I told you we couldn't go up there," Dean said, shooting the words directly at Jackson.

Okay, so half a point for having that much common sense at least. He still was a jerk for leaving the little girl alone. "Well, you can soon enough. We are taking Dani home."

Dean climbed out of the booth and Jackson stood to block his way out of the lounge. "What do you mean, *we*? What does any of this have to do with you, *friend*?" Dean spat the word, stabbing his finger into his chest.

Jackson didn't flinch. "I care about Dani and Abby."

Dean laughed. "That's right, I forgot. You've had a hard-on for my wife since junior high."

Elementary school. "Ex-wife."

"Well, man, she's all yours, but Dani is still my daughter."

"A daughter you wanted nothing to do with. You still

don't. This dad of the year bullshit—arriving at the last minute to take her to the dance, looking like a hero—save it. No one's buying it. You only did it to impress Abby, and she's not fooled by you."

"No? She's moved on to you, huh?"

"It's none of your business anymore," she said, behind him.

Jackson turned to see her and a tearful Dani, holding her mother's hand.

He hesitated. There was so much more he wanted to say to Dean, but it wasn't worth it. The guy wasn't worth it.

"Let's go," he said to them.

Abigail too looked ready to tear Dean's smug expression from his face, but she nodded. "Come on, Dani."

"I'm going back to court, Abigail. I want time with Dani—she wants that, too," Dean said behind them.

Abby turned and Jackson placed a hand on her arm, glancing quickly at Dani. There was nothing he'd rather do than take the guy out, but the little girl had already had a crappy evening and she didn't deserve to be seeing, hearing, or witnessing any of this. "It's not worth it," he said quietly.

At her side, Dani let go of her hand and walked back toward her father.

Oh no. She couldn't possibly be changing her mind about leaving, was she?

"Dad, I used to think you were the greatest hockey player ever, and I wanted to be just like you, but Mom's the real hero. She'd never put anything else before me," she said.

Tears gathered in Abby's eyes as Dani turned and headed back toward them. "Can we go home now?" Dani asked.

Abby nodded, and Jackson shot one final look at his former best friend before following the girls out of the lounge.

*   *   *

Abigail closed Dani's bedroom door quietly an hour later, after Jackson had carried the exhausted little girl into the house.

"She okay?" he asked.

"She's asleep," Abby said with a nod, smothering a yawn with her hand. "Thank you again. I'm glad you were here tonight. I wasn't thinking straight, and I would have driven out there to get her."

"Of course you would have. You might have also punched Dean in the face," he said, rubbing her arms.

She managed a weak smile. "It was certainly tempting."

He pulled her toward him, wrapping his arms around her. She didn't fight; she was too tired to keep fighting the feelings she had for him. She was finally seeing him exactly for who he was, and the excuse that she wasn't ready for another relationship was falling short the harder she fell for him. The way Dani had hugged Jackson tight and thanked him for being there that evening made it obvious the little girl was no longer annoyed by their growing attraction, either.

"I'm sorry," he whispered in her hair.

"You have nothing to be sorry for."

"I do. I was so quick to judge the situation, to believe Dean and not give you any credit. And then tonight, after seeing you both at the dance with Dani, I thought maybe I needed to back away, that maybe you still had feelings for him." He smoothed her hair back from her face. "But I just couldn't do it. This time I was fighting for you, fighting for us."

"I'm glad you had a change of heart," she said, leaning on tiptoes to reach his mouth.

"That's the thing, Abby. I've never had a change of heart. It's always been you."

"Make love to me, Jackson," she whispered against his lips.

This time there was no questioning whether or not she was sure. Pushing open the bedroom door, they stumbled inside and Jackson fell back against it as it closed, drawing Abigail's body toward his, his hands gripping her ribs as he kissed her exposed neck.

She shivered and pushed her hips back against his already full erection and turned her face toward him, claiming his mouth with her own. Her hips rocked forward and backward, teasing his cock, forcing his grip on her waist to tighten even more. "If you don't stop moving that way, I can't be held responsible for the bruising your ribs may suffer," he murmured.

She bit his lower lip and he swung her body around until her breasts were pressed firmly against his chest as he deepened the kiss. His hands slid down the length of her back and cupped her ass, lifting her slightly until his cock pushed against the fabric of her yoga pants between her legs.

God, she could barely contain her desire for him. That evening she'd felt so many different emotions, and they all cumulated in this crazy need.

Unzipping his jeans, she lowered herself to her knees. Tugging his underwear down over his hips, she gently slid her tongue from the base of his cock all the way to the tip, licking the pre-cum that glistened at the head. He groaned and she continued the flicking and licking, circling his cock slowly, massaging his balls with her right hand.

"Abigail, you are driving me insane," he growled.

"That's the point," she said with a teasing smile at him.

Gripping the back of her head with one hand, he

separated her lips with the other, forcing the length of himself into her accepting mouth.

Immediately, she closed her lips over him and began sucking and licking hungrily. He tasted so good, and she felt her own body ache with desire as she dared to glance up at him. The look of pleasure on his face as he leaned his head back against the door made her even more eager to make him feel incredible.

But placing his hands on her shoulders, he reluctantly and gently stopped her. "I'm going to come. Let's slow things down," he said, his voice strained. Pulling away, he helped her to her feet and carried her to her bed.

"What if I don't want to take things slow anymore?" she asked, cupping his face with her hands and staring into his eyes. She didn't. She was ready to be with him. She couldn't stand not being with him anymore.

"We will go fast tomorrow. Tonight, I'm savoring this." Setting her down gently, he lowered himself on top of her and, starting at the base of her neck, he rained kisses and soft little bites from her ear, over her neck and across her shoulder. Shivers danced down her spine and she trembled. It felt amazing being with him with no reservations, no doubts, no fears.

His hands cupped her breasts, squeezing her erect nipples until she moaned in a mix of pleasure and pain. He was far too sexy, and everything he was doing felt far too amazing to take it slow the way he wanted. Her body craved his touch everywhere, all at once.

Removing one of his hands from her breast, she forced it down, inside her pants, and between her legs. "Touch me, please," she begged as she spread her legs and arched her body toward him.

"I can do better than that," he said with a slow smile.

Moving downward, he knelt between her legs and removed her pants and the thin white thong, tossing it aside.

Exposed and completely vulnerable, her legs trembled on either side of him, and the anticipation of his touch was almost too much. She needed him, wanted him. "Jackson…"

He gently touched her, opening her folds, tracing the shape of her and licking the wetness from his fingers. "You taste so good, Abby," he said, continuing to tease and torment her throbbing, aching body.

She whimpered as she stroked her own breasts. "Please, Jackson, I need you inside me…please," she begged.

When he slid two fingers inside her at once, pressing the palm of his other hand to her pelvis, she cried out.

"Shhhh…" he whispered, leaning forward to kiss her flat stomach. "Think you can take another one?"

She bit her lower lip as she nodded. "Yes, please…" she said, tightening her interior muscles around his fingers as he inserted the third. The pressure was so intense, she knew she wouldn't last much longer. "Jackson, Jackson, Jackson…" she repeated his name over and over, clutching at his shoulders.

He left her then, and she trembled, her breath labored as she watched him remove a condom from his wallet. Returning to the bed, he ripped it open and slid it on quickly before lying back down between her legs. He paused briefly before entering her. "Ready?" he asked.

Oh God yes. She nodded eagerly, lifting her hips as he plunged deep inside her. His moan of satisfaction as his hips pressed against hers drove her close to the edge. She gripped his shoulders as she rocked her pelvis back and forth, searching, fighting desperately for release. "You're so incredible," she whispered, as a whirlwind of emotions brought her to climax. Her body shuddered and she held him tight, enjoying the intense sensations rippling through her. Jackson Westmore was perfect.

"You're the incredible one," he said, raising his body to look at her. He touched her cheek softly. "I've loved you for so long, Abby."

Her breath caught as his lips crushed hers, preventing her from answering. He loved her. He'd always loved her. Happiness filled her heart and because she couldn't say it, she poured every emotion she had for him into the kiss.

He held her against him as he pushed deeper, faster, quickening the motions with his hips, his lips never leaving hers, his heart beating in rhythm with hers.

She loved making love to him. Loved watching him make love to her.

She wrapped her legs around him and pressed her body closer, until every inch of him was touching every inch of her.

He groaned as he came, and she moaned in pleasure as she felt him throb inside her. Resting his head against her forehead, he struggled to catch his breath. "Okay, so maybe that wasn't exactly slow," he said with a smile.

"Slow is completely overrated," she said, as she hugged him tighter, never wanting to let go, terrified by what that meant, but ready to trust her heart, which was leading her to him.

* * *

Jackson lay wide awake in the dark room, his arms wrapped around Abby as she snuggled closer. He kissed her forehead and she glanced up at him with sleepy eyes. "Thank you again for everything tonight," she said quietly.

"Thank *you*, pretty girl. That sex was pretty awesome," he said kissing her nose.

She hit his arm. "Yes, it was, but I actually meant for everything else."

He nodded. "Of course, Abby. I'm glad I was here." He knew she was strong enough to have dealt with the situation herself, but he hoped his support had shown her just how much he cared about her and Dani. How much he wanted to be there for them—always.

"Do you ever wish you had that life—the one Dean has—with all the women and partying, being a local god to the sports fanatics?"

He traced a hand along her bare arm. "The only life of Dean's I envied was his life with you." The scene in the hotel bar that evening had been empty and meaningless. These guys never knew if the women liked them for who they were or if they liked the idea of being with a star athlete.

"Do you still wish you were playing hockey?"

That was a tougher question to answer. "Some days I do. Other days I don't. I quit the Eagles for a lot of reasons. But mainly, it was because when Dad got sick I couldn't deal with not being here. Even just a couple hours away, it was impossible to get back here to see him or to help Mom often enough. The training and game schedules were exhausting, and my mind wasn't in it anymore after I'd gotten sent back down from the majors. I was starting to wonder if chasing the dream was worth missing out on the last few months with him." He'd decided they weren't.

"Dean missed a lot: birthdays, anniversaries, Christmas... I never let him see how much it bothered me, but it was tough. Nine months a year, Dani and I were essentially on our own, and then when he was home, it was hard to integrate him back into our routines, our schedules..."

"Ben says that's why he's never settled down, and Asher is so caught up in the game, I'm not sure he even realizes there's more to life," he said, playing with a strand of her hair. "So, I guess the answer to your question is I think everything happens for a reason, and there was a reason I didn't make it as far as my brothers and Dean."

She kissed his chest. "Well, I can't say I'm disappointed. I really don't think I could ever live that life again...love another pro hockey player," she said through a yawn, snuggling closer, her eyes closing.

He held her tight, replaying her words in his mind as she drifted off to sleep. Everything happened for a reason, and maybe he'd finally discovered the reason he'd never made it to the NHL—life had other plans. Plans that suited him just fine.

CHAPTER 19

❧

The sound of voices woke her the next morning. Abby blinked several times before her eyes flew open, the events of the evening before flashing like a flipbook in her mind—the dance, the bar, the drive to Denver, and the night of passion with Jackson that had continued until the first signs of morning had cracked through the bedroom window.

Rolling over, she saw he was no longer in the bed, and the clock on the table said 9:35. She lay still, listening once more as she heard his voice, coming from outside on the deck.

Who was he talking to? Dani? She cringed, wondering how this all looked to her daughter. Sure, she'd been grateful to see him the night before, but having him there in her house when she woke up might be a different story.

But then she heard the toilet flushing in the bathroom down the hall.

Must not be Dani he was talking to.

"I really do appreciate the invite," he was saying. "But I don't think I'm going to try out."

Try out? For what? Getting out of bed, she moved closer to the window. Standing with her back to the wall, she listened, feeling guilty for eavesdropping on his conversation, but desperate to hear.

"Yes, I realize that there will be limited spaces…I'm just not sure I want to play professional hockey anymore," he said.

Her mouth went dry. Who was on the phone? Obviously someone presenting him with an opportunity to try out for a team…And he was turning it down?

A mixture of panic and relief made it difficult to breathe. She should be happy he was saying no to whatever opportunity he was discussing, but she just felt sick. She'd assumed hockey was a thing of the past for him. He was twenty-nine, and he seemed happy with coaching and his business. Hadn't he said a hockey career wasn't something he'd consider anymore?

That was certainly the impression he'd given her the night before.

"Yes…I know what I'm turning down," he was saying and her heart shattered at the sound of disappointment in his voice.

He could say what he wanted, but he still wanted to play.

"Thank you, Coach Turner…if I change my mind, you'll be the first to know. Thank you again, sir."

Coach Turner—the head coach for the Colorado Eagles. Jackson had just turned down an opportunity to try out for his old team. She'd heard Dani talking about minor league players being called up to play a lot recently…but truthfully, she paid very little attention to the sport anymore.

Her mind raced. Was this the first call from Coach Turner,

or had Jackson been mulling this decision around for a while? If so, why hadn't he said anything? And if not, why was he making such a hasty decision?

Hearing the front door open, she moved away from the window quickly and sat on the edge of the bed. Her emotions were a whirlwind as a million thoughts ran through her mind. He couldn't not take this chance on his dream, not when she knew deep down he still wanted to play. But yet, she knew if he did follow his dream, she wasn't ready to follow it with him. She had a new life here in Glenwood Falls with Dani. And she'd just gotten her full-time position with the school.

The night before it had felt like they'd turned a corner, that they'd left the past behind. She'd realized it was okay to let herself go with him; she'd felt safe, secure, loved...

She'd realized she loved him.

Oh God. Had she made a huge mistake? If he was still hoping for a career in hockey, then how could they be together? She'd said herself she could never love another hockey player. Never live that life anymore. The stress it put on a relationship was tough. The stress it put on a family was tough. She couldn't put Dani through that again. And at least Dean had a semipermanent contract in one city. Who knew where Jackson's career could take him. Moving all over the country wasn't an option for her at this stage in her life.

She fought for a breath as she stood and paced the room, panic setting in. Damn, what had she done? What did she do now?

It was time to distance herself. She'd gotten too close, too fast. Her head hurt and her heart ached even more. She swallowed the lump rising in her throat as the bedroom door opened.

"Good morning, pretty girl," Jackson said, coming into the room and falling onto the bed.

The sight of his easy smile, the relaxed happiness in his eyes, and the way his black T-shirt fit snug across his chest and shoulders, the short sleeves stretching across his biceps, made her new resolution to once again cool things between them feel like an impossible task. "Hi," she whispered, hating the weakness she heard in her voice. She needed to be strong if she was going to push him away.

His smile faded slightly. "You okay?" he asked, standing and reaching for her.

She moved out of reach, needing to put some distance between them before she could say what she needed to say. If he touched her, held her, kissed her, she'd never be able to do this.

"Abigail?"

"I heard you on the phone just now," she said.

He walked toward her. "Well, then you heard me say I'm not planning to try out." He placed his hands on her shoulders and bent at the knees to look in her eyes.

"But why wouldn't you? This is an opportunity of a lifetime—to get this second chance, especially at your age," she argued, moving away. His touch was dangerous. It weakened her resolve, and she had to do this. She refused to be the reason he didn't at least try out.

"Hey, that hurts a little," he said with a small, nervous sounding laugh. "Look, Abby—you've been perfectly clear the hockey life is not what you want for you and Dani anymore, and I understand that."

Her heart raced and her mind reeled. What was he saying? That he wasn't going to try out because he thought that's what she wanted to hear? She cleared her throat and forced her voice to remain steady as she said, "I don't know why you think you need to take Dani and me into consideration for any decision you make."

His face fell and the look of confused hurt almost broke her. Summoning every ounce of strength, she continued, "I think you should try out." The lie felt like peanut butter stuck to the top of her mouth.

He frowned. "You do?"

"Yes. I mean, this is the career you've always wanted, right? A second chance doesn't happen every day."

He looked as though he was weighing the intent behind her words. "But you've said you're done with all of that…"

She forced a hard expression, praying all of the feelings she had for him were hidden deep inside and nowhere on her face. "I am. But my life decisions have nothing to do with yours."

He stepped back as though she'd slapped him. "So, what you're trying to tell me is you'd be okay with me trying out because you're not considering a life with me anyway?"

Floor, just open up and swallow her now. She swallowed hard as she nodded. "That's exactly what I'm trying to tell you."

His eyes narrowed. "You don't mean that."

God, how had she let things get complicated? All she'd wanted when she'd moved back to Glenwood Falls was to get her life back on track—build a new home, create a new life for her and Dani, and she'd been succeeding in that.

Why had she once again allowed her heart to get involved, possibly jeopardizing everything she'd worked hard to achieve? Why had she once again fallen for a man who could break her heart? Whether it was now or later, he would.

"Jackson, we both knew this—us—was a long shot, and

now you have another chance at your dream. You should take it, because that's what you've always wanted."

"What if that's not the most important thing anymore?" he asked, a note of desperation in his voice, pleading with her not to break his heart.

She swallowed hard. She knew that while he may believe that now, hockey was always the most important thing, and she wasn't ready to repeat past mistakes. He may care for her, may even love her, but the game always won in the end. If she did take a chance on him—and he decided not to try out—he'd only resent her in time. "Don't give up your dreams for a woman who doesn't share your feelings," she said as firmly as her quivering voice would allow.

He stared at her for a long moment. The silence was excruciating, and she wasn't sure how much longer her legs would hold out or the tears would stay lodged in her chest. "I think you should go."

"Abby…"

"Jackson, I thought I could do this, but I can't." She turned away from him and shut her eyes tight, a part of her hoping he would wrap his arms around her and make her believe this time could be different, that she could trust him, love him, have a life with him. The other part of her knew that no matter what he said, some things just didn't turn out the way you wanted them to.

He must have realized that, too, because a second later, she heard the bedroom door close behind him.

CHAPTER 20

❧

*O*kay, I've got *Pretty in Pink* and *The Princess Bride*. Which one should we start with?" Abigail said, holding up the movies two nights later.

Taylor and Dani sat on the sofa staring at her like she'd suggested they watch porn.

"What?"

"First of all, those movies are ancient," Dani said.

Ancient? They were from the late eighties…

"And they are all mushy-gooey-grossness," Taylor said, wrinkling her nose.

She sighed. So much for a girls' night sleepover party. "Let me guess, you want to watch *Slap Shot*—again," she said, rolling her eyes as she reached for the movie the girls watched every time they were together.

They nodded eagerly.

She put the DVD in the player and said, "I'll go get snacks."

"Do you want us to wait for you?" Dani asked, pausing the movie as the opening credits started.

"You know, I think by now, I could probably act it out, so no, go ahead and start without me." Going into the kitchen, she put a bag of popcorn into the microwave and reached into the fridge for the homemade fudge Becky had given them for the sleepover.

Even though it was a school night, she'd suggested the sleepover because Neil had arrived home that afternoon from his tour overseas, and the couple had barely been able to keep their hands off of one another long enough to say goodbye to their daughter.

And Taylor had been plenty relieved to be out of the house for her stepfather's homecoming, too. Abigail couldn't blame the girl. The sight of the happy couple so disgustingly in love had made her nauseous as well, for other reasons.

Since the dreadful morning-after conversation with Jackson, she hadn't seen or spoken to him. She'd avoided the arena the night before, letting Dani go to the practice with Taylor instead. He hadn't called or texted, and she was almost relieved; avoiding him was easier when he wasn't trying to get her attention.

And while she was thrilled for Becky and Neil, seeing two people so in love when her own shattered heart was barely holding together was absolute torture. She hadn't worked up the courage yet to ask Becky or Taylor if Jackson had decided to try out for the team or not, and she wasn't sure she was ready to hear the answer anyway. She'd know soon enough.

She carried the popcorn and a plate of the fudge into the living room. "There you go," she told the girls, reaching for a handful before settling in her chair near the window, where she planned to grade homework assignments. Watching a hockey movie wasn't high on her list of things that could make her feel better, either.

Half an hour into the movie, the doorbell rang.

Oh thank God, something to save her from having to listen to the girls' delivery of the dialogue before the actors on the screen could say their lines. She rushed to the door, planning to keep whoever it was—delivery guy, Jehovah's Witness, whoever—there as long as humanly possible. Her eyes widened in surprise. "Becky?"

Her friend stood on the step, wearing yoga pants, Ugg boots, and a fall jacket that refused to close all the way over her belly. Mascara-stained cheeks suggested the night hadn't gone the way she'd hoped. "Do you have room for one more?" she asked, before a sob escaped her.

"Of course! Come in," she said. "Should I tell Taylor you're here?"

"Not yet. Can we just chat in the kitchen?" she asked quietly, sniffing.

"Yeah. Pretty sure the girls won't notice I'm gone."

"*Slap Shot*?" Becky guessed.

"Yep."

In the kitchen, Abigail placed the container of fudge on the table. "Tea?"

"Yes, please." Her friend sat with a heavy sigh.

A minute later, Abigail joined her. "What happened? You two were acting like hormonal teenagers grossing everyone out two hours ago," she said.

"Everything was great until I told him about the business." Becky removed a tissue from her pocket and blew her nose.

Crap. Without much contact with him when he was overseas, Becky hadn't been able to tell Neil a whole lot about the business before actually going ahead with it. And not that he should have been able to talk her out of it, but he did have a right to know about something as big as this, when it affected his future as well. "I take it he wasn't as supportive as you'd hoped?"

"Not at all. He said he didn't think now was the right time to be taking a risk on something like this."

He didn't understand. "And of course you explained it wasn't a risk at all, because you already have four orders to fill for the L.A. store and possibly new business for the New York location next year?" Becky wasn't taking any risks. She had most of the clothes needed to fill the first two orders already made, and Jocelyn had sent the payment for the first one. Besides, the clothes were a hit. The jacket and dress she'd originally sent had sold in an hour, according to Jocelyn. And the first full order had almost sold out as well.

Becky nodded, popping a piece of fudge into her mouth. "Yes, and he said he didn't know where I thought I'd have the time to make clothes with a new baby in the house and all of the responsibilities I have with Taylor's commitments…"

Abigail didn't know Neil. From what she'd heard and seen so far, he was a great guy, but this lack of support was surprising and disappointing.

"I told him all he saw when he looked at me was a baby-maker housekeeper who keeps shit together while he's off saving the country." She sniffed.

Abigail offered a sympathetic smile. She'd been there. Especially at eight months pregnant when hormones often clouded common sense. However, in this case, she wasn't sure her friend was exaggerating. Neil did sound like he expected her to hold down the fort without considering she may want a life and career of her own, outside of her family. "I'm sorry. I didn't mean for the idea to create conflict between you two."

Becky shook her head. "Don't you be sorry for a thing.

You've been so wonderful and supportive, and I want this new business, for me." She took a tissue from her pocket and blew her nose loudly. Then a determined look replaced the sad one as she said, "And Neil is just going to have to deal with that."

* * *

"She said she was doing it with or without my support, and I had to just deal with it," Neil said, chugging back his second beer in twenty minutes.

Jackson sat across from him, exhausted from six hours of training for the tryouts happening in three days in Loveland. "Look, you knew how strong-willed Becky was when you married her. Did you really think she'd respond well to the caveman attitude of 'I'm the man. You're the woman. Cook, clean, and pop out babies while I support you'?" His buddy had been away far too long if he thought his sister wouldn't chop his balls off for that macho attitude. He was struggling not to tell Neil just how he felt about him not supporting his sister's new passion, but he kept his cool. The man had just come back from a war zone; he'd give him time to readjust before setting him straight.

"I just thought those kinds of decisions were supposed to be made together." He swirled the beer around in the mug. "I mean we are a team, right?"

"Yes. But think about this from her point of view. A lot of the time, she's a team of one, holding everything together while you're away." The way Abby must have done all those years with Dean. He understood why she wasn't eager to return to that life, but damn it, he hadn't been asking her to.

"What am I supposed to do?" Neil asked and he tried to focus on his friend's problems. "You know the tours overseas pay better than regular duty. I don't want to be over there, away from her and Taylor. I was so worried the whole time that something could go wrong with the pregnancy and I wouldn't be here." He slumped back in the seat. "But we need the money."

"Even more reason to be supportive of this new business. Abby says the store owner in L.A. is in love with Becky's clothing. She wants to feature it in both stores. This could be something for her—for both of you. Maybe if it does well, the money won't be as important," Jackson said, his thoughts once again returning to Abby. In two days he hadn't heard from or seen her; it became obvious she was avoiding him when she hadn't even shown up to watch hockey practice the night before, and he knew when to back off.

For the first time in his life, he'd been honest and gone after what he'd wanted, and he'd made a fool of himself. He needed to get away for a while, and that was the primary reason he'd called Coach Turner that morning to see if the spot on the tryouts was still available.

Across from him, Neil ran a hand over his buzz cut. "I'm terrified, man, okay? While I was away, I had a lot of time to think about Becky, Taylor, and the baby and what if something happened while I was away. If this business puts her under stress…"

"Hey, relax. I get it, but nothing happened. Becky and the baby are fine. Better than fine." A lot in thanks to Abby.

Neil sighed as his shoulders slumped. "I was an asshole, wasn't I?"

Jackson nodded. "Yep."

He pushed the beer away. "Let's go. I have to go tell her that and beg her to forgive me so we can get back to…"

Jackson covered his ears. "Stop. That's my sister." And the last thing he needed right now was to hear about anyone in love. The temptation to reach out to Abby was killing him. Going back and forth about his decision to try out was torture. But she'd told him she didn't want him, so what choice did he have? He tossed several bills onto the table and grabbed his coat. "So, back to your place?" he asked as they headed outside.

"No, she left first. Went to Abby's I think. Do you know where she lives?"

Damn it. "Yeah, I know the place quite well, actually," he said, climbing into the truck. Leaving the parking lot a minute later, he headed straight toward the one person he'd been struggling to stay away from.

* * *

The doorbell rang just as the credits were rolling on the television. "Wow. I haven't had this many people stop by my house since we moved in," Abigail said, pushing herself up off of the living room floor, where she and Becky had been going over the last-minute details for her baby shower on Wednesday. She'd calmed down quite a bit, but she still refused to go home.

Opening the door, she wasn't entirely surprised to see Neil standing on the other side. She'd expected he'd come to his senses sooner or later and come in search of his wife, but the sight of Jackson next to him *was* a surprise. "Hi," she said awkwardly.

"I'm here to get Becky," Neil said.

She straightened. "First, I think you need an attitude adjustment…" she started as Jackson punched his shoulder.

"What Neil meant to say was, can we come in?" His gaze locked with hers, and her pulse raced.

They'd been doing a pretty impressive job avoiding one

another in the last few days, and she hadn't realized how badly she missed seeing him or hearing his voice until he was standing right there. She swallowed hard, as she reluctantly nodded and stood back. "Sure, why not?"

Neil rushed inside, past her, but then hesitated in the hallway.

"She's in the living room. Start with an apology," she said, closing the door behind Jackson.

As Neil went in, immediately both little girls ran out and headed toward Dani's bedroom. Smart kids, she thought. One of two things was about to happen in the living room, and neither one was something *she* wanted to witness, either.

Instead, she headed for the kitchen.

Jackson followed. "Can I hide in here with you?" he asked.

"Technically, it's your house," she said, then she took a breath. Now was as good a time as any. "Actually, I'm hoping to change that. I've decided we would like to buy the place, if you're still willing to sell."

His face clouded. "I am."

"Right. I guess with the tryouts in a few days, there's a chance you won't even be in Glenwood Falls much longer..." Becky had delivered the news about his decision to try out just moments before. Playing on the team would require him to live in Loveland, and if by some chance an NHL team called him up during the season, he could end up living anywhere.

But not here. With her. She forced a deep breath. She'd made her decision to let him go; now she had to follow through with it. He deserved this chance.

He nodded. "Listen, Abby, I'm..."

"Don't. Please." They couldn't start talking about them, or she'd likely beg him to stay. All she wanted to discuss with him was how much he was selling the house for. "I can get my bank to wire the payment to you as early as Monday morning. I just need to know how much." With the divorce settlement from Dean, she was prepared and willing to pay any price he wanted for the house.

He looked pained as he nodded. "I'll have an appraiser stop by tomorrow."

She nodded. "Great." It was anything but great. She loved the house. She knew she wanted to buy it, but living in it without him, she would always be reminded of how close they had come to something wonderful. Sleeping alone in a room where they'd made love, where he'd told her he loved her for the first time, would be heartbreaking. She hoped that in time, the pain would ease.

"We're leaving!" Becky said, popping her head in around the corner.

Abigail forced a smile. At least one couple had made amends. "See you at the baby shower."

"That's if I get out of bed in time," she said with a wink.

Jackson shuddered and she might have laughed at his disgusted expression if her heart hadn't been aching so much.

A moment of deafening silence later, he shoved his hands into his jeans pocket and turned to leave. "I guess that's it then. See ya, Abby."

The urge to call out to him, to ask him not to go, not to try out for the team was right there on the tip of her tongue. The temptation to cross the kitchen and wrap her arms around him and not let him go was strong. But she stood where she was, silent, as she let the man she was in love with walk away for a chance at his dreams.

CHAPTER 21

❦

GOOD LUCK, COACH WESTMORE was written across the banner hung on the wall of the Slope and Hatch. Behind a long table, the kids from the team and their parents all waited for him after practice the following evening. Possibly the last practice he would coach that year.

The involuntary lump that rose in his throat was embarrassing and unexpected. "You tricked me," he told Taylor, rustling her hair.

"You mean you really didn't know?" she asked, looking pleased to have been able to fool him about the surprise gathering.

He hadn't suspected a thing. No one had said a word, and he hadn't thought that anyone knew his plan to try out, other than Darryl and his niece. Apparently, they'd spread the word. "I had no idea," he said. "You masterminded all of this?"

"Me and Dani," she said proudly.

His gaze went to the other little girl at one end of the table and he winked at her before letting it move on to Abby, looking uncomfortable and nervous next to her daughter.

Uncomfortable, nervous, and beautiful. Damn her for looking so irresistible at a party meant to say goodbye. Though he was surprised she was there at all.

She smiled in greeting, but it fell short of her eyes.

"Come on, you get to sit here," Taylor said, leading him toward the opposite end and pulling out his chair. A new Colorado Eagles jersey lay across it, his name on the back.

Wow.

He didn't trust his voice, so he just fist bumped the kids around the table, avoiding the eyes of their parents, who would no doubt recognize the emotional wreck they'd just reduced their coach to.

He sat in the chair and picked up the jersey. "Thank you guys…and girls," he said, finally. "This was nice of all of you." He didn't even mind the extra layer of pressure it added to the already stressful tryouts ahead. "Now I have to get back on the team, huh?" he joked, but suddenly failure wasn't an option. Not with so many people believing in him, hoping he would succeed.

"The jersey was Ms. Jansen's idea," Taylor said, sitting in the seat next to him.

His gaze searched for hers at the end of the table, but she refused to look at him. And while he knew he should be grateful for her support and the thoughtful gesture, it just felt like one more way she was telling him to move on.

The last few weeks had played over and over in his mind, but he'd yet to come to any sort of conclusion that made sense, that made moving on without her easier. He knew she was lying about not having feelings for him, that she was scared. He understood that. He just wished she'd have enough faith in him—in them—to take a chance.

"To Coach Westmore," Darryl said, standing and holding up his mug of soda.

The kids all held up the glasses and echoed the sentiment.

He raised his own and forced a smile. "No pressure," he said.

*   *   *

"I can't believe everyone brought me fabric," Becky said the following day once the baby shower was over. She sat in the nursery in the new deluxe comfort rocking chair, her gift from Neil, and propped her feet up on the matching ottoman, as Abigail hung an animal-themed mobile above the crib.

"I told you everyone is supporting the new business. Besides, they're all at various stages of pregnancy themselves. Don't think for a second they don't have ulterior motives. Before long, they will all be hitting you up for your latest and coolest Baby Chic," she said, climbing down from the step stool. "There."

"What about you?" Becky asked.

"Dani is too big for baby clothes," she said.

Becky tossed a stuffed elephant at her. "You know what I mean. Do you think you'd eventually want to have more kids?"

She hesitated. "I don't know. If I ever found the right situation…the right man," she said, playing with the tag on the elephant's ear. Jackson had left that morning for try-outs, but he hadn't been far from her thoughts or her tortured heart all day. She wished him luck, and no part of her hoped he didn't make the team. Okay, maybe just a tiny, teensy, weensy selfish part.

Becky eyed her. "He would have stayed."

Damn. Were her feelings for Jackson and his decision that obvious? She cleared her throat. "There was no reason to."

"Of course there was. Try bullshitting someone else. That look you get on your face when he's around is the same look he gets about you." She shook her head. "I just can't believe he's repeating past mistakes all over again."

"It's not like that. Besides the fact that he deserves to go after this shot at the career he's always wanted, there's the fact I'm still his best friend's ex-wife. There's rules about that." She wasn't about to tell her friend they'd already broken those rules—twice—and that they'd both been willing to throw away the rulebook for a shot at a future together before this opportunity had presented itself.

"Forget that! Dean was an asshole. You know that. Jackson knows that. You two deserve happiness—together," Becky said. "Don't tell me you don't have feelings for him."

She sighed. "Fine. I have feelings for him." Lots of feelings, deep feelings, strong feelings. "But it would never work. Dean really left a scar with his betrayal, and as often as I tell myself it's not fair to make someone else pay for the trust Dean destroyed, I just know I can't go through all of that again. Every time he went away with the team, I'd be worried and wondering if he was messing around…" She set the stuffed toy inside the crib. "I can't risk my heart like that again."

"Jackson is not like Dean," Becky said, softly.

Abigail gave a weak smile. "Dean wasn't like Dean in the beginning, either." The game had a way of changing things, and long road trips away from home…Not all men were like Dean, that was true, but after being with one who was, and suffering through the damage he'd caused, she wasn't ready to do it again. "Besides the trust thing, I'm just not willing to be a hockey wife again." Not even Jackson's?

"I think you both just like being miserable," she said through a yawn.

"And I think you should get some sleep. This baby is going to be here any day, and then you won't get the chance again for, what, two years?" she asked, grateful for the opportunity to change the subject.

"You suck. You better help me with this business, Abby." She looked anxious as though maybe realizing for the first time how much work she was committing herself to.

"I will. Stop worrying. You're going to be fine. Better than fine." She helped her friend to her feet and gave her a hug.

"What about you, Abby? Will you be better than fine?"

She forced a fake smile as she said, "One day, I will be better than fine, I promise." She just wasn't sure when that day would come. But she had faith it would.

* * *

Jackson sat on the bench in the Eagles' locker room at seven the next morning. Tryouts started at nine, but he'd been sitting outside the arena in his truck for over an hour, waiting for the doors to be unlocked. He needed time alone to reacquaint himself with his former home rink. The place he'd spent hours and hours practicing and playing and waiting.

Waiting for the big break that never came.

The cold, dark stadium, filled with the echoes of past players competing to be the best, to get to that next level in their dreams, used to fill him with motivation. The familiar mottos on the inspirational posters on the walls; quotes from the greats—Gretzky, Orr, Hull—used to pump him up, remind him what was needed to succeed. Hard work, dedication, mental toughness.

But today, the posters, the silence of the empty locker room, and the chill in the air only reminded him of his previous failed attempt and the foolhardy longshot hope of a better outcome this time.

What was he doing here?

He stared at his tryout jersey hanging on the hook near the locker they'd assigned him. The masking tape across the front of the locker with his name on it only further served to remind him this tryout was no guarantee of a future in the game. The next day, the tape could easily be removed, and another name could take its place.

He ran a hand through his hair, fighting the urge to pack up and go home.

He had to see this through. He thought about the kids on his team who looked up to him and wanted him to succeed; all of his own childhood hopes and dreams had reflected in each of their faces as they'd wished him luck two days before. Even if he didn't make the team, he had to give it his best shot—for them.

Removing his shoes, he slipped his feet into his skates, letting them find comfort in the familiar. He laced them, untied them, then laced them again.

As he stood and pulled his jersey down over his head, the name on the back caught his attention. He was a Westmore. And Westmores showed up to win, or they didn't show up at all.

A dull ache in his chest made it difficult to breathe. He'd shown up for Abby and failed. What made him think this tryout would be any different?

He shook off the self-doubt crippling him. This time he refused to let anyone down.

* * *

He must have made the team.

Dani's high-pitched squeals could be heard all over Abigail's parents' house. All morning, the only thing Dani had talked about was the fact that today was decision day.

"Taylor says the team has two spots open. She said Coach told her there were fifteen guys at tryouts yesterday. She said his odds of getting a spot were like one in a hundred, but he's really good. He'll make it. Don't you think, Mom?"

Oh God, what a loaded question. Instead of answering, she'd threatened to put her daughter to work peeling potatoes for dinner if she stayed in the kitchen any longer.

But now, Dani rushed back in. "He made it. Coach Westmore made the team," she said, out of breath as she jumped the height of herself in the kitchen.

"You would think *she'd* made the team," Abigail's mother said, carrying the bowl of potatoes to the sink.

"That's wonderful," Abigail said, forcing a smile as she glanced up from peeling carrots. She wished she sounded more genuine and less heartbroken. But all day she'd been a mess. No matter how she tried to keep herself busy, her mind had constantly returned to Jackson and the tryouts and how she felt about everything. If he made the team, he would be staying in Loveland, and the chance of them being together and trying to make a long-distance relationship work seemed improbable. The East Coast Hockey League games were usually from Thursday to Sunday and practices were earlier in the week. He'd be lucky to have much time off, and she had a full-time teaching job now; she couldn't just abandon her own life to make the two-hour drive often enough for either of them to be happy for long. Then if he got called up, things got even more complicated.

But if he didn't make the team…then what?

But now it didn't matter—he'd made it.

"Tell Taylor to pass along my congratulations," she said.

"I will," Dani said, immediately texting her friend back.

When she left the kitchen, her mother touched her shoulder. "I'm not going to ask how you really feel about it, because I think the way you are attacking that poor carrot says it all. I'm sorry, darling," she said, grabbing a second peeler and starting to help.

Abigail shook her head. "I really am happy for him." He was getting another well-deserved shot at his dream. Everyone deserved that chance. She was starting over—building a new life—and he should be allowed to follow his heart as well.

"Happy for him, maybe, but sad for you?"

She sighed. Her feelings for Jackson had come out of nowhere. And his confession of love had surprised and confused her. But her mind wasn't foggy anymore, and one thing rang true more than anything else: she'd fallen in love with him.

"Yeah. Maybe a little sad for me."

Her mother's smile was encouraging. "You have to do what makes you happy. If being in a relationship with a hockey player isn't what you want anymore, then being with Jackson will never bring you the happiness you want. Sometimes love just isn't enough, sweet girl."

She swallowed hard. Her mother was right. She didn't want the hockey life anymore. The problem was a life without Jackson didn't appeal to her, either.

CHAPTER 22

~∞~

*J*ackson cradled his cell phone between his ear and his shoulder as he laced his skates two weeks later. "What's going on with the team? Taylor said she hasn't played a game since I left and neither has Dani," he asked Darryl above the noise in the locker room in the arena. Their game against the Alaska Aces was starting in fifteen minutes, but he'd just gotten off the phone with a tearful Taylor, and that wasn't like his niece. He needed to know what was going on back home.

"Oh, man, I hate to tell you this—you've got enough to be focused on…" his friend said.

"Tell me. It's worse if I don't know." Not that he could do anything about the situation. Even though he was only two hours away, he may as well be on a different planet. Coming in late to the season didn't give him an excuse not to pull his weight with the team, and he had more to prove than the other guys. He trained and practiced before everyone else, and later than everyone else. Admittedly, it was taking his almost thirty-year-old body a lot longer to adjust to the grueling early morning workouts, practice, drills, and then game schedule than it had when he was twenty-two. But then, he hadn't expected this to be easy. Being selected for the team among the group of twenty-somethings who had shown up that day—all eager, all motivated, all driven to make it—had shocked the hell out of him.

And now he was working hard to prove they'd made the right decision bringing him back.

If only he could quiet the persistent nagging in the back of his mind that asked whether or not he had made the right one.

Staying busy and draining himself physically and emotionally also helped him keep his mind off Abby. She'd sent her congratulations through Taylor, but that was the last he'd heard from her.

"I couldn't take over the team, the school sport programs are taking up so much of my time, so Kurt Miller stepped up, and he hasn't played the girls at all. He has no intention of playing them. Obviously he's hoping they'll quit."

Jackson clenched his jaw. He'd been worried the league would replace him with Kurt, and they had. "Have you tried talking to him about it?"

"Of course, man. He's not hearing a word I say. Sorry, Jackson, but with you not here, the team isn't doing so well. Even Dex is frustrated and not playing his best anymore."

"That's because Kurt's not playing the girls," he said a little too loudly, earning looks from the other players. He sighed. "I'll see if I can make some calls tomorrow, try to get him replaced." He'd been a coach for the league for a long time. He hoped he could have some influence over the issue.

"That's not going to help Dex," Darryl said.

No, it wouldn't. The poor kid had talent. It was a shame his father was an asshole. "Well, what do I do?"

"Jackson, I know you care about this team and those kids, but you're not the coach anymore. You're moving on to your own goals. Focus on those and forget about all of this back here. Otherwise you'll drive yourself crazy, man. There's nothing you can do; that's why I didn't tell you about all of this myself."

He sighed as he disconnected the call a moment later, knowing his buddy was right but feeling terrible and helpless. He hadn't expected this odd sense of homesickness he was experiencing or the longing he felt to hear a familiar voice or see a familiar face.

One in particular.

"All right, game time," Coach Turner said, coming into the locker room.

As he reached for his jersey and pulled it down over his head, Jackson forced the Atom team out of his mind and chased away images of Abby. None of that would help him win the game. And right now, this game against Alaska was the only thing he had any control over.

*　*　*

His feet had been in his skates for over nine hours. Sweat pooled on his lower back under his jersey, and his legs were moving on autopilot. He hadn't slept more than four hours a night in weeks, and his joints creaked and felt stiff when he tried to get up every morning.

But it was all worth it, he told himself. After all, this shot meant everything to him, didn't it?

"Westmore, Coach Turner wants to see you in his office,"

the assistant coach said, sticking his head into the crowded locker room after the game.

All his teammates stopped talking, stopped moving, probably stopped breathing based on the dead silence that fell over the room. All eyes stared at him.

"Okay, I'll just hit the showers…"

"He needs to see you now."

He swallowed hard, placing his hands on his knees to push his seizing muscles to a standing position. They'd won eight games straight. He'd assisted in nine of the fourteen goals, and he'd done his job protecting the goalie. If the coach was finally realizing he had recruited an almost thirty-year-old player, at least Jackson had had a good run. "Okay," he said, trying to hide what a struggle it was just to walk to the other side of the arena to Coach Turner's office.

He knocked once and the coach nodded him in. His cell was cradled against his shoulder and ear while he typed furiously. "Yes. Sending it all to you now. Tomorrow… Phoenix…Okay." He disconnected the call. "You're being sent up."

He what? He stood there staring at that man, wondering if he'd heard him right.

"Don't thank me or anything," Coach Turner said in the silence.

Shit. He hadn't actually said anything. "Sorry, um, thank you…I mean, I…Can I sit?" His legs had decided not to support him anymore.

Coach Turner, a thin man who'd always looked old, even when he was young, nodded his balding head. "For like thirty seconds, then you need to get to the airport."

Airport? That night? So much for the next two days off. He'd been planning on going home. After that call from Taylor and the talk with Darryl, he wanted to check in on the team, talk to the head of the minor leagues.

"Westmore, you hearing any of this?"

He blinked. "Yes, sir."

"You're going to play in Phoenix under Coach Foster. They just had their best defensive player taken out with a stick to the shin—broken in three places. They asked if I had an experienced player they could use as a third line if needed tomorrow night. You're it."

He still couldn't quite wrap his mind around what the coach was saying. Maybe because he still believed getting this far had been a fluke or some weird obligation the organization felt to the Westmore name. "Okay…Yes…Thank you," he said.

"Westmore, snap out of it! You're going to play an NHL game."

Was he? Or would he sit on the sidelines again—so close to the action, and not getting a chance to prove himself. He'd been in this position before and it had broken him. Could he really survive the disappointment again if things didn't work out? Especially while his heart was still aching for another dream that had been within reach. "I'm just…"

"Surprised? Confused? Exhausted? Hoping they don't bench you again?"

"Yes."

"Well, add rested and focused to that before tomorrow night. This is your shot, man. You're not a kid anymore—make the best of it. Now go before I change my mind. Truth is, I don't want to lose you from my team," he grumbled, indeed looking as though he might change his mind about sending him any second.

He nodded as he stood, no longer even feeling his body. "Yes sir, Coach. Thank you. I won't let you down," he said.

"Westmore."

He paused and turned back.

"Don't let *yourself* down."

*   *   *

When the text message from Becky arrived, Abigail was surrounded by Christmas presents, wrapping paper, bows, and ribbons, in the middle of her bedroom floor, trying to get an early start to her holiday preparations. Christmas was three weeks away, and she wanted this year to be extra special. But after reading Baby on the way! she'd stuffed everything back into the walk-in closet and had woken Dani, and the two were on their way to the hospital within minutes.

"How is she?" she asked Neil when they saw him pacing the hallway.

"Trying to suffer through without the epidural."

Good God, why? She'd gladly accepted the needle to the spine when the contractions on Dani had been at their worst. "She's a superstar," she said, glancing at Taylor, who'd come out of the room, looking slightly green.

"You okay?" she asked the little girl whose eyes were wide.

"I'm not going back in there," she said.

Abigail laughed. "I'll take a shift with her if you guys need a break."

Neil held up the back of his right hand to show four nail-shaped flesh wounds. "Don't let her hold your hand."

"Thanks for the warning," she said with a smile. "Dani, do you want to go in and say hi?"

Taylor was shaking her head. "Don't do it, Dani."

Dani laughed. "I'll stay out here."

"Okay." She walked down the quiet, nearly empty hospital corridor and went into the room. "Hi."

"Oh thank God you're here," Becky said as she sat on a stability ball, rolling it around in front of the bed. She clutched the sheets in front of her as another contraction started, and she panted through it. "Remind me again why I'm doing this."

Abigail just smiled, and two hours later, Becky held the reminder—a beautiful baby girl—in her arms wrapped in a pink blanket, the wool hat too big for her tiny head, as Abigail reentered the room after waiting out the final moments in the waiting area with the girls while Neil helped his wife through the delivery.

Also on Becky's lap was her laptop, and Abigail stopped short of approaching when she heard Jackson's voice coming from the screen. "She's perfect, sis."

Her heart raced at the sound she hadn't realized she'd missed so much until that moment.

"It's Jackson Skyping in from Phoenix," Becky explained, glancing up at her. "He got called up and couldn't be here."

Called up? Already? Wow. "That's incredible," she said, hoping she sounded sincere. Praying her further breaking heart wasn't evident in her voice. "Tell him congratulations." She forced her attention to the baby girl in her friend's arms and not the screen on her lap. Jackson was in Phoenix, playing for the NHL…His dream was coming true. So why did it feel as though hers were falling apart? She had to pull it together and start moving on.

He was.

"Tell him congratulations yourself," Becky said with an evil grin as she turned the computer monitor toward her.

Panic rose in her chest as she glanced at the old sweatshirt she wore and quickly smoothed her hair behind her ears. No makeup on, and she was about to see the man she was in love with for the first time in a month. Perfect. Thanks, Becky.

"Hi," he said, smiling nervously as she accepted the laptop from Becky. Of course he looked amazing, if tired, in a white T-shirt, the hotel room in the background reminding her of all of the important times in her past when she'd had to Skype with Dean, while he was in a faraway hotel room, instead of there with them.

She swallowed hard. "Hi. Congratulations—Arizona—that's wonderful."

"Thanks, we won last night."

"Well, congratulations again…" She felt like a moron. There was so much she longed to say to him, so much she longed to hear him say, but here they were at a standstill. He had his life to live, she had hers, and she wasn't sure they could meet in some cyberspace middle.

"They're keeping me up for one more game for sure. It's tomorrow night against Colorado."

Her heart stopped. He would be in Denver the following evening, playing in the NHL?

"If I reserve you tickets, would you and Dani be there with Taylor?" he asked, sounding unsure. "I mean, Becky won't be able to go and I…I'd really love it if you could be there."

Oh no. How was she supposed to go to his game? Watch the man she loved doing what he loved, knowing his decision to do it meant no chance at a future together. "I don't…"

"I miss you, Abby," he said, staring straight at her through the monitor.

In the bed, pretending not to listen while she cuddled her baby girl, Becky shot her a look.

She wanted to tell him she missed him, too. That she loved him. That maybe she was ready to figure out a way to make things work. The desperate feeling of wanting to say all of that, of wanting to hold him, kiss him, be with him was so strong…The realization that once again she could be in a situation where she felt like this while he was always out of reach, faraway in some hotel room, made her hold back the words. "Dani would never forgive me if I didn't take her to your game. So, yes, we will be there."

He looked disappointed, as though he'd been expecting more, hoping for more, but he smiled as he nodded. "Great. I look forward to seeing you…both."

"Okay, I'll pass you back to Becky now," she said, handing her friend the laptop, and in exchange accepting the little pink bundle. Settling into the chair next to the bed, she cuddled the little girl into her chest and smiled down at the sleeping precious child as tears gathered in her eyes.

Thank God for little babies. They could easily be blamed for tears.

* * *

Turning off Dani's bedroom light a few hours later, Abigail stared at her own little girl, wondering where the time had gone. It seemed like not so long ago that Dani had been a baby girl in her arms…She sniffed as she turned to go.

"You okay, Mom?" Dani asked, sitting up, wiping her tired eyes.

It had been a long, exciting night. "Yes, I'm great, sweetheart."

"Thanks for agreeing to take Taylor and me to the game tomorrow night. I know it's probably hard for you to go," she said quietly.

Abigail went back into the room and sat on the edge of her bed. "I'm happy for Jackson. This is a wonderful opportunity."

Her daughter nodded. "You know, Mom, if you wanted to move to Phoenix, that would be okay with me. I mean, I'd miss Taylor and Grandma and Grandpa, but if you love Coach Westmore, then it's okay."

Abigail hugged her daughter tightly. "I love *you*," she said, kissing her forehead. "Now, try to get some sleep. Big day tomorrow." She tucked her daughter back in, noticing the wooden jewelry box Jackson had made for her on Dani's bedside table. "Where did you find that?" She'd assumed her mother had put it away, knowing it held the wedding rings.

"It was in one of my boxes. I found it while I was unpacking, and Grandma said maybe I should just keep it in my room," Dani said.

Abigail picked it up and opened it. The rings caught the light of the moon coming through the open curtains, and she took them out of the box. "The rings are yours—they'll probably pay for college," she said with a soft smile, "but I think I'll keep the jewelry box, if that's okay."

Her daughter nodded sleepily. "He must have loved you to make you something so pretty," she mumbled, rolling over and closing her eyes.

Abigail held the jewelry box to her chest. Her daughter didn't know just how right she was.

CHAPTER 23

❦

"$\mathcal{H}$ow do you feel about playing against your brother this evening?" the reporter asked Jackson outside the locker room at the Denver stadium. The camera lights and the microphones shoved so close to his face were making him claustrophobic. He didn't understand how the other players were so calm and cool during these pregame interviews.

He was far from calm and cool. He was freaking out a little. Actually he was freaking out a lot. He took a deep breath and hesitated, weighing his answer. It should have been an easy one—repeat the same sentiments he'd heard Ben and Asher repeat over and over again. He was going to kick his brother's ass. He knew Ben's weak areas. It would be the same here tonight as it had been on the pond in Glenwood Falls when they were kids…All of these responses lined up to be used, but he was far too anxious to say any of it. Instead, he cleared his throat, and said, "I'm not sure. I guess I'll know when I get out there."

The reporter looked a little confused by the answer, but she glanced at her cameraman quickly and moved on. "You played for the Eagles years ago, and this opportunity presented itself back then—but you were benched and didn't actually play on NHL ice—is that why you took a break for a while?"

Jeez. They really knew how to put people on edge. "I… uh, I guess so. I don't know." Could they just play hockey now? The longer he waited for the game to begin, the longer he sat in the hotel room waiting to go, the longer he sat under these bright lights and glaring questions, the more uneasy he felt.

The game in Phoenix had been different; no one had known he'd been called up, no one knew who he was, and no one had expected him to play as well as he had, not even himself.

This game was different. The pressure was on. The pressure from the media, the pressure from the team, the pressure on himself…His chest hurt.

"Okay, one more question: Do you think we will see that amazing assist effort from you tonight like the other night in Phoenix?"

Finally, an easy one. "You bet." He may feel ill, he may be uncomfortable, he may be struggling with the fact that his second NHL game was on an opposing team in his hometown, against his star player brother, whom he'd yet to talk to about all of this, but none of that mattered—he would play his best game out there that evening.

As he climbed down from the hot seat and headed toward the locker rooms, he couldn't shake the nagging feeling that he should at least talk to Ben. Ben was the NHL player, this was his career, he was leading in points in the league that season, and Jackson couldn't help but struggle with the idea that playing his best could result in a defeat for Ben, a slide in the rankings…

Damn it. Asher didn't give a shit about those things. He played to win against everyone—*especially* Ben.

But this was Asher's life, too.

He still felt like an outsider, a fake, someone they just hadn't figured out didn't belong there yet.

He let out a deep breath as he entered the busy locker room. He had to get out of his head and get his focus back. The team in that room counted on him to bring his A game as he had two nights before.

"Hey, Westmore! Don't go easy on your brother out there," Olaf Herman, a first line left wing said, as though reading his mind. "Because believe me, he won't go easy on you."

* * *

"Okay, you two need to stop bouncing," Abigail said a little more harshly than she intended.

It didn't matter. Dani and Taylor ignored her anyway, continuing to chat excitedly as they waited for the stadium lights to dim and the national anthem to be sung.

In her own seat, Abigail was numb. Her body and mind couldn't decide how to feel, how to act, or what to say, so she'd gone through the motions that day in a fog. Her palms sweat but her mouth felt dry, and the soda she sipped as though it held all the answers wasn't helping.

The main lights went down and spotlights lit the arena. Everyone else in the stadium besides the three of them and Jackson's mom—sitting in the owner's box as an honorary guest—had no reason to care about the Coyotes skating out onto the ice.

But when Jackson appeared, a round of deafening applause rattled the stands.

She could see his expression from where she sat, and the look etched across his face caused an instant lump to surface in her throat. He looked so surprised and honored by the fans' reaction. Here he was, living his dream.

And as much as she hated to admit it, he looked damn good out there, like he belonged on the ice, like this was what he'd been made to do. In full hockey gear, the number thirteen on his back under his last name, he glided effortlessly across the surface as though he'd skated on it a million times. If he was nervous, no one could tell.

She was nervous. Incredibly freaking nervous.

"I am so proud of him!" Taylor said, her smile wide, and Abigail nearly choked on the emotions welling up in her own chest.

When the home team skated out, the fans continued their cheering and all around her the stadium was alive.

As the anthem ended and the lights came up, the Arizona Coyotes skated past on their way to their players' box and Jackson's gaze met hers.

He winked at her as he passed, and it was in that moment she knew.

Hockey player or not, she loved him. And hockey player or not, she wanted to be with him.

Now she just had to wait until this game was over so she could tell him. She suspected she was in for the longest three periods of hockey of her life.

* * *

The first two periods of the game were uneventful, with both teams trading scores until the home team took the lead at the beginning of the third period.

Jackson watched the majority of the first forty minutes from the bench, playing only one two-minute round toward the end of the second, resulting in an assist for the second goal of the game. The stadium's reaction to it had made a tornado of emotions well up inside of him. The cheering support from the fans had been exhilarating, and the look on Abby's face had made him feel prouder of himself than he'd ever felt. He'd made it. He was good enough—for hockey and for her.

Ben, of course, was on fire that evening, and getting to watch his brother play from a players' box was reward in itself, but he was itching to get out there again. His mom watched from the owner's box, and there were three other women in the stands he wouldn't mind skating past again.

"Westmore, you're in next. Let's see what you can do against your brother," Coach Foster said, tapping him on the helmet.

He shouldn't be surprised they decided to play him on Ben's line. After all, Ash had the best chance out of any defensive player to go head to head with him. Guess now it was time to find out if he could take on his brother as well.

The line changed, and holding his stick firmly to calm the slight shaking of his hands, he skated onto the ice. As before, the crowd cheered briefly to acknowledge one of their own, but he barely heard it as he approached the left side of the goalie, skating after a loose puck. He shot it right toward the other defenseman and the young man skated behind the net with it before passing to their right wing at the red center line.

Carson caught it expertly and skated toward Colorado's

net, where he took a fast, short, powerful swing at it, shooting the puck at lightning speed just to the right of the goal post.

The Avalanche's defenseman collected the puck and passed it to Ben.

Jackson's eyes were on the play and briefly met his older brother's as Ben took control of it.

Here we go.

Hanging back near his goalie, he could feel the electricity in the stadium as fans started to cheer their family name. For which brother—maybe both—it was uncertain. It didn't matter.

For the first time in his life, Jackson was going head to head against his brother on NHL ice. It didn't get much more real than this.

His legs felt like they were on fire as adrenaline soared through him, and all of a sudden he was a young kid again, experiencing the thrill of the game.

Ben skated toward their net, dodging the offense, past the blue line…

His famous move was the last-minute high shot to the left corner of the net.

Jackson positioned himself to block the shot, careful not to obscure his goalie's view. They all knew Ben's signature move, but this time, his brother surprised him by passing the puck.

He must have surprised his teammate as well, as the guy missed the pass, and the other Arizona defenseman took control of it, immediately sailing it across the ice to Jackson.

The puck hit his stick and he hesitated.

His brother was headed straight toward him.

The body check was one he'd taken from Ben a million

times. He knew where he would hit, the impact of the hit, and how to defend against it.

But he didn't.

Instead, a second later, his left shoulder hit the boards and his world was rocked momentarily as his brother stole the puck.

Ben grinned as he skated away toward the net. "Welcome to the NHL, little brother."

* * *

The sound of the home fans cheering and celebrating their team's third win in a row was in stark contrast to the solemn, exhausted haze lingering over the players in the Arizona locker room.

"We played well tonight. They played better," Coach Foster was saying, giving what Jackson assumed was his customary "we lost, it's over, let's regroup and refocus before the next game" speech.

Jackson was barely listening.

While the coach went over the game play by play, period by period, in his mind, so did he.

He'd felt good out there, just as he had two nights before in Phoenix. Once he'd settled onto the ice in the third line, he'd fallen into a rhythm. He hadn't let the home crowd cheering for the opposite team get to him. He hadn't wavered in his defense, even when the opposition skated toward him with the puck, closing in on his goalie. He hadn't let his conflicted heart mess up his confidence or skills.

He'd played his best game.

Until he faced off with Ben. He almost hadn't recognized the look in his brother's eyes as Ben skated toward the goalie, toward him. He knew he was about to be taken out. He also knew he could defend it. A part of him also knew he could have kept that puck.

But in that brief moment, he'd seen all the years of dedication Ben had put into being the best—the sleep he didn't get, getting up early for practice, the parties he hadn't attended, instead putting the time in at the arena. And then everything Ben was missing flashed in his mind—the time in Glenwood Falls with the family, the time to focus on a relationship with one woman, not a string of one-night stands, the life events he missed out on or saw only in Facebook pictures, the last few months of their father's life.

And in that brief second which had felt like it spanned a lifetime, he realized why he'd never made it to the NHL before: he hadn't wanted it bad enough. Not the way Ben and Asher did.

And even now, after having a taste of the life that realistically could be his if he continued to work his ass off, he still wasn't sure he wanted it as bad as his brothers did.

In fact, as an image of Abby's smile appeared in his mind, he knew he didn't.

There were just some things in life he wanted more.

* * *

"Mom, quit bouncing!" Dani said teasingly as the three of them waited in the players' lounge with the other families, while the players spoke to reporters, showered, and debriefed after the game.

She'd waited countless times for Dean in a similar lounge. Never had she felt so nervous. Never had she been so anxious. And never had it taken so freaking long. She paced in front of the bar, where Dani and Taylor sat sipping virgin margaritas, laughing and recapping the game with Jackson's mother, Beverly.

Come on…And they say women take forever getting ready.

The door to the lounge opened and she turned, holding her breath, as several players entered.

She looked past them.

No Jackson.

"Seriously, dear, you're going to wear down the floor. Why don't you have a seat," Beverly said, pulling out the bar stool next to her. "Trust me, he'll be here," she said with a wink.

Oh God. Everyone else had been so right about them. Why had it taken so many years for her to open her eyes to what had always been right in front of her?

She sighed as she sat, but then jumped back up again when the door opened and Jackson, wearing the required suit and tie, walked in. His messy gelled hair and his still flushed cheeks nearly buckled her knees.

Despite just watching him play, it felt like forever since she'd been near him. Since she'd been close enough to touch him, to smell the soft cologne she'd been missing so much. His gaze met hers and she stopped breathing.

He was hot. Plain and simple. And if they were alone at that moment, talking would have had to wait. Unfortunately, with so many people around, talking about anything important still might have to wait, and she prayed there was an opportunity to say everything she needed to.

Oh, but God, what she wanted most of all was to jump into his arms.

His niece beat her to it. "Uncle Jackson!" Taylor said as she and Dani rushed forward.

"Hey guys! Sorry, I didn't win," he said, with a grin,

accepting their hugs, looking above their heads to smile at her.

She held up a hand in a small wave and struggled to get enough air into her lungs as he approached.

"Hi, Mom," he said next, leaning forward to hug the woman.

She kissed his cheek. "I'm so proud of you," she whispered.

Abigail wanted to look away, to give mother and son the privacy of the moment, but she couldn't tear her eyes from him, just as she hadn't the entire game.

She was almost about to tug on his sleeve like an impatient toddler, when he finally turned to face her. "Hi."

She swallowed hard and cleared her throat, but still no sound came out when she tried to say the word. Her cheeks flushed and she yelled at herself to get it together. There was too much to say, and too little time to say it. She couldn't waste a second of it tongue-tied like a love-struck teenager. God, had he felt this way around her all those years?

Luckily, he spoke again first. "Can we go someplace a little less…nosy?" he whispered, leaning toward her.

The smell of his cologne was intoxicating, and she had to clench her fists at her sides to stop herself from reaching out to touch his face. She nodded. "Do you think they'll let you leave?" she asked, nodding toward his mom and the girls.

The door opened and Ben entered, his movie star smile in place.

"They won't even notice now," Jackson said with an easy laugh, taking her hand.

Her heart raced as his fingers interlocked with hers and she squeezed his tightly as he led her out to the lounge deck area, overlooking the ice below. The lights were off in the stadium, and the deck was empty. The perfect place, the perfect opportunity to tell him how she felt.

"Abby, I…"

"Wait. Please, can I go first?" she asked, afraid she might once again lose her nerve if she waited any longer.

He nodded, taking a step closer. Releasing her hand, he wrapped his arms around her waist, drawing her into him. "As long as I can hold you while you talk, because I can't wait any longer to have you in my arms."

She moved even closer, finding courage and strength in his words. "Jackson, I know what I said about not wanting this life anymore. I know I said I just wanted a normal, everyday, quiet life in Glenwood Falls. That I could never…love another hockey player." She paused. "But…"

He lifted her chin, staring into her eyes. His expression begged her to continue.

"But, the thing is, I love you. It doesn't matter if you're a coach, a player, a Zamboni driver. I love you. And if a hockey career is what you want, then I'm in. Whatever it takes, wherever that leads, I'm in." She stared up at him, praying he still wanted her in his life. Hoping he hadn't changed his mind or his heart since being away.

"Abby, you don't want that life anymore."

"I want you."

"Shhhh," he said, placing his finger against her lips.

"The thing is, neither do I."

Her mouth gaped. "What? What are you talking about? You've made it. You're playing in the NHL the way you always wanted."

He shook his head. "The way I always *thought* I wanted. I love hockey, and these last few weeks just reinforced how much I love this sport…"

"Right. So don't throw it away. Don't give up this second

chance at your dream because you don't think I'm ready to commit to it as much as you are. I saw your face tonight when the fans cheered for you. This is where you belong." She touched the stubble along his jaw.

"I'm not giving anything up. I've just realized that the dream I really want a second chance at is a life with you." He silenced her again before she could argue. "A *real* life with you. A home with you and Dani. Not being away for months at a time, never being able to settle in one place permanently, missing out on life events and only getting to experience them through a computer." He shook his head. "That's not the life I want."

She wanted desperately to believe every word because it was everything she wanted to hear, but she wasn't convinced. "Jackson, I mean it when I say I'm a hundred percent supportive of this. Please don't walk away from this for me, because you can have both."

He smiled as he lowered his lips to hers, placing a soft, gentle kiss there before pulling her into him even tighter and kissing her again, harder, with a sense of wanting, yearning, passion that matched her own. "I don't need both. I don't want both. All I want, all I need is you, Abigail Jansen."

She swallowed hard, happiness overwhelming her as she squeezed him, never wanting to let go. Still…"So, you really don't want to play hockey anymore?"

"I do want to play hockey, with Dani and Taylor on the frozen lake behind the house and with the boys on Tuesday nights. What I don't want is to play in the NHL or the AHL, or any other team that prevents this…" He paused to kiss her again. "From happening every day…" He kissed her nose. "All day…" He kissed her forehead. "For the rest of my life."

"Are you sure?" she whispered.

"I've always been sure. It just took a little while to get enough courage to tell you," he said. "Come on." He took her hand and brought it to his lips. "Let's go home. I want to make two dreams come true in the same night." His expression was full of desire as he pulled her in closer.

"I think I can help you with that," she said, standing on her tiptoes to kiss the man she loved.

He held back just a little. "Say it again."

She smiled. "I love you."

"It's about freaking time," he said, as his mouth found hers.

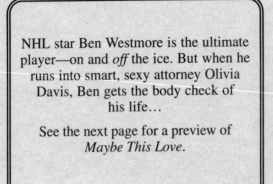

NHL star Ben Westmore is the ultimate player—on and *off* the ice. But when he runs into smart, sexy attorney Olivia Davis, Ben gets the body check of his life…

See the next page for a preview of *Maybe This Love*.

$\mathscr{I}$ guess there could be worse ways of finding out you're married."

His beer bottle paused on its way to his lips, Ben Westmore shot a glance across the booth. "Do you not hear something wrong with that sentence?"

His brother Asher drained the contents of his own drink and set the empty glass on the table inside Airways, a restaurant in the Denver airport. "Look, man I think you're sweating this whole thing for nothing. There's no way that marriage certificate you saw was real." He flagged a waitress as he put his baseball cap on over his hockey hair.

"You think it's a joke?" He studied the blurry image on his iPhone. That spirally signature at the bottom looked a lot like his...

"Of course it's a joke. This is *you* we are talking about." Asher reached for his jacket. "And I've got a plane to catch."

The waitress smiled at him as she set their bill on the table. She'd been smiling at him since they'd walked in. Nothing new there. Captain of the Colorado Avalanche and MVP in the league that season, he was one of the more recognizable hockey players, and his reputation as a playboy was one he wore as a badge of honor. Getting a pretty woman's attention was easier than winning a game of pick-up hockey against eight-year-olds.

He glanced back at the phone. Had he inadvertently, unknowingly married one of them?

Not a chance. He hit DELETE and tucked the phone away.

"How was everything?" the waitress asked, still not tearing her eyes from him.

The required uniform was basic black pants and white blouse, but *her* black pants were leather and hugged her curves as though they were painted on, and her blouse was open at the top far enough to give them ample view of the lace bra she wore underneath. The messy bun her blonde hair was gathered in looked ready to come undone at any moment, and in another place and circumstance, he'd be more than willing to be the force that shook it loose.

But unlike the night before on the ice, today Ben was off his game a little.

"Everything was perfect. Unfortunately, we have to go," he said.

She looked slightly disappointed as she asked, "Will you be paying together or separate?"

"Together," Asher said. "The least you can do is buy the drinks after taking me out of the NHL playoffs," he grumbled.

The waitress finally turned to look at Asher. "You're *both* players?"

Ben tossed a hundred-dollar bill on the table to cover the fifty-dollar tab and stood. "Yes, this is hockey's greatest secret, right here," he said, draping an arm around his brother's shoulders. It was true. The Avalanche may have beaten the Devils the night before, taking them out of the playoffs early in the second round, but it hadn't been from lack of ability, skill, or effort on his brother's part. Out of the three hockey-loving, hockey-playing Westmore brothers, Asher was arguably the best. Not that Ben would ever tell him that.

"But didn't he just say your team beat his?" She shot him a teasing smile, and the temptation to continue the conversation well into the night—at her place—was strong, but he was still in Colorado, and he didn't mess with women in his own state. Too close for comfort.

"Bad goalie on his team," Ben said, grabbing his leather jacket. "Thank you, you've been lovely."

"Wait…your receipt," the waitress said.

No doubt with her phone number on it. *Keep walking,*

Westmore. He pretended not to hear as he led the way out of the lounge and grabbed his baby brother for a quick hug. "Sure you can't stick around for a few days?"

Now that the New Jersey Devils were officially out of the playoffs for that season, his brother was free, unless he got an invitation to play in the World Championships scheduled to start the following week. Which Ben suspected he would.

"I'll be back in a few days. I just need to wrap up a few things in Jersey," he said, slinging his hockey bag over his shoulder.

"Like getting rid of that playoff beard?" His brother looked more like a bushman than a hockey player the longer his team had advanced.

Asher ran a hand over it. "You're just jealous because I can actually grow one."

Ben laughed. It was true. A thin covering of stubble was all he could hope for, despite not having shaved since the start of the playoffs four weeks ago. "Anyway, clean yourself up before Mom sees you."

His brother shot him a look. "Pretty sure once she finds out the mess you may be in, I'll be able to do no wrong. Later, man," he said with a wave as he headed toward security. "Make sure to bring home the cup."

That was the plan. After successfully taking his own brother out of the running for the Stanley Cup—no one else stood a chance of getting in the way.

His team that year consisted of a lot of young players, and while they played hard and fast, they looked up to him as a veteran in the sport to lead them to a victory. He was up for the challenge. At thirty-two years old, he'd been in the NHL playoffs three times before in his career. This was his year to win. The Colorado Avalanche's year to win.

His cell phone rang as he headed out of the airport. Kevin

Sanders, the team's lawyer, reminding him of the "mess" Asher had mentioned. No doubt the guy was calling to see why he hadn't responded to the lame attempt at what he hoped was a joke he'd emailed him earlier that week.

"April Fool's Day was two weeks ago, man. That email wasn't funny," Ben said, answering the call. The lawyer, a well-known prankster who liked to mess with the players, had sent the email attachment of the copy of a marriage certificate from Happy Ever After, a wedding chapel in Las Vegas, dated December 31 of last year. The spirally signature—a fairly accurate forgery of his own—at the bottom had caused him a brief moment of panic, until he realized he was being punked.

Still, he'd been worried enough to show it to his brother that evening. But Asher was right—it couldn't be real.

"I wish I *were* kidding," Kevin said, sounding annoyed. "But unfortunately this is no joke."

Ben scoffed, though his heart was a jackhammer in his chest. He couldn't exactly claim to remember New Year's Eve in Las Vegas with several of his teammates well enough to say a hundred percent that this marriage certificate was just a really good fake. But…"Quit messing around, man. There is no way that thing is real. I would have had to have been unconscious or drugged to get married." Full stop.

"Well, you look conscious in the video from the chapel."

"What video?" The cool, early-spring mountain air made him shiver as he stepped through the revolving doors and he raised the collar of his leather jacket higher around his neck.

"The one I just received from the owners of Happy Ever After."

His gut tightened. There was footage of him in a wedding chapel in Vegas?

"And unfortunately, if you were drugged, the evidence

would be out of your system by now, so we will be submitting a drunk and stupid case," Kevin said.

"What case?" If the guy was messing with him, he could stop anytime. This shit was not funny.

"Your divorce case."

Crossing the airport parking lot, he climbed in behind the wheel of his Hummer, slamming the door. "I have no idea what you're talking about. I'm not married." The guy obviously couldn't admit to a prank fail.

"According to a Ms. Kristina Sullivan and the Happy Ever After Chapel in Las Vegas, you are. Now, shut up and listen."

He sat confused and annoyed as Kevin took him through step by step, making sure he was aware of the predicament they found themselves in. For four months, this Ms. Kristina Sullivan had remained quiet, and now after the ninety-day annulment period, she'd resurfaced to ruin his life, claiming she wanted a relationship with her "husband." Kevin had immediately brought it in front of a judge, but the woman had lawyered up, turning what could have been a minor inconvenience to a full-fledged shit-storm.

"This is bullshit. I don't even know this woman."

"Since when has that ever mattered to you?" Kevin asked.

Ben ran a hand through his hair. It was true that he liked the company of women. His reputation was one he couldn't dispute, but *married*? Hell no. Right? Damn, he wished he could remember that night clearly enough…or *at all*…to be sure.

"Ben—this is not going to just go away quietly or quickly," Kevin said when he was silent.

He sighed. "Fine. What do we do now?"

"We'll file the required papers to start the divorce process and just pray that this Kristina Sullivan chick doesn't contest them. In the meantime, her lawyer is requesting a face-to-face."

Fantastic. He wouldn't have been able to pick out his new "wife"—he cringed at the thought of the word—from a police lineup if his life depended on it, and now he would have to sit across from her and ask that she be reasonable enough to let him out of this shit-show without too much headache? He had his doubts this meeting would go smoothly. "When's the meeting?" he asked, stabbing the button to start the vehicle. He didn't have time for this. In four days, he planned to lead his team to a four-game, shut-out victory in the third round of the playoffs. He couldn't afford stupid distractions like this.

This Ms. Sullivan better prepare herself for a battle, because he was pissed. He didn't know what kind of game she was playing, but he wanted nothing to do with it.

"Tomorrow morning at eleven," Kevin said. "I'll email you the address to the law office."

"We're meeting at *her* lawyer's office? Isn't that already setting a precedent, giving them the upper hand?" Home ice was where his team felt at ease, comfortable, more confident. The opposition always held an advantage when they met on their ice.

"This isn't hockey. It's a boardroom. Trust me, I can do my job anywhere."

"I hope so." Because if not, it was game over before it even began.

"Hang in there. Keep breathing, and we will figure this out," his lawyer said through the speaker phone on the dash.

Where was that note of optimism two minutes ago when the man was explaining in fine detail just how bad of a shit-storm Ben's life was about to become? "Can we figure it out quickly? Like before the next playoff round?"

"I can't work miracles, Ben. Talk to you tomorrow."

Disconnecting the call, he swore under his breath. So much for it being a joke. This was the last complication he needed right now. But one thing was for certain, there was no way he would let a little thing like marrying a woman he didn't know in a ceremony he couldn't remember prevent him from hoisting the Stanley Cup that season.

No way in hell.

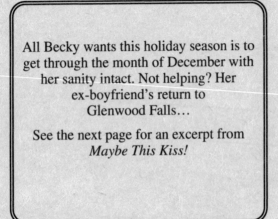

All Becky wants this holiday season is to get through the month of December with her sanity intact. Not helping? Her ex-boyfriend's return to Glenwood Falls…

See the next page for an excerpt from *Maybe This Kiss!*

$\mathcal{N}$eed some help?"

The unexpected sound of a deep male voice made Becky jump and lose her balance once again on the wet floor. Two hands gripped her shoulders to steady her, and she immediately wished he had let her fall. Feeling her cheeks on fire, she turned to face Neil.

His profile picture did not fully capture the hotness standing in front of her. Time had been far too good to him. The young, boyish face had been replaced by a rugged handsomeness that would turn more than one head in the small town, and she immediately felt a pang of irrational jealousy. His solid, square jaw with just the right amount of stubble had always been her weakness, and his dark brown eyes held a look of uncertainty mixed with a friendly familiarity as though no time at all had passed since she'd last gazed into them.

Becky folded her arms across her body, putting up a physical barrier to match the internal one that had immediately sprung up around her heart at the unexpected feelings spurred by the sight of her ex. "What are you doing here? How'd you get in?" Small town or not, she never left her door unlocked. After having a police officer for a husband, she'd known not to adopt a false sense of security.

"Your daughter let me in." He surveyed the mess of the laundry room. "Washing machine problems?" he asked, removing his jacket to reveal a tight, black T-shirt haphazardly tucked into one side of a hip-hugging pair of jeans.

"Oh no…it's no…" She clamped her lips together. She couldn't even remember the question. What was it about his big, muscular arms that turned her brain to complete mush?

Maybe the fact that she still remembered what it felt like to be wrapped up in them?

"Let me look," Neil said, moving her away by her shoulders and stepping carefully into the water on the floor. It sloshed under his boots and soaked the frayed hem of his faded jeans.

Riding boots. He'd always talked about owning a motorcycle. An adrenaline junkie from an early age, he'd owned his first dirt bike at fourteen and the sight of him on it had done crazy things to her teenage hormones. She remembered sneaking out after curfew to ride on the back of it, holding on tight to him as they sped along the empty dirt roads at night, stopping to make out near the riverbank…"That's not necessary. I got it under control."

He ignored her. Opening the lid, he looked inside, then reached into the water, up to his biceps. Sexy, toned, still-tanned-from-the-Miami-sun biceps.

"Really, I'm sure you have places to be. I'll call someone if it's something I can't fix on my own." Since ending his pursuit of a hockey career, Jackson flipped houses for a living and was quite the handyman. He was her go-to for these kind of things.

"It's okay. I'm here anyway," Neil said, not sounding all too pleased about it.

Well neither was she. She certainly hadn't been expecting a visit from the hottest man to ever leave her weak in the knees. And she definitely would not have invited him in and allowed him to see her messy laundry room. But here he was. Standing in a puddle of water, his arm disappearing in her washing machine, looking like a sexy gift from handyman heaven.

And she was wearing Star Wars pajama pants and a holiday-themed sweatshirt featuring Grumpy Cat that said DASHING THROUGH THE SNOW…GET THE F*CK OUT OF MY WAY.

Not exactly the way one fantasizes about running into an ex.

She was going to have to have the "don't open the door to strangers" talk with Taylor again.

"I think I found the problem," he said, pulling a thin piece of black, lacy fabric from the machine. "These were wrapped around the agitator." He opened the thong, stretching the thin waistband between his hands. "Nice."

Her mortification obviously knew no bounds. She yanked them out of his hands and tucked the wet fabric under her arm. She'd worn them under duress earlier that week when she'd had nothing else clean. They were horrible. The lace, the string between her ass cheeks...She shuddered at the memory of how they'd ridden up past her jeans when she'd bent over at the grocery store to pick up an apple that had rolled off the fruit display table, and she'd caught the fifteen-year-old stock boy, Al, staring.

She should have burned them instead of washing them because she would never wear them again. "Thank you for discovering the problem," she said through clenched teeth. "Even though I said I had it under control."

He ignored her comment. "Why don't you plug it back in and see if that fixes things?"

Well, another thong wouldn't be caught in there, if that's what he was hoping. A memory of the lingerie she used to wear for him flashed in her mind—matching bra and panty sets, one-piece teddies...The look in his eyes seeing her in those things had made her feel like the sexiest woman in the world. And the way he'd slowly remove the garments from her body had sparked a passion, an intensity, an undeniable need...

Her eyes met his now and she could see her own thoughts reflected in his expression. He glanced away quickly, but it was too late—she knew that look well. She wasn't the only one struggling with the past.

She plugged in the machine and it hummed as it resumed its cycle as though nothing had happened. As if the ground beneath her feet hadn't just trembled.

"Great," Neil said. "Just FYI—You're supposed to put those things in a garment washing bag."

"Suddenly a connoisseur of women's delicates?" Damn, that sounded jealous even to her ears.

"Twelve years is enough time for anyone to change."

Was it? Then why did things feel so much the same when she looked at him? Too much time had passed, too much life had happened for both of them—she couldn't claim to know the man he was now. Yet, her heart insisted it did.

Before she could say anything, his hands were on her face. Her eyes widened at the feel of the rough palms against her skin. She opened her mouth to speak, but his lips pressed against hers before she could process what was happening.

What was he doing? What was *she* doing? That was the better question as her arms circled his neck. And how did the sensation of his mouth on hers feel so damn familiar after all these years?

Shockingly, the anticipated urge to pull away didn't appear. Instead, she was more conscious of him than she had ever been of anything in her life. Caught in the moment, her sensitivity to every aspect of him was magnified—the glimpse of chocolate brown beneath his half-closed lids, the light stubble across his jaw, the faint trace of a scar above his right eyebrow that hadn't been there years before. His lips were soft, yet demanding, as though searching for answers, and she willingly opened herself up to anything he might find.

When he pulled away a moment later and his lips brushed across hers, she reached for him instead of letting go. All traces of common sense had vanished as the sensations took over.

He hesitated briefly before connecting their mouths again, his hands tangling in her hair. Pressing her hands to his chest, she felt the contours of his muscles, hard and smooth, through the material of his T-shirt, and her body tingled with a longing she hadn't felt in four years, two months, and ten days. Or maybe it was longer.

The thought caused her to step back.

He moved away quickly, his hands falling away from her.

"Damn. That was awful," he muttered, running a hand over his face and chin.

"Wow." First, he kissed her out of nowhere—a mind-blowing, knee-weakening kiss that had stirred long repressed emotions and desires—and then he insulted her?

"Not the kiss itself…just the kiss. I should get out of here." He turned to leave. "Sorry about that." Without waiting for a response, he left the room and headed toward the front door.

She caught up to him as he was stepping outside, and she shivered as the early December mountain breeze blew her light brown, shoulder-length hair across her face. She tried to tuck it behind her ears, but her wispy bangs flew right back into her eyes. Unfortunately, they didn't block the sexiest view on the planet—Neil Healy walking away toward his motorcycle.

How much longer could he get away with driving that thing anyway? Come on snow!

As he reached for his helmet, he paused. "About what just happened…"

She shook her head. "We really don't have to talk about it." In fact, she'd be willing to never talk about it. Her flushed expression was already saying far too much.

"Okay." He went to put on the helmet, but stopped again.

Oh God, just drive away. For some reason, she was unable to close the door and go inside.

"But I want you to know I didn't mean to insult you by saying the kiss was terrible."

Awful had been his exact wording. "It's fine, really." He looked ready to try to explain again, so she continued before he could. "I should get back to cleaning up."

Neil nodded slowly. "He's a lucky guy," he said, a hint of jealousy evident in his voice.

She blinked. "Excuse me?"

"Whoever that thong was for. He's a lucky guy," he said, putting on his helmet and revving the bike.

She wondered what he'd think if he knew this "lucky guy" was fifteen-year-old Al at the grocery store and that Neil's unexpected, untimely kiss was the best action she'd actually gotten in years.

ABOUT THE AUTHOR

Jennifer Snow lives in Edmonton, Alberta, with her husband and son. She writes sweet and sexy contemporary romance stories set everywhere from small towns to big cities. After stating in her high school yearbook bio that she wanted to be an author, she set off on the winding, twisting road to make her dream a reality. She is a member of RWA, the Writers' Guild of Alberta, the Canadian Authors Association, and the Film and Visual Arts Association in Edmonton. She has published over ten novels and novellas with many more on the way.

You can learn more at:
    JenniferSnowAuthor.com
    Twitter @jennifersnow18
    Facebook.com/JenniferSnowBooks

Fall in Love with Forever Romance

TOO HOT TO HANDLE
By Tessa Bailey

Having already flambéed her culinary career beyond recognition, Rita Clarkson is now stranded in God-Knows-Where, New Mexico, with a busted-ass car and her three temperamental siblings. When rescue shows up—six-feet-plus of hot, charming sex on a motorcycle—Rita's pretty certain she's gone from the frying pan right into the fire... The first book in an all-new series from *New York Times* bestselling author Tessa Bailey!

SIZE MATTERS
By Alison Bliss

Fans of romantic comedies such as *Good in Bed* will eat up this delightful new series from Alison Bliss! Leah Martin has spent her life trying to avoid temptation, but she's sick of counting calories. Fortunately, her popular new bakery keeps her good and distracted. But there aren't enough éclairs in the world to distract Leah from the hotness that is Sam Cooper—or the fact that he just told her mother that they're engaged... which is a big, fat lie.

Fall in Love with Forever Romance

MAYBE THIS TIME
By Jennifer Snow

All through high school, talented hockey player Jackson Westmore had a crush on Abby Jansen, but he would never make a move on his best friend's girl. He gave her the cold shoulder out of self-preservation and worked out his frustrations on the ice. So when Abby returns, newly divorced and still sexy as hell, Jackson knows he's in trouble. Now even the best defensive skills might not keep him from losing his heart...

LUKE
By R.C. Ryan

When Ingrid Marrow discovers rancher Luke Malloy trapped in a ravine, she brings him to her family ranch and nurses him back to health. As he heals, he begins to fall for the tough independent woman who saved him, but a mysterious attacker threatens their love—and their lives. Fans of Linda Lael Miller and Diana Palmer will love the latest contemporary western in R.C. Ryan's Malloys of Montana series.

Fall in Love with Forever Romance

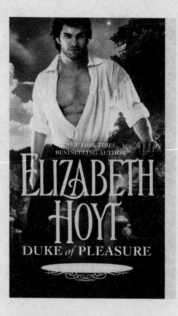

DUKE OF PLEASURE
By Elizabeth Hoyt

Sent to defeat the notorious Lords of Chaos, Hugh Fitzroy, the Duke of Kyle, is ambushed in a London alley—and rescued by an unlikely ally: a masked stranger with the unmistakable curves of a woman. Alf has survived on the streets of St. Giles by disguising her sex, but when Hugh hires her to help his investigation, will she find the courage to become the woman she needs to be—before the Lords of Chaos destroy them both?